EBUT

THAT

Nidhi Upadhyay is an engineer-tu   ...um
spent her days matchmaking senioi   _ ...eir dream jobs and
her nights reading thrillers, until her husband borderline bullied her
into writing one. She lives in Singapore with her doting husband and
two exceptionally loving but polar-opposite boys. *That Night* is her
debut novel.

that night

FOUR FRIENDS

TWENTY YEARS

ONE *HAUNTING* SECRET

Nidhi Upadhyay

EBURY
PRESS

An imprint of Penguin Random House

EBURY PRESS

USA | Canada | UK | Ireland | Australia
New Zealand | India | South Africa | China

Ebury Press is part of the Penguin Random House group of companies
whose addresses can be found at global.penguinrandomhouse.com

Published by Penguin Random House India Pvt. Ltd
4th Floor, Capital Tower 1, MG Road,
Gurugram 122 002, Haryana, India

Penguin
Random House
India

First published in Ebury Press by Penguin Random House India 2021

10 9 8 7 6 5

This is a work of fiction. Names, characters, places and incidents are either the
product of the author's imagination or are used fictitiously, and any resemblance
to any actual person, living or dead, events or locales is entirely coincidental.
The occult practices and beliefs mentioned in the book are purely a work
of fiction, and the author and publisher do not endorse any opinions and
practices mentioned in the story.

ISBN 9780143451877

Typeset in Adobe Garamond Pro by Manipal Technologies Limited, Manipal
Printed at Thomson Press India Ltd, New Delhi

www.penguin.co.in

MIX
Paper
FSC   FSC® C010615

For Maamaji, who wanted me to write a book but left too soon

For my family, who kept me going

Prologue

The fog was as thick as a block-out curtain. I could see nothing. The realization came as a relief. No one could see me, too. I walked out of the hostel gate. The damp seemed to sit in the air. Trees I passed shook icy droplets down, and the bushes smeared me with the cold. I dropped on my knees and began to dig. The chill in the grass blades seeped through my woollen shalwar and settled in my bones.

I dug deeper and faster.

The soil in the field felt finger-numbing cold and it was settling underneath my nails, forming cold and dark crescents. I buried the coin and the Ouija sheet, and let out a sigh of relief.

I had buried the demons.

But on this sinister night, someone, somewhere, had unleashed another demon.

A set of eyes stared at me with unsatiated hunger. The morbid darkness in those eyes washed over me with a wave of panic. I ran back to the hostel gate, but it was closed.

I was locked out.

I assessed the height of the gate; it was too tall to climb. And to get past the barbed wires on the top of the gate wasn't an easy feat either. I cast a slow, calculative glance—the vast and dark woods surrounding the hostel felt like a stormy ocean. No matter how fast I swam, I was destined to drown. My undermined reflexes concluded that escape wasn't possible.

So, I surrendered to the devil.

1

Trick or Treat

December 19, 1997
Girls' Hostel
Institute of Technology, Kurukshetra, India

Silence fell across the room like an elongated shadow. I felt a presence draw near, raising bumps on my skin. My sense of reality teetered between the real and the surreal. But before my logical mind could take over, the coin started to move again. It stopped and moved, following a rhythm that was significantly visible, even under the candle's dim light.

Katherine's shaky hand jotted down the words, letter by letter, as indicated by the coin. She read it aloud for us with a tremble in her voice, 'Revenge. And I am here to get it. Look outside your window.'

'Open the curtain,' Anjali said. Her voice had a slur; fear and alcohol both were to be blamed.

Katherine pulled the pale jacquard curtain to one side and moved closer to the window, holding the candle in her hand. The droplets of mist on the windowpane gleamed in the candlelight shining on it. Something scribbled in red caught my attention, and Katherine's unblinking gaze confirmed my suspicion. She moved the candle closer to the glass. The word 'HELP', written with a red lipstick, made me cringe in disbelief.

The sceptical frown on Katherine's face meant that we were on the same page. She walked to the window, touched the glass and rubbed her thumb against her index finger. Nothing. The words were scribbled on the outside of the window, and it was a recent scrawl. Else, the stark temperature difference on either side of the glass would have coated the lipstick mark with layers of damp, making it run like a syrup.

I stared at the windowpane; the letters began to dance. I blamed the droplets in my eyes for this little dance. But no, it was the flame in Katherine's hand that was flickering. She used her free hand to guard the flame and moved it closer to the red scribble on the glass, illuminating the word 'HELP'. The 'H' had started to bleed, making a red trajectory, adding a more sinister feel to the already eerie scribble.

Katherine placed the candle on the windowsill and cupped her hands to peep outside the window. She had clearly underestimated the utter blackness of nighttime in the woods.

Our college campus was situated miles away from the never-ending lights of the city, and the girls' hostel was further away from the rest of the campus. The building was practically perched upon a piece of land at the cusp of the woods. Even if it were a full moon, its silvery rays would not have penetrated the dense fog. The few streetlights installed sparsely were not enough to tame the wilderness of the forest around us.

'I can't see a thing,' Katherine said, trying to stem the tide of fear.

A shiver ran down my spine too, causing a tremble.

'You can't break contact, or it will haunt us all!' Riya warned and pointed to my hand. My finger had lost the grip on the coin. Anjali's, Natasha's and Riya's pointers were still resting at the edge of the coin. I got a handle on my nerves and placed my pointer firmly on the coin. It started to move. The coin jumped from one letter to another and made me reel in disbelief.

Was one of them moving the coin or was the tug in the coin bound by some unseen force?

But the movement was too swift for any of them to pull through without getting caught, especially, with that level of alcohol running in their veins. They weren't moving the coin.

Then who was?

My question was answered in Katherine's faint voice. She was reading the sentence that was carefully constructed by stringing the letters indicated by the coin, 'I want to talk. Can I come inside?'

Katherine looked at all of us with shock in her eyes, as if one of us had the answer to the turn of events that her logical mind could not comprehend. My suspicion that it was all a prank evaporated after reading Katherine's troubled expression. I hastily swallowed the tears stinging the back of my eyes, but the growing fear soon made itself felt in every part of my body, blurring the boundaries of the real and the surreal.

'Are you here?' Anjali asked.

Her controlled demeanour again raised the alarm in my head.

They are fooling you.

But before I could jump to any conclusion, the coin moved and spelt out the word 'Yes'.

'Where are you?' Anjali asked, throwing a furtive glance at the window.

The room was cloaked in silence. Yet, I heard a thud, a loud continuous thud. It was my heart beating in my ears. Boisterous and erratic. I stared at the coin. It was still, as the air around us. Everyone was holding their breath, waiting for the coin to move, until Riya's husky, deep-throated growl shattered the silence.

'I am here, inside her,' Riya said in a voice that wasn't hers.

Twenty Years Later

October 31, 2017
Natasha Gupta Lim
Raffles Place, Singapore

Natasha's weekly sales report needed another hour, but the notification on her smartwatch caught her attention: Trick or Treat Party.

She dismissed the alarm, turned her eyes away from the incomplete sales report and looked outside the window. A patch of crimson cloud over Marina Bay Sands looked like the mast of a sailing vessel. The shades of pink in the sky hinted at sunset. It was a perfect evening to be home with her kids, to witness the sun take a dip into the sea. But Natasha's new role as sales head had robbed her life—and her twins' lives—of these tiny pleasures. Before her guilt could again drag her down the rabbit hole, the ring of her phone pulled her back.

'Mommy, are you coming for the Halloween party?' Ryan asked.

Natasha looked around. Everyone in office was still glued to their seat. But she had promised her twins to be home for trick or treat.

Today is my day to be a good mother.

'I was about to call a cab, munchkin,' she said and half-heartedly dumped the laptop in her bag. Kids or work, whichever side she swayed, the abandoned side always weighed her down. And a kids' Halloween party in her condominium wasn't exactly a valid excuse to leave work early.

She booked an Uber and got into the lift. It made a weird clacking sound as it descended from the eleventh floor. A moment later, the lights in the lift flickered and died. She switched on her phone's flashlight. The dust motes dancing in the slice of light stirred something uncomfortable within her.

Natasha pointed the flashlight and located the emergency call button on the lift's control panel. The lifeless buttons cemented her anxiety. She unlocked her phone to call for help, but the last bar of the signal had disappeared.

Calm down, it is just a lift breakdown. Help will come soon.

A few deep breaths and she felt better. Natasha pressed the emergency call button again and this time made an attempt to talk into the dead microphone, 'Hello! Can you hear me? The lift is not moving. Is someone there?'

Her loud, irregular breathing punctuated the eerie silence.

She angled her phone closer to the lift's door, hoping to get a signal. Her reflection on the lift's stainless-steel door startled her. She was about to scream for help when the power was restored. She hissed out a steady stream of breath when the lift touched the ground.

'Uncle, the lift wasn't working a minute ago. The call button wasn't working either,' she said to the old man seated at the security desk. Her tone hovered between complaint and fear.

'Cannot be. No one complain, mah,' the old security guard said, and pointed to the people alighting from the other lift.

Natasha turned away and walked to the taxi bay. Her taxi was here.

'*Kaisi.*' She overheard the guard muttering under his breath to his colleague. It felt like the sting of a wasp. Kaisi was the word her mother-in-law often used to describe Natasha's borderline paranoia regarding her kids. But there was no way for the guard in her office building to know that she was married into a Chinese family and had picked up most of the local slang.

She ignored the guard's comment, the way she had ignored her mother-in-law's remarks on her hyperactive motherly instincts.

I have already paid the price for not being cautious. Twice.

She took a deep breath, walked to the taxi bay, checked the car number and perched on the car seat. The phone in her bag buzzed for her attention much before she could get over the guard's comment.

'Hey, you left for home, already? I thought you brought forward the eight p.m. team call to six.'

It was Andrew, her boss.

'But . . . I didn't . . .'

Andrew didn't give Natasha a chance to complete her sentence.

'We received the meeting change request from you. Anyway, let's not waste any more time. We have everybody on the call. Please log into the call, all right?'

Andrew's voice was cold and curt. Natasha was left with no choice but to transform the car's back seat into her office desk. Her laptop, the sheaf of sales report and her moleskin notebook were all out before she could log in to the call. The crawling traffic on the Marina Coastal Expressway meant that the call would get over before the car ride.

But tonight, nothing in Natasha's life was going as per plan.

She was still juggling with the team's sales numbers when the driver swiped his phone's touchscreen and completed the trip. Natasha packed her makeshift office into her bag and stepped out of the car. She had to walk away from the playground to finish this call without getting bothered by her boys. But there was no need to hide from them.

The Uber had brought her to a wrong destination.

Natasha muted the call and tapped on the car's boot before it could drive off.

'This is not 26 Siglap Road,' she said when the driver rolled down the window.

'Your destination is 426 Siglap Road. See,' the driver said and pointed to Natasha's call history on his phone.

'But how is it possible? I selected the destination as 'Home' from the Uber app,' she said. She was about to convince the driver to drop her to the right building when her boss threw a question at her.

'Natasha, any news on the Thailand placement?'

Andrew's vexed tone had again eclipsed every other worry from her world. She unmuted the call and watched the car speed away. Natasha soon finished the call, changed the home address on the Uber app and booked a new cab. She was about to pull out the earphones, to dump them in her bag, when a message notification appeared on the phone screen: 'Are you here?'

She assumed it to be the driver's message and texted back, 'Where are you? Yes, I am in front of this old, yellow gate.'

She waited for a minute for the driver to respond, and when no response came, she launched the Uber app. There wasn't a driver nearby. The system was still finding a ride for her.

Natasha had responded to an anonymous message. She tapped on the message icon to apologize for her hasty response when another message from the same sender flashed on her phone screen: 'Stay there. You love calling upon the dead, don't you? All you need is a Ouija board. And that much I can do for you.'

Before Natasha could reread the message, her phone screen turned black. An app had launched itself. The umber-coloured screen, with the word 'Spirit' written on it, looked way unfamiliar. She stared at the three tabs displayed on the screen—Scary Stories, Start Séance and More. She quit the app.

Did Rick download this crap or . . .? And where the hell am I?

Natasha turned around, drinking in the unfamiliar surroundings. The road was lined up with affluent houses, except for this battered yellow Mughal–Gothic structure. It stood out like cotton patchwork on a silken tapestry. She carefully studied the yellow-and-green pillars supporting the palisade wooden gate. A lingering air of neglect and abandonment hung around the building.

The partially open gate beckoned Natasha to enter, but the surrounding green barrier-screen concealed what lay beyond. She decided to stay away but studied the arch more intently. The Arabic writing engraved on the yellow-and-green arch revealed nothing to her about the building. Her gaze drifted to the pillars supporting the arch. The green text on the bright yellow pillar must have been prominently visible once, but the peeled-out paint and the dry weeds erupting from the mortar had partially effaced its design. She googled the phrase 'Kubur Kassim', written in Roman letters on the pillars.

Kubur Kassim was a cemetery, a Muslim burial ground. It was considered one of the most haunted places in Singapore and was clearly an object of interest for ghost hunters in town. She scrolled further down and spotted a video. Before Natasha could exit the search app, her phone's screen turned sepia green. A loud, eerie tune playing in her earphones startled her. She pulled out the earphones from her ears and hit the pause button.

The ghost-hunt video had stopped but the music from the video was still playing in her head, giving her chills.

Natasha wasn't scared of ghosts. But her landing here was more than a coincidence, and the context of the messages from that stranger had sent a rush of weakness in her legs. She dialled the number that had texted her. The country code indicated that it was a local number.

The call went unanswered.

Before she could dial again, Uber's notification flashed on her screen: 'Yay! We found you a driver!'

Natasha had just tapped on the map to track the car when a loud 'Boo!' startled her. A throng of kids dressed in Halloween costumes were out for trick or treat.

She laughed at herself. Of course. This was a prank—a Halloween prank.

But why would someone mention the Ouija board? And what if this wasn't a prank?

The thought caused a subtle distress to churn in her stomach. She walked away from the graveyard and waited for the taxi. In the cab, she took a deep breath to calm herself down, but what the extra oxygen couldn't do, her twins' smiling faces did. The boys were eagerly waiting for her at the drop-off point of her condominium.

Ian and Ryan's collective embrace grounded Natasha, erasing the stress of the lift malfunction and the weird trip to the cemetery. She was home—exactly where she wanted to be.

The twins' identical Transformers costumes were looking sharp. In no time at all, they dragged her to the playground, which was decorated as a spooky castle. The door-to-door adventure afterwards gave Natasha no time to think about her trip to the graveyard.

Rick was still at work. Without his help, the dinner–bath–bed routine was more exhausting than usual, thanks to the sugar high. Once the kids were asleep, Natasha replayed the events of the day in her head.

The lift breakdown. The change of home address. The app and the message about playing Ouija. Something about her evening felt off-kilter. She unlocked her phone to read the messages. There weren't any. She swiped her phone screen, looking for the Ouija app. The app had disappeared too.

The incidents had no whiff of the past, yet her mind drifted back in time. She typed her friends' names, one by one, in the search tab. They were all on social media, just a click away. A click on the 'Send Friend Request' tab could cover that distance. Her hand momentarily hovered over the tab, and then she put the phone away.

Their silent presence was enough for Natasha.

Anjali Kapoor
23 Park Street, London

A notification of a new WhatsApp group caught Anjali's attention. She shook her head in disbelief.

Will she ever stop trying?

Natasha had created a WhatsApp group and named it 'College Friends'. Anjali was on a work call when the group was created. It was a slow-paced call, the kind that allowed Anjali to clean her desk or clear her mailbox. But today, Natasha's message had made Anjali put the spadework on the back burner. She tapped on 'Group info'. Anjali Kapoor, Natasha Gupta, Katherine D'Souza and Riya Banerjee were all together, just like college. Back then, they had lived every moment in the hope of creating memories that would bring back laughter and love for a lifetime. But a single night had altered their universe. Now, reliving those moments made Anjali sad. The others probably felt no different and that's why they had all let the passage of time dig a gulf between them.

However, Anjali's frequent travel to Singapore had brought Natasha and her together. But none of them had talked to the other two for ages.

Then how did Natasha manage to get all the numbers?

Anjali couldn't resist clicking on their WhatsApp profile pictures. Natasha's display pic was the first to get her attention. Her light-brown eyes looked more profound on her now-chiselled face, and her new hairdo had added a contrasting lowlight to her natural blacks; she looked more attractive than ever. Anjali couldn't help but notice Natasha's strange WhatsApp status: 'When in doubt, choose the kids.'

Next, she clicked on Riya's profile picture. It astounded her. The beautiful, fashionable Riya looked nerdy in her WhatsApp DP. Her oversized, black-rimmed glasses hid her doe eyes, and her cascading black hair was stuffed into a bun. Even on her worst days, a woman as pretty as Riya couldn't look like this; she had to make an effort to look so ordinary. She had definitely donned this new 'intellectual look' to match her new profession. At least Riya's sense of humour was still unchanged: 'I am not perfect. I am a limited edition.'

Katherine had changed over the years, too. She had lost a lot of weight, and her long, unruly curls were replaced by a pixie-style cut. The highlight streaks of caramel complemented her dark black hair very well. Katherine's choice of subtle make-up had accented her dusky complexion and her sharp features in the pic. A tiny crucifix hanging from a slender gold chain was the only thing familiar about Katherine. Her WhatsApp status was typically glum too: 'I need a break from my own thoughts.'

Of the four women, Anjali was the only one not to upload a picture or set a status.

When was the last time she got a candid picture clicked? And lately, she had started avoiding the mirror too.

I would rather be anyone else but me.

The last work call of the day got over with self-loathing looming in her mind. Anjali wilfully dragged herself back to her empty apartment. The salmon sandwich from

Pret was her dinner tonight. These days, her culinary creativity was limited to picking a new kind of sandwich from the stores; anything more was impossible since her separation from Sid. For years, he had saved her from the grind of meal-planning, and over the last month, Pret had come to replace her husband.

Anjali had no plans for Halloween this year, so she settled in with a *Friends* rerun and a cold sandwich. Last year, Sid's Halloween party had made him an instant hit with the kids in their new neighbourhood. This year, no one would show up at her door as she had unplugged the doorbell and was pretending to be caught up with work.

Her mom's call shattered her pretence.

'Hey, Anju. Sid called. When were you planning to tell me all this?'

Anjali sighed. Sid had again won the race—the race of being the responsible one. She felt like letting her guard down, but a quick analysis of her mother's misplaced loyalties stopped her in her tracks.

'Hi, Ma. Sid told you?' she asked, keeping emotions out of her voice.

'Yes. Yesterday. I waited for a day. Don't I deserve to know, Anju? Sid at least called and told me about it all.'

Her mother's tone was cold and distant, with an undercurrent of anger. This was not the right time to ask her to pick sides. Anjali had to buy time.

'Ma, I can't wrap my head around it yet. I want to think it through,' she said.

'Anju, Sid is devastated. Do I need to remind you how much he adores you? If you ask me, all you guys need is some quality time together and things will go back to normal. Take some time off from work, focus on him and on having kids.'

There it was—her verdict. For Sid, and against her. Like always.

Her mother had declared Anjali guilty even before listening to her side of the story. There was nothing new in that, but the feeling gripped her like an ache from a half-healed wound.

'Anjali, Sid is coming to New Delhi this weekend. Why don't you come too? We can sit together and sort this out.'

She had forgotten about Sid's upcoming trip to India. But there was nothing she could do.

'Ma, there is a merger. I am working this weekend. I will come in December.'

'Well, I don't want to impose, but everybody back home will blame me for your upbringing. They will say: like mother, like daughter.'

Words bubbled in Anjali's throat, but she swallowed them back.

Pulling one thread out will unravel the entire tapestry.

'Ma, listen. I have a call in three minutes. I will call you back,' she said and ended the call.

The dreaded call with her mother was over with minimum damage.

All thanks to Sid.

Anjali dumped her barely eaten sandwich into the bin and hit the play button to resume the show. Her mother's phone call had killed her appetite for food and entertainment. But she thought the canned laughter might help break the oppressive silence enveloping the house. Her empty apartment felt too silent without Sid. She felt his absence as keenly as she had felt his presence.

Tears smarted her eyes. Again. She felt an aching need to cry, and it was as though her chest had caved in.

Not anymore.

Tonight, she had come home with a prescribed tranquilizer. She popped one and waited for a free-fall into sleep. She teetered on the edge, feeling the ache subside.

She woke up with the metallic taste of a nightmare lingering in her mouth. The dark woods, the damp winter night and a shadow approaching her were the only things she remembered at first, and then she recalled the sight of blood flowing down the stairs, like red leaves through the October air.

The sound of footsteps in the woods had jerked her out of sleep. Or was that part of the dream too? It was her phone vibrating on the nightstand. Anjali squinted to read the message, her eyelids still heavy with sleep.

'Anjali, hiding something on purpose is just the same as lying. People around you deserve to know the truth.'

The tone of the anonymous message washed away all the tranquilizer from her brain. She read the message again, as if it was a continuation of her dream. A blink and it would disappear. But the text was still there, as concrete as the aftertaste of her dream. Anjali sat up in bed, tapped on the sender's number and hit the call button. The phone was switched off. She saved the number and launched WhatsApp, but the number didn't have a WhatsApp account.

She dialled the number again. Nothing.

For some reason, Anjali's drowsy mind connected the anonymous message with the WhatsApp group created by Natasha. Was it mere coincidence? Or had something triggered Natasha to find all the numbers and create that group?

She had to put her doubts to bed. Else, she wouldn't be able to sleep tonight too.

It was early morning in Singapore. Natasha must be out, running. Alone.

Anjali dialled her number and wondered how Natasha had turned into a complete health freak in the last couple of years, losing the extra kilos and looking much better than ever. 'Morning, madam. How much more weight have you lost?' Anjali asked.

'How much more do I want to lose is what you should ask,' Natasha said, breathing heavily into the earphones.

'Are you sure that you are promoted as a sales head and not the brand ambassador of the company? Looks like your KPIs have changed.' Anjali teased Natasha, and her own anxiety relaxed into a grin.

'Midlife crisis, my friend. You tell me.' Natasha stopped mid-sentence and said, 'Oh my god, Anjali . . . that theme song, I am hearing it after ages. Sid still watches *Friends*?'

Anjali let the silence fill the gaps for her. She was in no mood to discuss Sid. The anonymous message came knocking at her conscience from nowhere: *Hiding something on purpose is just the same as lying. People around you deserve to know the truth.*

Anjali decided to omit the truth and asked, 'Natasha, why are you waking up the old demons?'

'Sorry?' Natasha asked, with evident shock in her voice.

'You created a WhatsApp group with the four of us in it, no?' Anjali asked and opened WhatsApp to reconfirm. Natasha was the administrator.

'Which WhatsApp group?' Natasha asked.

The wind blowing into the microphone had stopped with Natasha's run. While Anjali waited for Natasha to launch her WhatsApp, her mind was already connecting the dots.

If Natasha did not create the group, who did?

'Anjali, I didn't create this group. I mean, how could I when I do not even have their numbers. Didn't have, I mean.'

The tremble in Natasha's voice made Anjali swallow hard.

She cursed herself for taking the tranquilizer. Her mind wasn't razor-sharp. Before she could try to clear her head, Natasha embarked on describing the strange text and the incident in the Uber that happened with her the previous night. Anjali didn't breathe a word about her own strange text. Knowing Natasha, there was no reason to light a bigger fire under her worry.

One step at a time.

'Could your phone be hacked?' Anjali asked.

'Makes sense . . . I actually didn't change the team call timing last night, but it was changed too, and so was my home address on the taxi app. But why would a hacker mention about the Ouija and talking to the dead? Unless it was one of us . . .' Natasha stopped for a moment to reflect, and then they both arrived at a name, almost instantly.

'Katherine,' they said in unison, waking up some old and beautiful memories of thinking alike and completing each other's sentences. Anjali had an aching need to pull them all in this call and start afresh. She knew it would take only a call to melt away the years between them.

Probably Katherine was trying to do the same.

'But it doesn't make sense. Katherine would be the last person to bring the dead out of the closet,' Natasha said and brought Anjali back to reality.

None of them would have done it. Because that night was hidden inside them like a splinter of wood, and for all these years, all four of them were careful not to touch it.

Riya Banerjee
Malabar Hills, Mumbai

Riya woke up at dawn, squinting at her phone screen. Her muscle memory again defeated her. Her fingers had launched the mail app much before her mind could register. She took in the rejections the way senior citizens in the park inhale oxygen every morning, feeling it in every cell of her body.

And the day has begun. With rejections.

She sauntered to her writing desk with a mug of steamy coffee in her hand. Her determination to write was at the brink of shattering much before it could come together. This was clearly not a writer's block. It was failure. Dark and depressing failure.

And the only cure to failure is success. So make it happen, damn it.

Riya straightened her spine and with a click made all the rejection mails from the literary agents disappear. They dropped from her mailbox and settled in the pit of her stomach, like a sinking coin finding its place in the depth of a calm river; still there yet not visible.

Riya's first book wasn't exactly a success, but her dream to have a stellar career in writing was the only thing that had kept her moving in this dark tunnel. She had already celebrated her first work-quit anniversary, and the numbers in her bank balance were dropping rapidly. All the marketing efforts to make her first book a success had swallowed her time and money like a sponge, and now, after a year, the euphoria was wearing out.

She had to pay bills, too, which her writing couldn't help her with. Not yet.

Riya had to make it big or quit. Soon.

Two weeks ago, she was this close to giving up when her fertile mind struck a gold mine. The story idea grew overnight, like a bean sprout, and soon she was scaling the heights without bothering about the beast waiting at the top.

Today again, the rejections from literary agents had not tipped the fine balance between her resilience and disappointment. Riya's steamy coffee had turned ice-cold, but her hands refused to stop typing, not until her sugar levels dropped to a point where whatever she wrote felt like crap. She then stood up and lathered the bread with butter and assembled a cold sandwich. A sprinkle of *namkeen* between the two layers was enticing enough a breakfast after hours of writing. Any type of meal that could keep her alive was a feast. Unlike her friends and colleagues, she didn't have to balance the proteins, carbs and fats from the food pyramid to plan a meal for her family, and her desire to keep her waistline slim had lost its charm after she decided to end the game of dating.

Riya was alone. Jobless. And a tiny bit desperate. It was how she felt this morning while nibbling on a stale piece of bread. When the spice in the namkeen couldn't overpower the taste of failure in her mouth, she used her phone as a distraction.

Her phone screen was loaded with Twitter notifications. These were responses to her latest tweet, one sent from her account, but she had no recollection of sending it.

'Four college friends. An innocent Ouija prank. But the victim winds up dead the next morning. #pitwar'

The tweet almost made her choke on her bite. Panicked, she logged in to her Twitter account to delete the tweet before it was too late.

And what was this #pitwar thing all about?

A click on the hashtag and the information untied the knot in her stomach. Excitedly, she read the details. PitWar was one of the many Twitter events organized to help writers get an agent for their unpublished manuscripts. She had almost deleted the tweet when the fifteen hearts on the tweet caught her attention. Riya felt ridiculously happy—she had fifteen manuscript requests without querying a single agent. Belatedly, the enormity of what she was facing caught up with her.

Her Twitter account had been hacked, and the mention of her new manuscript meant her computer was hacked too.

And there wasn't a finished manuscript to send. All she had was a partial recount of that night. But someone had read what she had been secretly writing and had shared the pitch using her Twitter account. Above all, she had fifteen partial manuscript requests. A task that her endless querying had not achieved with her other completed manuscript.

Maybe my account has been hacked for good.

That night had changed her life once. It was about to change her life again, only if waking up the demons was considered an auspicious start.

Riya quit the Twitter app and was still wondering about it all when a new WhatsApp group notification caught her eye, sweeping her world again. This was not a case of simply conjuring a story out of her own mind.

The WhatsApp group was as real as her tweet, and she had no role to play in any of it. Only if secretly writing about that night was discounted.

Katherine D'Souza
38 City Apartments, New York

Katherine turned around and found a long-haired girl in a tattered white dress in her kitchen.

'I am Sadako from *The Ring*. Cool, no?' Janice, her teenage daughter, asked through a layer of white makeup.

Katherine swallowed back the swear word that had almost escaped her lips. She flashed a faint smile and asked, 'Where's your brother?'

From the doorstep, twelve-year-old Aaron waved a plastic knife. He was waiting patiently, wearing a black T-shirt and dark jeans. Besides the knife, his only prop was a 'Scream' mask. It was where Aaron's imagination began and came to an end, year after year.

'You could be a little more creative, Aaron. It won't hurt,' Janice said.

Katherine ignored the bickering of her teen–tween kids, checked her phone once again and set out to drive them to the party. She was not a Halloween enthusiast, yet she had picked a short, red lace dress for herself. Janice insisted on adding a devil's headband with red horns—a bit over the top, but it was Katherine's only ticket to exit the party without annoying her daughter, a project that required more effort every week.

She parked the car and gave herself a quick glance in the rear-view mirror. Out of habit, she tugged the hem of her dress towards her knees. A tidal wave of under-confidence always hit her when she approached an unfamiliar social gathering.

She flashed a fake smile at Janice and rang the doorbell. A lady dressed in a witch costume answered the door. Katherine thanked the host and handed her a box of homemade witch-finger cookies. This year, Janice had made them look more realistic by staining the almond nails with raspberry syrup.

'Sorry, I have a work call. I will be back in a couple of hours to pick them up. Hope it's okay?' she asked the host and caught Janice rolling her eyes. Of course, Janice knew it was just her mom chickening out again, but tonight Katherine had not bothered to be polite about her exit. She had kept up the pretence of normality for hours; anything more was not possible.

The WhatsApp group created by Natasha this morning had turned her mind into a sauna room. A gnawing sense of trepidation fogging the windows, making every movement and sound blurry with fear.

Katherine parked the car and entered the coffeehouse, which was as festive as her outfit. She resisted the fancy Halloween cookies, ordered a black coffee and unlocked her phone. There was no traction on the WhatsApp group. She vacillated between initiating the conversation or quitting the group, but neither was an easy decision to make. She dumped the phone into her bag much before her mind could turn into a basket of thorns, making thinking painful.

The envelope in her bag served an easy distraction: an offer letter.

A full-time position with her fastest-growing client was hard to resist. So was the money. But she knew what Samir would say—or rather, not say. *If you want to run the show on your own, you can do whatever you want.* Samir was neither a hands-on dad nor did he have any plans to be one. He earned double the money made by his peers, so that in his free time he could follow sports or news. Loading the dishes in the dishwasher or monitoring the kids was not how he liked to spend his evenings, so he left everything to her.

However, Samir had never quite stopped Katherine from taking up a job—it was fine by him if she could outsource all the housework or could train herself to live with a bag full of dirty laundry and a messy countertop in the kitchen.

An assignment-based freelance job worked for her. If she planned her day well, she had time to scrub the bathroom floor, be a helicopter mom to her kids and still get her creative juices flowing. She always had a steady list of clients and enough work to keep her days filled. But occasionally, an offer like this made her regret her decision to not work full time.

With a huff of annoyance, she pushed the offer back into her bag. She wasn't ready yet.

I will never be.

She wished she were cut from the same cloth as her college friends. Anjali was already a partner in one of the fastest-growing consulting firms in London, Natasha was heading the Asia Pacific sales team for a multinational corporation and Riya had beaten the other two to fame with her stellar writing.

I am the only underperformer.

A new text message pushed away her unruly, dark thoughts. It was from Aaron.

'Mom, please pick me up. This party is no fun.'

She replied, 'Okay, honey. Wait outside.' She wanted to ask him why he had insisted on going in the first place. Why did he always pretend to be someone he wasn't?

Her questions felt like an epiphany. Suddenly, she wasn't feeling that bad about putting away the offer letter. It would haunt her later, but not in the most unpleasant way. A sweet regret.

An hour later, Janice texted Katherine: 'Mom, almost done!!! You can start now. We are in Emma's backyard, playing the last game of the evening. Bring Scaredy-Aaron along for the final game at least!!!'

She knew Aaron wouldn't want to go. He was already in his pyjamas.

'Going to get your sis. See you in a bit,' she shouted over her shoulder and locked the house.

When the doorbell at Emma's wasn't answered, Katherine walked around the side of the house. It led her to the pitch-dark backyard. She could barely put one foot in front of another, and the eerie silence wasn't helping either. Was anyone actually here? And why were the lights out? She spotted a tiny halo of a candle and geared herself for a round of a spooky game.

Before she could orient herself to what she was seeing, voices in unison broke the deafening silence hanging in the air.

'If any holy spirits are passing by, please announce your presence.'

This can't be happening.

Katherine walked towards the game of Ouija, a buzz of fear rushing through her.

As she drew near the intoning voices, she spotted Janice's hand settled on the Ouija. Katherine almost jumped out of her skin.

'Janice, let's go,' she said, her voice inflected with mild panic.

Several irritated-looking teens rounded on her, the boring adult.

'One more attempt, Mom.' Janice pleaded.

'Aaron is alone. Shall we?' she said through gritted teeth. With a tug on Janice's shoulder, she drew her daughter away from the game. Janice's friends groaned in disappointment.

Katherine could have handled their exit better. But fear had warped her thinking—or was it guilt, or the formation of the WhatsApp group? It was fortunate that she had stopped Janice from playing the game of Ouija tonight; she wished she herself had done the same twenty years ago.

As they walked away, Janice swearing to never speak to her again, Katherine felt something zip down her spine. *Fear*.

2

The Ghost in the Wires

Riya Banerjee
Malabar Hill, Mumbai

The hearts on Riya's tweet throbbed with the possibility of newness, robbing her of peace and acumen. A twenty-year-old promise had lost its weight years ago, and so had the love between them. Her friends were all happy. She too had a right to be happy.

And this was her only chance.

Riya had reluctantly sacrificed her dream of living in London to take care of her ailing mother. She was in the final year of her post-graduation degree when her mother was diagnosed with cancer. Riya finished her course and flew back to India to take care of her teenage sister and mother. Her appointment letter with a leading technology giant and her long-distance relationship with Adam were still valid after her mother's death. But she didn't have the heart to leave her sister behind. How could she? Especially when her sister looked upon her the way a nestling looks at the mother bird, with its beak open.

Riya stayed back in India, first for her sister and then for reasons she couldn't remember now. She had labelled everything that had happened to her as bad luck. But luck had turned around.

Now, it was her time to reclaim whatever she deserved.

Riya's dream to get this story published was as fragile as an eggshell, but those fifteen hearts on her tweet had cemented her determination. However, the timing of her tweet and the creation of the WhatsApp group felt too contrived.

And how did Natasha manage to source my number?

In her moment of insanity and loneliness, she had once messaged Katherine to add her as a social media friend. But Katherine's icy cold reply to Riya's friend request had deterred her from approaching others: 'Let's not start again what we ended back then. You might have forgotten but I haven't, that you left us alone when we needed you the most.'

Riya very well knew that others also shared the same sentiments. Why create the group then? Something was amiss. She decided to wait and watch. Minutes transmuted into hours, yet there was no traction. She clicked on their WhatsApp pics and then stalked them on all the possible social media sites. Nothing.

The ding of the doorbell brought Riya's detective work to a standstill. If the maid were to be left to her own devices, Riya might end up eating bread and butter for her next meal too. She gave a set of instructions to the maid, plugged her almost-dead laptop to the charger and ran a bath for herself. After a relaxing bath and a proper meal, she logged in to the system and the new wallpaper on the screen made her jump out of her skin.

It was a photograph of all four of them sitting on the corridor wall of their hostel wing. They were wearing the same grey hoodies they had bought together on a trip to Chandigarh. Riya was sitting with her hands folded neatly across her chest; Natasha was behind Riya, with her chin tucked into Riya's shoulder and her arms thrown around Riya's neck; Katherine and Anjali had copied Natasha's pose. They looked like nesting dolls in grey hoodies, arranged in a line according to their heights. The memories of the hostel rolled back full throttle—the endless singing and dancing, the leg pulling and the night outs on the hostel terrace. Those three years of Riya's life contained all her best moments. She had lived them again and again.

Riya stretched her hand out to touch the photo and a realization jerked her out of her stupor. She hadn't brought this photo with her. In fact, she had never gone back to get anything from the hostel. All she had as the souvenir of their friendship was the grey hoodie that she had brought along with her during that winter break.

Someone had hacked her laptop despite the anti-hacking software she had installed after the Twitter hack. And the hacker had access to this photo too. The minimized windows confirmed her suspicion. Her unfinished, semi-finished and yet-to-develop story ideas were all in there, including the story arc of 'That Night'.

She launched the Scrivener app, with her heart working like a sledgehammer. All the projects were there except 'That Night'. She typed 'That Night' in the search bar. No results popped up. She began shaking her legs to defuse the anxiety. Riya calmed her nerves, opened a search window and typed 'Ouija'. A Scrivener file appeared in her search window, bringing a fresh batch of oxygen into her lungs. Her hours of hard work were still there. Only, the file had been renamed to: 'The Game of Ouija That Killed!'

Riya felt a strange sensation in her limbs, like she had stepped into quicksand.

She had not yet reached the end of the story. How, then, did the hacker manage to reach this conclusion? Was there too much foreshadowing, or did she inadvertently give away the end? She began to read, to find out what the hacker had found.

* * *

That Night: December 19, 1997

It was my third year in the college, but my first introduction to a full-fledged winter in north India, and the weather was hitting me hard. The lowest temperature I had ever seen and felt in Calcutta was still in double digits. Kurukshetra was way too cold, the kind that was plunging me into depression. No fleece sweater and no down jacket was able to warm my shivering body. The cold was as much in my mind as in my skin.

The others complained too. But they whined about the tiny gaps in the windows through which the cold would seep in. They were all accustomed to this cold—all except me. I was constantly cursing the unexpected exam delay that had left us shivering in this bone-biting cold.

With every passing day and each downward dive in temperature, I started to regret my decision of choosing the Institute of Technology, Kurukshetra. Three years too late, though.

Our college was in a village thirty kilometres from the city of Kurukshetra. Away from the hustle-bustle of the city, this village had its laid-back rustic charm. And in the middle of nowhere, there was this newly constructed building that had been my home for the last three years. A hostel building surrounded by barbed-wire walls, a big iron gate and two uniformed guards stationed at the doorstep—this was the perfect setting for the thriller lover in me. And the cherry on the top was my room facing the dark woods.

I had relished this cabin-in-the-woods kind of setting for the last three years. But that year winter arrived early, and with a vengeance.

Katherine, my roommate, had managed to source an electric heater for the room, but my body wasn't used to this chill wind that would bite me every time I stepped out of the room. The breeze in the open corridors, the ice-cold toilet seats and the mind-numbing icy water in the faucet, everything was working against my resolve to stay back and finish the last couple of exams. While the others in the hostel just complained, my teeth chattered endlessly. I counted minutes to the winter break, to go back and enjoy Mom's daal bhaat and the weather that did not kill you with every breath.

But that fateful evening, the cold turned beastly.

'*It must be snowing in Shimla,*' *I heard the guards speculating, warming their hands at the little bonfire they had created near the gate entrance.*

'*Where are you going? The hostel gate is about to close,*' *one of the guards informed me as I was about to step out to pick up my dinner from the college canteen.*

'*Going to pick my dinner. Will be back before eight. It's only seven.*' *I turned my wrist to show him the time.*

'*Madamji changed the closing time, as the sun is setting too early. And why do you waste your money when your parents have paid for your food in the mess?*' *one of them asked.*

'*Because the menu today is watery chana daal and hard-to-chew roti,*' *I said and walked back to my room. I had been holed up in my room for the last two days, preparing for the electromagnetic theory exam. Consequently, I had missed the early-closing-hours notice.*

I braved myself to walk to the mess and swallow the dinner I hated the most, but the tangy aroma of the chana daal pushed me further away from the mess. I decided to live on a packet of biscuits for a night. But I realized my mistake a couple of hours later into the night when I began to shiver incessantly.

'*You shouldn't have skipped dinner. I will go and see if someone has some food to share. Also, I will get you some tea,*' *Katherine said and jumped into action. Soon, Natasha and Anjali were roped in too.*

The four of us had turned into best friends in the very first week of college. Katherine was my roommate, and Natasha and Anjali were our immediate neighbours.

My mischievousness, Anjali's calm head, Natasha's protective instinct and Katherine's unconditional love had glued us with an invisible bond. We used to spend our days and nights together in the hostel and college, and whenever the hostel's madness became unbearable, Katherine would summon her elder brother, Mathew, to take us all home. Mathew would happily drive us back to Katherine's home for a warm meal or a sleepover at their place. Katherine's parents were from the outskirts of Goa, but she was born and brought up in Karnal, where her father was a scientist at one of the Central government research institutes. As her parents' home was the closest to our hostel, it invariably became our safety net, where we showed up uninhibited in times of sickness, boredom or just for a home-cooked meal.

But in the thick of the night, going back to Katherine's house was not an option. So, while I shivered constantly, my friends decided to divide and conquer. Katherine went to hunt for some bites to nibble on, Anjali volunteered to get some warm water and Natasha sat next to me, radiating this maternal calm that always made me feel close to home.

Twenty minutes later, Katherine barged into the room with a look of accomplishment gleaming on her face. She had something bottled up inside the pocket of her hoodie.

A whisky bottle and a pack of peanuts!

I stared at her in disbelief. She ignored the look on my face, handed me the peanuts and poured some of the golden liquid in my drinking cup. A potent, smoky, malty smell filled my nostrils.

She looked at Anjali and Natasha for support.

'My granny used to give brandy to keep us warm. This might actually help,' Anjali said and took the cup from Katherine. She drank it in one go, wiped her face with the back of her hand and returned the cup to Katherine.

Katherine refilled it and extended it to me. I looked at Natasha, who was the moral compass of our group.

'Take a sip or two. Maybe it helps. Just a sip or two,' Natasha said, treading carefully. Anjali read my temptation and said, 'Don't think too much. Nobody is asking you to finish the entire bottle.'

I could do anything to beat the cold that was searing my bones. Yet, I was not convinced about drinking in the hostel room, that too two nights before the toughest exam.

'Where did you get it from?' I asked, munching on the peanuts.

'From the warden's room. I went to her, to request for the keys to the mess. She was in the washroom, so she asked me to take it from her cupboard. There were a few bottles lined up in a bag next to her cupboard.'

'From the warden's room? Are you out of your mind? She will come to know that you took it,' Natasha said with a frown.

'Not really. Not tonight at least. I don't think it's her bag. It's a military bag, and she is definitely not alone tonight. I saw a pair of men's boots near her bed. I think she hid with her boyfriend at the first knock on the door,' Katherine said and flashed a naughty smile.

The hostel was almost empty that night as most of the exams were over. Natasha and Anjali were supposed to go back home too, but the unexpected thick fog had deterred them from travelling that evening. Katherine and

I had our last exam scheduled in two days. The warden might have felt the need to relax her vigilance and focus on her love life. After all, it was only a few girls and just one corridor to watch.

'Take it and don't worry about her,' Katherine said and placed the cup in my shivering hand, nudging me to take a sip. This wasn't exactly the ideal way to experiment with alcohol, but the cold in my bones was shredding my judgement apart. Speedily.

'Drink this and go back to finish revising your course. Don't waste time,' Anjali said.

I looked at the cup with such temptation that Katherine bent forward and placed it on my lips. I took a sip and a burning sensation hit the pit of my stomach, blurring my guilt away. Anjali and Natasha observed me closely while Katherine fixed me another drink. The knot of cold in my bones started to open bit by bit. I was oddly light on my feet by the third round, a lightness that lifted into an uncontrollable giggle.

The impending exam was soon forgotten under the spell of alcohol.

Anjali and Katherine were on the second round, while Natasha was still sipping her first drink like it was scalding tea. She had conservatively thrown the latch on our room's door and was constantly reminding us to keep the volume down.

'The guard downstairs might not hear us, but the girls next door will. Sania will surely complain,' Natasha warned us a couple of times. We started singing loudly when she warned us again, and it was as if her warning had conjured Reet, our neighbour, to our room. Natasha threw a quilt on us, slid the bottle under the bed and switched off the light at the first sharp knock on the door.

I peered out from under the quilt and saw how Natasha had sensibly jammed the door with her leg, to keep Reet from coming in.

'How's Riya? Did she manage to eat something?' Reet asked, with genuine concern in her voice.

Natasha nodded, probably to avoid exhaling the breath that reeked of alcohol.

'Sania's mother came this morning and brought some home-cooked food for all of us. But she is in a foul mood, not willing to share any.'

Reet's words against Sania sent a jolt of shock to my fuzzy brain. Reet and Sania had moved in together in the second year, after a couple of rounds of unsuccessful room-sharing stints. They had both taken to each other like fish to water, which had come as a surprise to me, considering their polar opposite natures. The tiny-framed Reet, with her warm smile, and the strikingly gorgeous and snobbish Sania were like water and fire together.

Sania was not only my peer in the programme; she was also my biggest competitor, as my desire to be the best in everything had often clashed with hers. This competition between us had killed any chance of friendship. We were both painfully aware of our feelings for each other, yet we were silent about them. But last year, Sania and my animosity had taken an unexpected turn when our project coordinator pointed out that our project reports were word by word the same.

Sania had copied my project report that I had inadvertently left unattended in the computer lab *one afternoon. But she wouldn't accept it. Consequently, we both had to rewrite the report. Sania's performance had dropped considerably over the last few months but stealing the project report was an unexpected low. I had not forgiven her. And the painstaking memory of rewriting the entire report overnight always rekindled my desire for revenge.*

Just when I was wondering why Reet sounded so pissed off with her beloved roommate, she said, 'My dad is here to pick me up. He got late because of the fog. Sania is alone and a bit gloomy. Call her over to study together, she might get some food along.'

Reet was still looking out for Sania and sounded concerned for her. But I had no such feelings for the mean girl who had refused to share food with a shivering classmate, that too when her mother might have brought extra food for all of us, which she always did.

The mention of unlimited supply of food in Sania's room lit up a million greedy neurons in my brain.

It had seemed like such harmless greed at the time.

* * *

Riya's computer flashed a low-battery warning and died on her. She plugged it back and waited for it to come back to life. The crisp first draft gave her a new high. She once again googled the name of the literary agents who had favourited her tweet. They were the big names in the industry, the most powerful gatekeepers who could open an entirely new world for her.

I will finish the story, come what may. And what are disclaimers in books for if they cannot save an author's ass!

Natasha Gupta Lim
26 Siglap Road, Singapore

'You are dropping them to school again?' Rick asked, in a cold voice.

Shouldering her work bag, Natasha ignored Rick's question and called a cab, keeping an eye on her phone for the Uber notification. She wasn't willing to give up. The big school bus, with its adult-sized seatbelts, wasn't exactly toddler-friendly. It felt like a harness around a child's neck. It was much easier for her to drop the kids off at school than to endlessly worry about their safety.

Rick sighed and left the house without kissing her goodbye. He didn't like the idea of Natasha obsessing about the kids' safety, especially when it affected her work. Rick had Natasha's best interests in mind; only his priorities were different.

Natasha texted 'Sorry' to Rick from the car and got an instant reply.

'Take it easy, babes. You looked all worked up this morning. I suggest you focus on your new role and stop fretting about the kids. And if something else is bothering you, please tell.'

She replied, 'Nothing at all.'

Rick hated it when she kept things from him, and he had made it clear at the very start of their relationship. His stinking-with-betrayal first marriage had made him a torch-bearer of truth in every relationship. Rick's soft looks and mild temperament could deceive others, but Natasha had seen the steely resolution beneath it. The theft of a ten-dollar bill had cost their previous house help her job.

'I can tolerate anything, but a lie,' were Rick's final words before he fired her, essentially getting her deported back to the Philippines. The only reason Natasha had not argued with him was that his words had set off a lightning bolt of fear in her own heart.

That night was her ten-dollar theft. But Rick wasn't looking for it, so he wouldn't find it. She had to make sure that he never did.

'Ma'am, is it where you want to alight?' the cab driver asked.

Natasha shook off her ruminations and walked into her office, leaving her fears outside the office door. The endless dings of her emails efficiently muted the alarm bells sounding in her head, and the faint rumble of office chatter soon silenced them completely.

After three hours of back-to-back meetings, Natasha called home, but today, the boys' back-from-school voices did not feel refreshing. The memory of the graveyard still clung to her like a sweat-soaked T-shirt.

Anjali's steely calm, Riya's art of putting the day behind her, Katherine's impetuousness or the combination of all three would have worked as a charm, drifting her away from the guilt that hurt like an old wound getting stabbed again. But the ghost of unspoken guilt hung over their friendship. A walk on their wild sides had tarnished everything.

She launched WhatsApp and got startled by a newly formed group, created by Anjali this time. Natasha had spent her workout hour cleaning up her phone. She had deleted the group that the hacker had created using her phone number. Also, she had installed a few basic anti-hacking tools to add another layer of security. However, the group was back and had formed a distinct shape. It was called 'The Ouija Group'. It had a display pic too: four hands playing Ouija.

She read the messages on the group and compulsively picked at a piece of dried skin on her lip.

Anjali: *I want to talk about that night. So that we can get closure on it and be friends again.*
Katherine: *Are you sure you want to talk about it? Here?*
Riya: *Hi Katherine and Anjali. How are you guys? Yes, Anjali, I agree we should get over this and be friends again. I miss you all.*
Katherine: *Anjali, remember we promised to never discuss it?*
Anjali: *I won't talk about Ouija. I want to talk about Sania and what might have happened to her.*
Riya: *@Anjali, I reckon you have a theory. Twenty years late though, but let's hear it out!*
Katherine: *WTF Anjali? I tried calling you. Why are you not taking my call? Riya, I called you too. Answer my calls, damn it!!!*
Katherine left the group.

Natasha had pinched her lip way too hard; it was oozing blood. She wiped it away with a tissue and read the message thread again. None of them would have opened this Pandora's box; so the hacker must have initiated the conversation, pretending to be one of them.

Natasha called Anjali. She was still online, but she didn't answer the call. Natasha texted her instead: 'Call me back!!'

Natasha's heart was beating in her throat. She sipped some water to moisten her parched throat. A minute later, she received Katherine's call.

Was she behind all this?

They hadn't talked in years. Time, family and careers had drifted them apart, and whatever efforts Natasha made to bridge the gap were all one-sided. Time had changed their friendship but had not touched Katherine's impetuousness at all.

'Is Anjali in India? Do you know? Can she possibly be at the same place as Riya?' asked Katherine, with her quick-as-mercury temperament. She was clearly beyond social niceties. Natasha kept herself calm and made an attempt to slow Katherine down.

'Hey! How are you? Anjali is in London. Are you in touch with Riya?'

But Katherine's train had already left the station.

'Someone hacked their WhatsApp accounts. The IP address shows the location as our old hostel in Kurukshetra. Do you know what that can mean?' Katherine asked.

Natasha swallowed the new piece of information with a lump in her throat.

Why was the hacker bringing the dead out of the coffin?

'Are you there, Natasha?' Katherine asked.

'So, someone at the college knows about that night?'

The silence on the other end of the phone line meant that Katherine was grappling for words. As was Natasha.

'Unless some other forces are at play,' Katherine said in a low whisper. Her words left Natasha perplexed. 'What forces, Katherine?' Katherine paused, stammered and then strung her words together. 'I caught Janice, my daughter, playing Ouija. I shouldn't have interrupted the game, but I did.'

It took Natasha a minute to understand that Katherine's guilt and her fear of the occult had connected the two events together. She couldn't hide her surprise and asked sarcastically, 'You are kidding, right? One moment you are telling me that all our accounts are hacked and another moment you are blaming it on the paranormal.'

This time Katherine didn't take long to reply. 'Well, you know how I feel about that night. About her.' Natasha shook her head in disbelief and said, 'Please, Kath. Let's try and reach Anjali and Riya, okay? We will work together, find the hacker, and get past this, all right?' She had no intention of ending the call this way. But informing Anjali and Riya was far more important than nursing Katherine's ridiculous superstitions.

How could Katherine still believe in all this?

She called Anjali again, and when the call went unanswered she called Riya after much contemplation. Natasha was surprised that even after twenty years, Riya's decision to take a lateral transfer, soon after that night, felt like a betrayal. There were so many questions Natasha wanted to ask Riya, so many grudges she wanted to put into words. But asking a question would start a domino effect, and this was not exactly the time for all that, so she decided to stick to the topic.

'Riya, Natasha here. Can we talk?' she asked.

'Yes, of course.'

'Your phone is hacked. I mean our phones are hacked.'

Riya took a minute before responding. 'Oh! That explains the formation of the group.'

'So you haven't read the messages on the group?' Natasha asked.

'What messages?'

'WhatsApp group messages. Are we not on the same page?'

'No, we aren't. My computer was compromised. But my phone . . . Hang on. Holy shit, the hacker accessed my phone too . . .'

But Natasha's panic didn't let Riya finish. 'Riya, what are you saying? Our other devices are hacked too? This is serious. I need to inform others.'

'Not sure if there is cause for panic. Because strangely, the hacker didn't mess with anything on my machine . . . other than . . . a piece of my writing . . .'

The pause between Riya's words was so oddly familiar. She was hiding something.

'What writing?' Natasha asked.

'Nothing that concerns you all,' Riya said in a defensive tone that sounded way too familiar.

There were twenty years between them, yet Natasha could sense deceit in Riya's voice.

Did Riya just lie to her? Or was it Natasha's own guilt that had forged a fresh pathway of suspicion through her mind?

Katherine D'Souza
38 City Apartments, New York

This isn't happening was Katherine's first thought. *This isn't Anjali* was her second, and *No way it's Riya* was the conclusive one.

Immediately, she called Anjali and Riya, all thanks to whosoever had put the contact details together. They didn't answer their phones, even though they were online, and that's when her doubts were confirmed.

A hacker. A hacker who was novice enough to mess with Katherine. She felt her adrenaline pumping like never before.

I will give this piece of shit a tough time.

Within minutes, Katherine was in Anjali's account and then in Riya's. Their Gmail accounts highlighted remote user activity. She launched the IP address hacker. Bingo. Riya's and Anjali's messages were originating from the same IP address. Now, all she needed to do was to track the location and get into the hacker's server.

She was determined to find the location and let the cyber police beat the shit out of the hacker. She would personally see to it that it happened. Katherine entered the IP address into the system and waited for it to pinpoint the server's location. However, the coordinates took the wind out of her sails: the location indicated her old hostel back in India.

The college server had to be almost inviolable, not something that any self-taught hacker could access for some cheap thrills or as part of an extortion plan. She used the primary set of tools to attack the server. Nothing moved. She upped her game with no success and stopped before she could set off any serious alarms. She wasn't going to jeopardize her professional reputation for this. Not yet.

'A ghost in the wires' was the symbolic phrase used for hackers, and she knew how to conquer them all. But the hostel's IP address had steered her fears in an unforeseeable direction. Her fears started to shift rapidly, like sunlight glinting off water. If the hacker was skilled enough to enter the college's platform, he or she would have cleared the tracks, leaving only the breadcrumbs they wanted Katherine to find.

So, leading her to the college was deliberate.

But why go back to college? Why mention that night?

The memory of that night made her shudder. She clutched the crucifix hanging around her neck, the four pointed edges of the cross pierced into her skin as she called Natasha and got another earful from her, for her 'illogical superstitions'.

But how come the hacker appeared exactly on the same day when she witnessed Janice playing Ouija?

A client call was due in an hour, but Katherine's mind was trapped, circling like a hamster in its wheel. There was only one way to calm it.

Smoke.

She drove to the mart, bought a pack of cigarettes, pulled one stick out and dumped the rest of the pack in the rubbish bin. Keeping the rest would have meant going back to smoking. One was enough to calm her mind. She was not an addict. Not any more.

It was Katherine's first cigarette in four years, and a crisp drag was enough to calm her nerves. The ease was short-lived, however. As she drove home, the lingering aftertaste of tobacco pushed her further down the rabbit hole.

It reminded her of Sid.

'Try this, KD?' Sid had asked when they were in their final year of engineering.

Katherine and Sid were childhood friends, and they knew each other's every thought as surely as lifelong ballet partners in a pas de deux. Unlike Katherine's average dusky Indian looks, Siddhartha Kapoor, aka Sid, was exceptionally good-looking, fair and tall. His astonishingly dark eyes and chiselled face radiated a charm and charisma that made him everyone's favourite, while Katherine lurked in his shadow, falling deeper in love with him. But Sid's popularity or army of friends never came between their friendship. He never left Katherine alone, especially after her mother's untimely death. Mathew, Katherine's brother, or Sid—one of them was always there with Katherine, following her like a shadow. And as luck would have it, Sid and Katherine's studying together had landed them in the same college too.

Or was it Katherine's secret power of intention?

Sid had started smoking by the beginning of the third year, but he had invited Katherine for a smoke only in the final year, around the job placement time, when her nervousness had hit the roof. She had been in a constant state of anxiety after Sania's death, but the ongoing placement drive had snapped a vulnerable nerve.

'This will help you relax,' Sid had said.

Anjali had tried stopping her, but Katherine ignored her friend and inhaled the first waft of nicotine into her lungs, just to give Sid company. Sid was right, as always;

the nicotine had magically relaxed her taut nerves. However, before Katherine could stop, smoking had become a habit.

Or was it her excuse to be alone with Sid for as much time as possible?

An email notification on her phone broke Katherine's train of thought and brought her back to the present. It was like a blow to her abdomen. A severe one.

Hello Katherine,

Did you see the teaser of Riya's latest? Let me make it easy for you. Here you go:
'Four college friends. An innocent Ouija prank. But the victim winds up dead the next morning.'
And guess what's the name of Riya's new baby? THAT NIGHT.
Did you contribute to the story? After all, you played a prominent role in the real story, no?

Sania Malik

The sender's name had caught Katherine's attention much before the content in the body of the email could. She inhaled and exhaled a few times to gather the little pieces of herself and switched to autopilot. She expanded the message header to see the sender's address, with tears stinging the back of her eyes. She wasn't surprised: WhathappenedtoSania@iotk.com, on the college's server.

Katherine drew out a breath, but it escaped into a sigh instead.

Anjali Kapoor
23 Park Street, London

Anjali read and reread the WhatsApp messages that were sent from her phone in the wee hours of the morning, when she was knocked out by her medicine. Whoever was impersonating her and Riya knew how they spoke. At least it was enough to fool Katherine, temporarily.

All of it had hit a vulnerable nerve.

One allegation and Anjali's hard-earned position would vanish. And it might hurt her divorce proceedings too. But, worrying about it wouldn't help. She had to know what was going on.

She picked up the Post-it from the table and followed the instructions she had noted down. Simple things, like deleting WhatsApp from her laptop, changing the password of her computer and reconfiguring a new Wi-Fi password, were easy enough. But the rest of the jargon-loaded statements were an array of herculean tasks. Anjali neither had the skills nor the desire to get her hands dirty. She was big on outsourcing. So the to-do list went into Anjali's work bag along with her computer.

There was one last thing she needed to do before deleting everything out of her system and her devices. She closed her eyes and uttered it aloud: 'Sania Malik, I am sorry.' Her words felt like a piece of hot coal simmering on the tip of her tongue. A moment longer and her breath would have caught fire.

She unlocked her phone, tapped on the college folder on her cloud storage and began browsing through the photos. She had recently scanned and uploaded all of them in an attempt to organize her old memories. Anjali swiped compulsively until her eyes lost focus and the images turned blurry. Her hand froze when Sania's fair skin, sharp features and arched eyebrows came alive on her phone screen. She swiped a little more and found another one.

The one with a hijab-clad Sania, her pretty face trapped in a scarf yet shining bright, like a ray of light filtering through the trees. This was a click from one of the hostel parties. Sania was standing with Reet, her roommate. She wore a subtle shade of pink on her lips and dark lines of kohl around her eyes, a finishing touch to nature's masterpiece. Anjali had never seen anyone so beautiful and yet so deceptive. Just as her head started to swim with nausea, a text message diverted her attention: 'Watching my photos won't help. Finding the reason behind my death might. Sania.'

Anjali felt the ingredients of panic brewing in her gut. The hacker was watching her live. The dirty game of blackmail was going way too far. She had to find the hacker before it was too late.

She hastily changed into her work clothes, ran a finger through her tousled black curls and sped to office. For once, she was glad that her home was a few blocks away from her office at the Shard.

Anjali logged in to her work machine and requested for IT security assistance. The desktop support team jumped into action and in a span of a few minutes, a fresh-from-college guy was gawping at her table and at the stunning view of London from her cabin. The young man was clearly inspired and envious at the same time.

'I need help in encrypting my personal machine and phone. I have already disabled the passwords, etc.,' Anjali said and handed him the devices. Anjali had taken backup, deleted all the apps with built-in passwords and all personal messages before handing her devices to this stranger.

She left the young techie to battle with the hacker while she went back to her mailbox. There was a merger in two days, and Anjali was already starting her day late. But before she could reply to the first mail, the techie had reached a conclusion. 'Anjali, your devices are attacked by an experienced hacker, or, I must say, a team of hackers. I found a difficult-to-spot malware. The hacker has invested some serious quid to continuously monitor you. I suggest I take your devices back, do an extensive clean-up, reinstall the operating systems and add a robust anti-spyware programme.'

A bubble of panic pushed itself up her throat. *I can't pull work people into my mess.*

'Ma'am, are you with me?' the techie asked and pushed his blonde hair back with his bony fingers. Anjali took a moment more to reflect on this, without giving away the panic brewing in her heart.

'Thanks, but this seems to be a lot of work, and I hate asking personal favours at work. I will handle it,' she said, forced a thank-you smile and gave this handsome, nervous man a moment to excuse himself.

Anjali let her facade drop only after the IT consultant had left the room, having recommended that she get the cyber-crime department of the police involved in this. She calmed her ragged breath, lifted her work laptop and read the two sticky notes placed under it:

> Anjali, hiding something on purpose is just the same as telling lies. People around you deserve to know the truth.

> Watching my photos won't help. Finding the reason behind my death might. Sania.

Anjali had deleted the texts from her phone before writing them on Post-its. She wished she could delete them from her memory with similar ease.

But Anjali might need a factory reset of her system, while others could do with selective cleaning. After all, she was guiltier than the rest. And now, someone other than her also knew about it.

December 19, 1997
Girls' Hostel
Institute of Technology, Kurukshetra, India

No literature class teaches you how to write a suicide note.

When you have to write one, your words fail you as much as your life does.

But what are goodbyes without a parting note?

Devils made me do it. But I got them first.

Alvida

3

Two Can Keep a
Secret If One Is Dead

Riya Banerjee
Malabar Hill, Mumbai

Riya's phone rang again. This time it was Katherine. Riya braved herself for a stormy conversation. There was a lot unsaid between them, and Katherine was the one who could nurse her grudges for eternity and express them too. Riya hoped against hope that maybe her jumble-of-nerves, once-a-lifetime-away roommate had a drastic mental makeover.

'So, you are hanging us out to dry once again?' Katherine asked instead of exchanging pleasantries.

Katherine hasn't changed, not even a bit.

Riya tried her luck with calming Katherine down. 'How are you, Katherine? It's been ages. It's so good to hear your voice.'

'Fuck being nice, Riya, and let's get straight to the topic,' Katherine said.

The only way forward in this conversation was to let Katherine's anger fizzle out. 'Okay, let's unload your gun. Shoot,' Riya said and waited for the blizzard of accusations to swamp her. But Katherine's words sounded like a melody instead.

'Your first book was a great read, unless that too was a story picked from real life. So how about you stick to fiction? And you seriously thought you could get away with publishing the story about that night? You seriously have some guts, Riya Banerjee,' Katherine said, inhaling sharply to announce her burning anger.

Life had not changed Katherine much; under the veneer of logical tech smarts, she was still ruled by her emotions. Riya was willing to take any bashing from Katherine, be it for leaving the college, abandoning her at the hostel or bringing the dead out of the closet.

Riya was at fault once again and there was no turning away from it.

'I was not planning to publish the story. I had just written it to get closure on that night,' Riya justified, grappling for words.

'And you will get your closure by announcing it to the world and tweeting about it?' Katherine asked and paused for Riya's response.

'I thought you must have figured out by now that it's the work of a hacker . . .'

Before Riya could complete her sentence, Katherine had jumped in again. 'Okay, let's assume that there is a hacker who tweeted the story idea, but you were the one writing it, right? No one would have known about it if you had not written it. Riya, get this straight, we are not characters from your book. We are real people, and we live a real life where the revelation of the past can shatter relations like glass hitting the floor. We have husbands, kids and jobs, and in case you have forgotten, your spinning tales had cost us a lot that night. And then you left us stranded . . .' Katherine said.

Katherine had again mixed up everything in her head, placing all the blame on Riya. Riya was willing to accept her mistakes, but she wasn't ready to shoulder the entire responsibility for that night.

'We all were equally responsible for what happened that night. And I did not return to the hostel because of my father's stroke. I am sure you would have done the same if you were forced into my shoes. Just the timing was bad,' Riya justified.

'No, Riya. I wouldn't have done any of it. Especially, fucking dig into the past, break a promise and turn that night into a money-making machine. And, not to mention, at the expense of others,' Katherine said.

Before the accusation in Katherine's words could sting her, a doubt crept into Riya's mind: Who told Katherine about her new manuscript? Was Katherine following her on Twitter? Was she stalking her?

Riya decided to spit out her doubt rather than letting it simmer in her heart.

'Okay, I did write the story. I thought about getting it published, too. It was my way of getting closure on that night. But why would I jump the gun and tweet about it? Moreover, I am not even halfway through the story, and I have not reached the point where we could get in trouble. But the hacker seems to have linked Sania's death to our playing Ouija. How can someone do that? Unless you read the story secretly and panicked. Katherine, are you behind the blackmail? Is this your way to stop me from working on this story? You are an ethical hacker, supposedly, and you could make things difficult for me at the drop of a hat.'

Katherine's reply came after a pause.

Was it shock or fear of getting caught?

'Holy shit, Riya. You think I am doing this?' Katherine's animated, loud, high-pitched voice pushed Riya to move the phone away from her ear.

'Maybe. I mean, you can hack our accounts like nobody else,' Riya said, giving Katherine a taste of her own medicine.

'Really, Riya?'

'Yeah, really, Katherine.'

'So nothing has changed, right? You are still good at twisting any logic with your carefully picked words,' Katherine said in a huff. But her soft tone indicated that her anger had evaporated considerably.

It was funny how a familiar comment passed between old friends could send you back to college life.

A sweetness welled up in Riya's mouth while she continued the charade.

'And you are still the calm and cool Katherine who saw the tweet and panicked?'

'What?' Katherine asked.

'My Twitter was hacked, and someone used it as a platform to reveal my story idea,' Riya explained.

'And you thought I did that to stop you? That would be the dumbest way to stop you from writing it, by announcing it to the world,' Katherine argued.

'Point well taken,' Riya said, but before she could finish, Katherine again cut her mid-sentence and said, 'But what's troubling me the most is: Why would someone go to the extent of hacking a college server to threaten us? That's not an easy platform to get into. The hacker is either a genius or is bloody serious about this.'

'You mean revenge?' Riya asked, mentally drawing up a list of friends and acquaintances she had left behind in college that winter.

'I don't know. Probably someone who was waiting up for us to make this one mistake,' Katherine said.

Riya felt a wave of guilt wash over her. 'And I had made that first mistake, by writing that story,' she said.

'Yes, you did.' Katherine's words sounded more like an acceptance than an accusation. Riya breathed in the sense of familiarity. Talking to Katherine was still the same, like there was no time lost between them, like they had just talked yesterday.

It felt like listening to an old favourite number. The lyrics had long been forgotten, or so she thought until she started singing, surprising herself by remembering every beat and every word. Katherine, Natasha and Anjali were that forbidden favourite song in Riya's life. The song she wanted to sing again.

Riya made another attempt to make it right between them.

'Kath, I didn't ditch you all. On the contrary, I had no say in the matter back then. My mother was hell-bent on the transfer and after seeing Baba half-dead, the least I could do was to come over the weekends to help her, and that would not have been possible if I'd stayed in

Kurukshetra. But I am sorry for leaving you guys alone,' Riya clarified.

Katherine paused for a bit, and then changed the topic.

'Delete the story, will you? And get some IT guy to add some extra security to your devices. I will send you the details. Okay?' Katherine said. The iota of doubt in Katherine's voice caught her attention. Or was it not doubt but fear? Riya decided to chase it.

'Sure. Katherine, can I ask you something?'

'Shoot.'

'Do you still pin the blame on the occult for what happened that night?' Riya asked, prodding gently.

'It's a matter of belief. You can question God's existence, and I can light a candle in the church every day; we both may be right or might not be,' Katherine said, her voice wavy with hesitation and self-doubt.

So Riya was right. Katherine was considering the play of the occult in this. What if the hacker knew about her deep-rooted fears too? Riya decided to put some sense into her.

'Kath, gods and devils are internal constructs. We did not call upon any demons that night. Perhaps we became one,' Riya said and heard a sigh at the other end of the line.

'Well, like always, let's agree to disagree and not discuss that night. Looks like the promise we made needs a vow-renewal,' Katherine said.

But Riya was determined to guide her back to the realm of rationality. 'You can reach the hacker faster than us. Technically, you are stronger than the three of us together. Please don't let your fears guide you.'

Katherine's pause was longer than usual.

'To be honest, the mention of Sania Malik in the hacker's mail did stir some dormant guilt, waking some illogical fears. And now that you pointed out that there were not enough clues in your manuscript to link Sania's death to the prank . . . So, yeah, my mind is going to places it shouldn't.'

Riya argued, 'It's easy for anyone to put two and two together. One trip to the college and Sania's suicide would come up. It's an urban legend, and I am sure it is exploited enough to scare the shit out of the newcomers in the hostel.'

'Could be' was all Katherine said. She sounded annoyed, upset and humiliated. The conflict of her own beliefs was eating her up, all thanks to the hacker. The geek surely knew which buttons to press on each of them: Katherine's superstition, Riya's ambition.

But Riya would not let that happen.

She tried again. 'As far as I know, a ghost cannot interact with your physical environment. It can only make you do things by messing up with your mind. It surely can't hack accounts and tweet. We have a hacker, Kath, and you can help us find them.'

'True that. So why are you wasting my time then? Talk to you later,' Katherine said with a chirp in her voice and disconnected the call.

Riya spent the next hour following the set of instructions that Katherine had sent in the mail to make her devices hack-proof. The last thing on Riya's to-do-list was to hit the delete button on her latest work. Riya fired a print and dragged the Scrivener project to her backup device.

Hold on to your horses, Ms Banerjee, there will be a right time for it. Soon. But the agents who have requested for the manuscript won't wait for the hacker to be found.

Grief rolled through her body; she felt an ache equivalent to that of a new mother holding a stillborn in her arms. Her baby was dead before it could come to life. Riya collected a pile of papers that had dropped to the printer tray and filed them into a transparent folder.

Memories of a stillborn.

Riya was taken aback by her own vulnerability. Where was the Riya who could rush into life and wrest from it what she could? This crisis had made her give up so easily. Or had it peeled off the mask of strength she had been wearing over her fragile edifice? She sat there shaking her legs with an impatience that was difficult to tame.

Probably, she should focus on writing her CV. But before she could explain her year-long break on her CV, Katherine's words rolled back into her memory. *Your first book was a great read.* So, Katherine did read her work and liked it.

Riya couldn't resist texting Katherine: 'Like you really read my book?'

Katherine was typing and Riya's heart was doing somersaults in her chest. She was that starved for friends, and for success and praise too.

'I found it in the trash bin. So, for the sake of old times, I rescued the book and managed to survive through all the 310 pages.'

'And?'

Why the hell was Katherine taking so long to type?

'And that's some decent story,' Katherine texted.

Some decent story coming from Katherine was equivalent to a five-star review on Goodreads. Back then, the four of them never praised each other. They only insulted each other and pulled each other's leg. It was a trait they had developed in the first six weeks of their ragging time in the college and hostel.

The four of them were each other's best critics, yet they never hesitated to stick their necks out for each other when needed.

A ping on her phone brought Riya back to the present.

'That doesn't mean you can write about that night. I am sure you can come up with something better . . .' Katherine texted.

But that's not how it works, Katherine!

A story is a demon that chases you until you trap it in words. Riya had to tame the demon. She stacked up the printed manuscript and began to read.

* * *

That Night: December 19, 1997

'How about we invite Sania for a board game?' I asked.

'Who can stare for longer is the only game Sania would know,' Anjali said. She was drunk as a skunk by now.

'Anything that can keep you guys from screaming and singing is okay with me. You are going to wake everyone up,' Natasha scolded.

'Have you guys ever played Ouija?' I asked. They all looked at me. Anjali shook her head while Natasha threw

a nervous smile at me. However, Katherine warned, 'Ouija and alcohol should not be mixed. In fact, it's no game to play at this hour and definitely not as a prank.'

Katherine had a strange belief in the occult which I could not fathom. But we weren't going to play Ouija, and that's all that was needed to win Katherine over.

'We won't call a ghost. We will just invite Sania and act like there is a ghost in the coin. A hungry ghost that needs food. You get me?'

Slow smiles spread across Anjali's and Natasha's faces, beckoning me to continue.

'Sania is religious. Hopefully, she'd be superstitious too, and her fears could deliver a fresh stock of home-cooked food into our hungry stomachs,' I said and looked at Anjali for support.

'If it can get you something to eat, I am game,' Anjali said.

Katherine looked at Natasha, who silently approved it. It was three versus one. Katherine gave in. She rummaged through her stationery supplies and handed me a chart paper, a marker and a fifty-paisa coin. I pushed away the piles of quilt from the bed, placed the paper in the centre and handed the marker to Katherine. Her hand momentarily hesitated, but she swallowed her discomfort and began to draw.

The first sign that appeared on the paper was a cross, similar to the crucifix hanging around her neck. Then she wrote YES and NO on the left- and right-hand corners of the paper. She paused to recall the details and then filled the paper with letters and numbers. The paper looked like a kindergartener's homework sheet, with A–Z and

0–9 all cramped in the centre—a twin arc of the alphabet, followed by a straight row of numbers just beneath the arc.

Katherine took her time to write the word 'Goodbye' under the digits. I had only seen an Ouija board once before in my life, and if not for Katherine, I would have missed out that tiny detail. But nothing ever escaped her sharp eyes.

'Only four people can play at one time, so I am not playing. You guys will have to take turns to ask the questions and . . .' But before she could complete her sentence, Anjali jumped in.

'You don't fool me for a second. You are just scared. Otherwise, if you were so against Ouija, you wouldn't have been able to draw the whole thing from memory.'

Katherine frowned. 'My granny used to communicate with the dead this way. Ouija is not a joke, and trust me, I have learnt my lesson the hard way. I almost got someone killed once. So yes, I am scared.'

Anjali groaned and said, 'The Drama Queen.'

I had never seen Anjali that angry and vocal. But none of us were acting the way we used to. The alcohol in our veins had made us different people.

'May I remind you all that we are not playing Ouija. We are playing Sania. And mind you, her roommate requested us to invite her over. We are just being exceptionally good neighbours,' I said and winked.

'Good neighbours like India and Pakistan!' Anjali said and broke into another fitful giggle.

Katherine looked at me nervously, tipped a stream of whisky into her cup and replaced the lid on the bottle.

Natasha walked to Katherine, took the bottle from her hand and placed it on the table. It was a message to stop drinking—we were all pretty messed up.

'I will just ask her once to come and be with us. Hopefully, she would agree because it's just the five of us on this floor tonight. I won't force her,' Natasha said and went to bring Sania. Natasha was the mildest among us, and her care and love was legendary, a quality admired by everyone at the hostel. Sania too. Moreover, Natasha was the only one in the group who could hold a conversation with Sania for more than a minute. And the look on Natasha's face meant she was willing to do anything to keep me warm.

She was going to bring Sania.

Katherine excused herself to the washroom. I knew she would drag her feet because she wasn't keen on playing. She believed in the spirits. Her faith in good and evil was equally profound, thanks to her mystically minded grandmother.

Natasha and Sania came to the room, but Katherine was still in the washroom. She was probably hoping that Sania's refusal would end this all before it began. However, I was in no mood to give up.

'You sleep in these? And tell me what's with your new look? Whose attention are you seeking?' I asked and tugged Sania's hijab down, exposing her silken dark-brown hair. The venom that I had collected for her over the three years was ready to come out. All thanks to the alcohol.

'At least it is better than wearing the same hoody every night. Did you guys manage a buy-two-and-get-two-free deal somewhere?' Sania asked with a wicked glint in her eyes and pointed to our legendary grey hoodies.

Before I could come up with a witty reply, she had caught the whiff of alcohol in the air.

'What's that smell? Are you guys drinking in the hostel? Riya, really, I thought you were worried about the EMT paper. Is this the secret for your extraordinary scores?' Sania asked mockingly.

Her remark was like a lit match in gunpowder.

'Try stealing my reports again, this time you might get lucky,' I said and shot a cold stare at her. But before Sania could react to my accusation, Anjali jumped in to defuse the tension, 'A little relaxation is good for the mind. One game and you can go to your room and continue studying.'

By now, Sania was almost leaving the room, she turned back and shot a furtive glance at the Ouija sheet spread on my bed. Her eyes jumped over us, gauging the scene like a hunter.

Katherine, who was listening from the doorway, said, 'Nobody will force you, Sania.' She had thrown another spanner. However, Sania's mind was visibly oscillating between thrill and fear.

'Come, Sania, you won't regret it,' Anjali said and gently nudged her to the bed. The slur in Anjali's speech was becoming increasingly prominent. Sania probably noticed it too. She took a step away from the bed and said, 'Anjali, you are not in your senses. I am scared of all this, so I'd better go to my room.'

I wasn't ready to lose out. The thought of revenge and home-cooked food was creating an evil concoction.

'We're going to play Ouija no matter what. You can be alone in your room while we play it, or you can hang out with us. Sometimes the spirits do wander, and our rooms are barely separated by this thin wall,' I said and tapped on the wall to bring home the point.

Sania caved. Glumly, she sat down on Katherine's bed and waved, as if to say, 'Do what you want.' Anjali grabbed the opportunity and said, 'Okay. So we are all set to go. Let's start with asking some serious questions, like about exams and their outcomes. Excites you, Sania? Do you want to know your grades much before you finish your exam? We do it before every term break and the predictions have never disappointed us. Isn't it, girls?'

Sania scanned our faces with a solemn intensity. She was still teetering on the border. I had to pull her to my side before Katherine could flip Sania's decision.

'How about we play one round with Sania. If she isn't comfortable, we quit. Agree all?' I suggested.

My proposition made it easy for all of us. Sania nodded a yes, making me dizzy with happiness. I signalled Katherine to light the candle and bring it to us. She lit the candle and turned off the light. The candlelight filtered through Katherine's unruly hair, casting a shadow on the wall behind her. It felt like a scene straight out of a paranormal thriller. I stole a glance to see the impact it had caused on Sania.

The hammer had hit the nail.

Her gaze danced along with Katherine's dancing shadow on the wall.

I had played many pranks in the hostel: from jumping out on girls from the dark corners of the hostel to rattling *my Kathak ghungroos outside someone's room in the middle of the night. But never ever had I messed with Sania so far. She wasn't the one who would take any joke in the spirit of the game. However, today she had walked into our trap willingly.*

Why?

I glanced at Sania's calm face to understand why she was here and noticed that Sania was studying the weakest link in our group. Before I could act on it, Sania asked, 'Have you played this game ever, Katherine?'

'My granny is a psychic, Sania. She can read the future and talk to the dead,' Katherine said and tilted the candle on the base of the inverted steel glass. The flame flickered as beads of molten wax bled from the candle. Katherine secured the candle on the base and placed the glass on the hardback cover of Murder on the Orient Express.

She knew that I hated it when someone played around with my books, but she was giving it back to me for starting the game of Ouija, which she hated in equal measure. I got up from the bed and suggested, 'Let's join the beds and make space to spread the Ouija sheet out.'

The engineering drawing board that had been out of use for ages came to rescue my Agatha Christie. I placed the board on the bed, pinned the Ouija chart on it and placed the candle next to it. By now, Katherine had lit another candle that sat neatly on her writing desk. She pulled the chair closer to the bed and perched on it. She was clearly avoiding sitting too close to the Ouija. Sania had read Katherine's hesitation too.

'You are not playing?' Sania asked.

'Only four of us can play at one time,' Katherine said, masking her discomfort and annoyance. Thankfully, the room was blanketed with enough darkness to hide Katherine's giveaway expressions. Also, her head was hanging low as she was busy scribbling something under the candlelight, I waited for her to finish and guide us. She placed the paper in my hand and said, 'You have to summon the spirit using this chant.'

I read it aloud, 'If any holy spirits are passing by, please come and honour the board. We call you for peace and love.' I placed the piece of paper given by Katherine in my lap, rubbed my hand and asked, 'Ready for the game, everyone?'

Before anyone could reply, I had placed my pointer on the coin, keeping the major chunk of the coin under my skin, leaving only a quarter of it for the others. I gently tugged at the coin; I could easily move it. We chanted the lines given by Katherine and then I asked the spirit, 'Are you here?'

The coin gently moved to 'YES' and caught Sania's attention. 'Can I ask the first question?'

She wanted everything first. And today, I would let her act like a queen. The joke would be on her, though.

'Will I pass my exams this term?' she asked hesitantly.

I moved the coin swiftly and authoritatively, making her happy. YES.

'Will I complete my engineering?' she asked, not letting the next person take a turn.

I imperceptibly moved the coin.

YES.

Sania's grades had suffered considerably over the last six to seven months, but to suggest she would not be completing the programme was way too pessimistic. Before I could read between the lines, Sania had asked another question.

'Will I get what I want?' Sania asked, with a little more faith in the game this time.

I didn't move the coin. I was too engrossed in reading her mind.

'Will I be loved and wanted?' Sania tried again.

She had hijacked the game. What else was expected from her!

It was time to take charge. I moved the coin to YES and then to NO. Sania's face was suffused with disappointment. She seemed vulnerable, but mercy was not my thing, not when I was hungry, and she had loads of food. I looked at Anjali, our eyes met, and I beckoned her to take charge and steer the game to the previously sketched script.

'My turn. Tell us something about you. Are you a male or a female?' Anjali asked.

I played along and gently moved the coin to F.

A wave of disbelief touched Sania's face.

Anjali geared herself to generate questions on the go. All I had to do was match her imagination, and it wasn't something new for me. We were used to completing each other's sentences and reading each other's silences too. And we had honed our skills by playing pranks on each other for the last three years.

'Why are you here?' Anjali asked.

I looked at Katherine. I was scared that she would blow it all. But her eyes were liquid with fear, as if she had felt a presence draw near. I was feeling a tiny bit bad *for messing up with Katherine's fears in the process, but everything was fair in love, war and hunger.*

And there was revenge too.

I let Katherine sway between common sense and the paranormal. Just then, the coin started to move. It stopped and moved again. Katherine pulled her chair closer to the bed and started writing the letters pointed by the coin, until it became a full sentence.

'Revenge. And I am here to get it. I am outside your window.'

The tremble in Katherine's voice was the last nail in the coffin. A soft sigh escaped Sania's lips, but Anjali was still in the game.

'Open the curtain, Katherine. Let her see us.' Distantly, through the alcohol, I remembered our discussing a scary turn of events. Maybe Anjali was still following the script. I wasn't sure.

Katherine followed the instructions and opened the curtain. She placed the candle near the window, illuminating the word 'HELP' written on the glass. The letters trembled in the faint light of the candle.

In truth, while Katherine had gone to the washroom, I had used a red lipstick to write the message on the outside of the windowpane. Now it looked blood-red in the flickering light, and the mist on it had made it a bit runny, giving it a dramatic feel, like someone had scribbled it with blood.

Sania and Katherine were both frozen in fear.

A silent giggle crawled up my throat. I swallowed it back. Nothing could beat the joy of seeing your script coming to life. Sania had begun shaking. She was about to step away from the Ouija and break the trance when I stopped her.

'You can't break contact, or it will haunt us all!'

It was time to bring all my theatrical skills to action.

'How can we help you?' I asked, bringing a realistic tremble in my voice. The coin moved and started to form another sentence, which Katherine soon read with disbelief.

'Can I come inside the room?'

This definitely was not part of the script, but I couldn't help getting a little creative. Katherine fell back into the chair like a dead bird.

The best way to fight your fears is to fight it out. I had hoped that this incident would help Katherine grow out of her irrational fears.

Wish I had known what was waiting on the other side of the night.

But back then I was happy that the game of Ouija was going to yield more than what we expected.

Natasha's gaze slid from Katherine's face to mine. Anjali's eyes were on my face, too. I gave away nothing. I wasn't risking Sania reading my expressions. My friends had to use their own discretion to validate whether this was a real manifestation or I had all of them wrapped around my little finger.

I knew I had them all because the tightly held coin had turned wobbly like a loose tooth in a socket, ready to dislodge any minute. I wasn't worried. Anjali and Natasha would catch my drift in a minute. The four of us knew each other's every tell and every quirk as well as we knew our own. Anjali got it first. Natasha's shoulders

relaxed next. I looked at Katherine, but she was blind to
our silent communication. Her eyes were locked on the
board just like Sania's.

'Are you here?' Anjali asked.

The coin moved to YES.

'Where are you?' Anjali asked.

In a husky, deep-throated growl, I answered, 'I am
here, inside her.'

* * *

A loud thud brought Riya back to the present. She turned
her head and found her maid pushing the nightstand, to
sweep under it. Riya's concentration was gone, but an
until-now-forgotten piece of the story surfaced in her
memory.

That night, in the middle of the Ouija drama, Anjali
had dropped a glass to catch Katherine's attention.
She had blinked her eyes. It was Anjali's way of telling
Katherine that they were still in the game. But what if
Sania got the message, too? What if she had decided to
play along, and what if she had told someone about the
prank?

In retrospect, Riya and her three friends were not
nearly as subtle.

The thought started to grow into full-blown suspicion.
That night, Sania must have told someone that they had
played a prank on her. But, unfortunately, the next
morning Sania was found dead. The bearer of her secret
might have blamed them for her death and was now
playing with them for some extortion or merely cheap

thrills or revenge. But he or she had no proof until the point when Riya had stupidly written everything down and barely changed the names.

Two names elbowed into her memory: Rahim Malik and Reet Singh.

Rahim Malik, Sania's distant cousin, was their senior at college and might have been on the campus that night. Sania would have somehow managed to phone him after the prank, maybe using the phone at the reception, complaining about them. Although Riya had never seen Sania interacting with him, she was not willing to take chances. Riya googled him, but before she could carry on with her line of investigation a text notification popped up: 'Answers you are finding are meant to be found within the group.'

Anjali Kapoor
23 Park Street, London

How the hell do people live alone?

Anjali wasn't excited about her newfound freedom. Her solitude confused her. With Sid, life was work, party, travel, drinks, and repeat. Without Sid, Anjali was lonely, running aimlessly, searching for food and company. Like an ant abandoned by its army.

Her thoughts were again running in a downward spiral. It was time to swallow her sleeping pill and get through another night. But tonight, she couldn't quite relinquish her grip on the day. She lay there, half-asleep and worrying, until a thud by the door jerked her out of bed.

Someone was in the house.

Anjali leapt to her bedroom door. It was shut and locked from the inside (to do so was her habit). She was safe. She placed her ear against the wood. There was a muffled sound of footsteps coming from outside; someone was rummaging through the things in the hall.

Her heart started to beat like a jackhammer. Had she not locked the main gate? Did she leave the window open?

The sound of heavy shoes pounded against the floorboard. The thump of her heart competed with the clacking of heels outside, and the one-knuckled knock on the door nearly made her pass out.

'Anjali, open the door. Why have you unplugged the doorbell? I need some papers. Did you move my files from the study?' Sid asked.

The fear-blindness passed. She was rattled, disoriented. Still scared.

'Please, Anjali. Open the door. The taxi is waiting,' Sid pleaded, with a sense of urgency. She gathered herself and opened the door. Her heart was still beating with the same anguish.

Sid's piercing gaze mapped her. The look on his face made her heart crack—it was a mixture of longing and regret. Her love stirred to life again. Distance had not extinguished it at all. He was still as handsome as she remembered, and today a peppery stubble traced the line of his jaw, radiating an air of dark sexiness.

Unloving Sid was as difficult as loving him. How am I even alive?

Before the silence between them could rip them apart or pull them together, Sid's words shattered it.

'You look cracking in my T-shirt,' he said with a fawning smile.

She felt a rush of weakness in her legs. She reminded herself: The idea of him is better than the reality.

Anjali chewed the inside of her cheek, partly in nervousness, partly in anger.

Sid read her mind. 'Don't be narky. I just came to get my passport; I have a flight to catch. May I?'

Anjali stepped away from the door before the tears could start to sting in her eyes. She didn't want Sid to go to Delhi, but she had no time or experience to help her mom run the small pita joint that Anjali's mother had started a couple of years ago. It was Sid's idea to start the joint, and he helped her mother in every way possible.

If he wasn't letting their separation affect her mother's business, Anjali had no right to complain.

She sat on the edge of the bed and watched Sid. He picked his files from the holdall bag in which Anjali had started packing Sid's things last weekend. His actions were swift and defined. She studied his face. The ruddiness that appeared after a drink or two was missing. He caught her staring at him; she looked away.

'I need my certs too. I have some interviews planned in Delhi,' he said.

She walked to him, bent over the bag and pulled out a file. She kept herself calm even though her heart was still hammering in her chest. Sid extended his arm to take the file but tucked her hair behind her ear instead.

A numbness crept into her body.

He came near her, touched the edge of the T-shirt she was wearing, and said, 'I want my T-shirt back. Now.'

His touch opened a new ache inside her.

You have gone down this street several times. Only to regret it later. Don't go there again.

'Please leave, Sid. Now,' she said. Her voice was as feeble as the squeak of a mouse. Sid ignored her request and walked to her. Anjali braved herself to push him away, but her hands were trembling. It would take all the self-control she had, to push him away.

'Anjali, why are you so stubborn? My life is hell without you,' he said in a soft, pleading whisper.

'Sid. Leave,' she replied in a voice that was barely audible to her.

Anjali closed her eyes and waited for the soft sound of Sid's footsteps to die away or for his desire to take over. And when Sid's footsteps retreated, she felt a fresh batch of oxygen flowing in her lungs. She hurried to the door after him. But this time, instead of opening it and shouting his name, she bolted it.

Anjali wiped the tears that had coursed down her cheeks and buried her face in her pillow. But Sid's fragrance in the linens added more life to her ache. She inhaled a little bit of him, turned around and lifted an old photo album she had found while packing Sid's belongings.

She had loaded all the photos on the cloud, yet she loved the tangible feel of the album in her hand. Tonight again, she escaped into her past, which was much more glorious than her present.

It was the second day of college. Anjali had just entered the college campus when she saw a handsome guy tugging at a girl's hair. They were too cool and too casual to be a couple. The mismatched clothes and oiled braids meant that Katherine was a fresher too. But before Anjali could steal a glance at Sid, he commanded, 'Eyes on the floor.'

She trained her eyes at her shoes. So what if it was only the second day of college? The dressing-down from the seniors had already set the ground rules—the most important one was to never look a senior in the eye.

'Introduce yourself,' Sid said with an air of confidence that only a senior could have. Anjali delivered her introduction like a pre-recorded message.

'Do you know this Bollywood number, "Tumse Milne Ko Dil Karta Hai"?' Sid asked.

'Yes, sir.' Anjali said.

'Then let's hear it out and pour some feelings into the song, like you are in love with me,' Sid commanded.

Anjali sang in a low whisper.

'Did not eat your breakfast today? You, Miss World, come here and sing along,' Sid said to a girl walking by with an orientation folder in her hand. Before they could finish the song, Sid had disappeared.

'Hi, I am Riya,' the girl standing next to Anjali had said. She was pretty as hell, even those mismatched clothes and oiled braids couldn't hide her flawless beauty. They walked to the academic building together and found a fair, plump and beautiful girl staring at the notice board. She turned around and said, 'You must be Anjali. I am Natasha, your roommate.'

'How do you know my name?' Anjali asked.

'The warden told me that my roommate is exceptionally tall. Took a wild guess that it must be you,' Natasha said. Before Anjali could respond to that, Katherine walked to them and said, 'And you must be Riya Banerjee. I heard I got lucky with the most beautiful girl being my roommate. Boys there want to swap rooms with me.'

'Sure, only if they agree to clean the room and wash my dirty laundry,' Riya replied, and they all high-fived each other almost impulsively.

And that day, with that joke, the four of them came together like the missing pieces of a jigsaw puzzle—sharing their all-India ranks in the entrance exam, their high school scores and the engineering branch they each got selected for.

'The guy who ragged you this morning wasn't our senior,' Katherine said at the dinner table in the mess. 'He is Sid, our batchmate. Must be with you and Natasha in the electronics branch,' Katherine said and looked at Anjali.

'You've got to be kidding. I thought he must be a senior. He definitely got me,' Anjali said.

'No, I am serious. He is my childhood friend and a pro in pulling a straight face, especially in a prank,' Katherine said with a tinge of pride.

'He will get it back soon,' Riya declared.

'Yes, he will,' Anjali said.

'Oh! I will give anything to see that happening,' Katherine added.

Natasha flashed her soft, subtle smile to confirm that she was in the game, and they high-fived each other again.

What started as a mission against Sid soon became an unbreakable friendship. In a week, they were thick as thieves—eating, sleeping and studying together. Before the first weekend at the hostel arrived, they knew every tiny detail about each other, and as the weeks passed by, the bubble of their intimacy grew thicker and thicker.

Sid's mischief had tied them with an invisible thread. And now, the hacker was pulling the strings of that thread to bring them closer to each other or break them apart. It was as though the mere thought had actually evoked the hacker. Her phone lit up with an anonymous message: 'Check your mail!!! Sid was not yours. You snatched him from her.'

Anjali's gut turned into a slipknot.

The new mail in her inbox was nothing but an attachment. A photograph of an old, creased-and-faded letter. A note to Sid written by Katherine:

SK,

Sometimes you have to put your friendship at risk to say I love you. But you are worth risking my whole life.

Katherine

Anjali had always respected what Sid and Katherine had, but someone was twisting that—while seeming to read her mind too. It could ruin Katherine's marriage. She wanted to call Katherine, but the passage of time had caused a gulf between them, and whenever Anjali took a step forward Katherine took two away from her. Anjali never knew what the reason for that was.

Probably this.

She jumped into action and called Natasha.

'Morning. Running already? Can we talk?'

'Metaphorically, yes! Running away from everything. You tell me. Sid is out, or you can't sleep?'

Anjali swallowed the reply and continued, 'Do you think Katherine ever had a thing for Sid?'

Natasha reacted almost instantly, 'Whoa! Where did that come from?'

'Our hacker friend just sent a note that seems like Katherine's confession of love. It's her long hand, from the look of it. Would you know about this note?' Anjali

asked and read it aloud for Natasha with the words
burning slightly on her tongue.

'But Katherine had torn that one up. I know for sure
that she never gave it to him,' Natasha said.

A wave of shock ran over Anjali. She overcame it and
asked, 'You knew about it?'

But Natasha's reply was brief. Something else was
playing on her mind.

'I came to know by accident. It's a long story. Listen,
we need to do something about this hacker. He is digging
up too much dirt. Rick will be difficult to handle if he
knows I've kept this . . .' she trailed off. 'It's just that it
has been so many years. He will think I've hidden a part
of myself from him, and it might not go that well with
him.'

Natasha had meandered away from the topic. But
Anjali's mind had developed some faint logic for all this.
'Nat, do you think Sid or Katherine can do this?' she
asked, shedding her inhibitions.

'Are you out of your mind? Why will Sid do that to
us? To you? And why will Katherine drag the dead out of
the closet?' Natasha questioned her assumption.

Anjali was slowly warming up to the idea of voicing
her feelings. The therapy sessions had helped her in this
regard. She braved herself and suggested, 'Do you think
Katherine and Sid can plan this together?'

'Anjali, what's wrong with you? You are pulling
innocent Sid into this. Moreover, the Katherine we knew
would never stoop to that level. What made you doubt
them?' Natasha asked. Her tone had a tinge of anger and
disappointment in it.

Anjali almost instantly uttered the words on her tongue before they could double back, and her silence could drag Natasha away from her and closer to Sid.

'Sid and I are getting a divorce,' Anjali said.

'What . . .?' Natasha asked, but Anjali didn't let her finish her sentence.

'It's been a while in the making. We really can't go on together any longer. I need some time to come to terms with it before I can announce to the world. Anyways, coming back to the topic: the hacker's timing on this is making me think that it's Sid. He wasn't much keen on going ahead with this divorce. You understand where I am coming from?'

Natasha gabbled, 'Oh god, Anjali! This is a shocker. I don't know what to say and where to start . . .'

At least Natasha wasn't blaming her, and it was a good start.

'How are you coping?' Natasha asked after a beat of silence. Her concern felt like drops of fresh rain in a scorching dessert.

She is my friend. She didn't ask about how Sid was coping. She didn't take his side like Mom.

'Well, I am the one who called it off. So, no surprises there. But I can be better. I am expected in Singapore next month, for my quarterly team meeting. By then, I think I will be ready to talk about what went wrong between him and me,' Anjali said in a calm voice.

She was glad that her voice didn't give away the storm brewing in her heart. Natasha, true to herself, said what was expected of her, 'I am here, and I am ready to listen whenever you are ready to tell.'

This was Anjali's chance to open her wounds and let them bleed for Natasha to see and tend to. But she needed time and courage.

'So, you suspect Katherine told him and now she is helping him to manipulate you?' Natasha asked.

'Well, Katherine can do anything for Sid, and she is an ethical hacker too,' Anjali said with suspicion weighing more heavily on her mind now.

Natasha was silent. Probably still processing all that had come down on her like an unexpected blizzard. Natasha's mind had reached the same conclusion as Anjali's. But in friendship, doubt was one side of a seesaw balanced by trust, and it too quickly tipped from one to the other.

'But I don't think Katherine and Sid are capable of doing this. Moreover, Katherine thinks that some paranormal forces are at play. Why would she feel scared if she is the one behind it? All this isn't making any sense, Anju,' Natasha said.

'What if this is Sid's desperate attempt to not lose me, and Katherine is just helping him to save our marriage,' Anjali suggested in a voice that was a pitch higher than usual. She was trying to justify her point. The seed of doubt was growing like a bean sprout in her mind and she wanted Natasha to water it.

'You are not thinking straight. Sid can achieve this by blackmailing you, why drag all of us? Let's not rush to a hasty conclusion. Let me talk to Katherine, okay? I will call you back.' Natasha's voice had an element of doubt.

But Katherine's love confession was a swarm of locusts unleashed to eat up whatever was left in Anjali's marriage.

Was Katherine doing all this to get Sid back in her life or was this Sid's way of getting Anjali back into his?

Katherine D'Souza
38 City Apartments, New York

Katherine woke up with a bitter feeling in her heart that refused to go away. She drove to the client site to run a network-vulnerability test, but the distraction didn't wipe away the blood-in-the-mouth tang on her tongue. Nor did the three glasses of water. The metallic taste was still there.

A bad omen.

As she waited for the tests to run, she inspected the palm of her hand. The mystic cross was still there, between her head line and heart line. It was a mark of her extraordinary intuitive powers—her grandmother had told her that. Katherine was reminded of her grandmother's words every time her hunch rang true.

That evening, Natasha's call translated the premonition into reality.

'Didn't you really tear the love letter you had written to Sid back at college? Anjali received something similar in her email today,' Natasha said. Katherine tried to hear past the rush of panic flooding through her. The blood drained from her cheeks as the words settled in her mind.

'She received what? Wait a minute . . . I had torn it in front of you. Don't you remember that?' Katherine asked. She didn't mean to raise her voice, but it didn't comply.

'But Anjali did get a note written by you for Sid. Did you write a few?' Natasha asked.

Katherine placed her palm flat against her stomach, trying to calm herself. 'I wrote only one. The one I tore the day Anjali said yes to Sid. You had seen it all. And why is Sid being dragged into this? Did she tell him about that night?' Katherine asked.

'Did you?' Natasha asked in return, almost in the same breath.

Katherine went ballistic at the allegation. 'What's gone in you, Nat? I am the last one to bring that night up. I have boxed up that memory and thrown it in the darkest corner of my mind. So much so that I stay away from all of you to keep that night away from me. And why would I leave a note like that lying around for anyone to pick and bring the dead out of the closet? Please tell Anjali to forward me the mail. I would like to see it,' Katherine said, keeping the edge out of her tone.

'I think you'd better clear the air and request for the forward on your own. I will ask her to give you a call,' Natasha suggested and ended the call. Katherine's stomach felt full of worry, like she was inside a nightmare.

No one could possibly reproduce a torn, two-decade-old note.

Katherine had written that note to Sid on the day of their high-school results party. Sid had recently broken up with a girl back then, and Katherine had planned to tell him about her feelings before it was too late again. But that very night, their all-India ranks were announced and their similar scores indicated that they were about to end up in the same college. So Katherine decided to stow the note away for college. However, in college, Sid's affairs started much before the studies could, giving Katherine no time to pluck up her courage.

It was only when Sid proposed to Riya that she got worried, but Riya turned down his proposal and Katherine once again placed the note on the back burner. Sid did try going out a few times, but it appeared that Katherine's love for Sid was stronger than Sid's charm. All his attempts to be with someone ended too soon, keeping her hopes alive every time.

However, in the final year of engineering, the note showed up in Katherine's certificate folder. That weekend, Sid had gone home for his birthday and was supposed to bring back her clean laundry, parcels of food from her home and her high-school certificates folder, which she needed urgently. But as expected from Sid, he delivered everything except the folder. Her certificate submission was due the day after, but Sid wasn't budging. He irritated her with his effervescent mischief, stretching the torture by handing one certificate at a time from her folder. By evening, she had recovered the entire folder. But then he waved something at her: an envelope. Panic shot through her heart.

How did the note reach here? It had been safely tucked in her jewellery drawer at home. Had she put it in the certs folder?

Katherine lurched forward to snatch it, but Sid held it high in the air, dangling it out of her reach. The charade carried on until Katherine was satisfyingly irritated and angry.

'Who do you think I am? A courier guy? And what's in this envelope with pink hearts? Why is it glued?' Sid asked and handed her the note finally. Katherine clenched the note in her fist and silently walked to the college canteen, to help Sid with his birthday party arrangements.

The three of them had learnt to keep up the pretence that everything was normal, but in truth, a thick layer of sadness had wrapped itself around them. The jokes they played on each other, the sleepless nights they spent chatting with each other were no more the glue that bound them together. Sania's death and Riya's betrayal had poked a hole in the fabric of their friendship, which was slowly being ripped apart.

However, Sid's 'small' birthday party soon became a full-on bash for his ever-growing list of friends. Anjali and Natasha looked happy. After Riya's departure, Sid had gently taken her place in their group, filling her shoes by cracking jokes that Riya used to crack with them.

'Don't you forget that you are an Indian girl. When you get married—that is, if someone agrees to marry you—you will be expected to do all this for your ugly husband and his ugly litter,' Sid said, flicking Katherine's braid.

She got up and poured some more soda in the half-empty glasses to just shut Sid up. He seemed unusually happy. She looked around. Everyone was happy. Anjali's smile and Natasha's guilt-free face lifted her spirits too.

Maybe things would become normal. Without Riya, too.

Katherine allowed herself to relish this moment. Sid again came and pulled her cheek in a happy way. There was something different about him today. A faint wave of hope flickered in her heart—maybe Sid had actually read the note and placed it back to save her the embarrassment—maybe he felt the same way as she did and was looking for the perfect moment to say so.

But before her heart could warm up to the idea, Anjali stood up and sat next to Sid and whispered something in his ear.

'Seriously, Anjali?' he asked aloud.

Anjali nodded. It was a shy nod. Katherine couldn't understand. She shot a questioning glance at Sid.

'Oh! Kath. I had asked Anjali out. She said yes. I am so happy,' Sid announced to the world.

Katherine's heart cleaved into two. It hurt so much that she could hear it breaking. A cracking sound. Like wood being shattered. And when she thought she couldn't take it any more the look on Sid's face brought her back to life. Sid was happy. Anjali was happy too.

The blush on Anjali's cheeks brought a smile on Katherine's face. Natasha was smiling as well. Katherine could not let her heartbreak ruin the moment. She hugged Anjali and then Sid.

'You'd better not break her heart, otherwise I will kill you,' she whispered in Sid's ears, holding his shirt collar.

'I have finally found a woman I want to marry, and this time I bet you won't doubt my choice, right?' Sid asked and tapped Katherine's cheek, bursting with happiness.

His words cut through Katherine's flesh like a thousand razor blades. She walked to the washroom, cried into her palms and came back like nothing had happened. After the party, she walked back to the hostel feeling both happy and miserable. For the first time in weeks, Katherine was glad that the warden had not found a roommate for her.

She locked her room and fell on the floor.

The note in her jeans pocket was on the floor, mocking her one-sided love. Katherine opened the note and began to read it in a slow whisper but loud enough to swallow the thud on the door.

Natasha had heard it too.

'I thought I'd locked the door,' she said and stifled the nascent tears in her eyes.

'It wasn't and I am glad for it,' Natasha said and hugged her. Katherine's need to break into a sob took over everything. 'I had planned to hand this note to him so many times. But I never had the courage to do it. This year it reached him accidentally, but he still didn't read it. So, I take it that it was not destined to be. Anjali and Sid make a good couple. And that makes me happy and sad, because unlike other times, this one time I do not want Sid to be fooling around. I want to see them together,' Katherine said. She had to string her words together around the fractured sobs.

'You go tell Anjali. This will be over before it starts,' Natasha said.

'You haven't fallen in love yet, Nat. It is always too late before you discover it. There is no way that Anjali can come back. It's a one-way street and for the first time, Sid seems to have made a good choice.'

* * *

The ping on her phone brought Katherine back to the present. It was Anjali's message: 'Can we talk in ten?'

What will I tell Anjali? And SK knows about it too? How will I face him ever again? Why was the hacker dragging all the dead out from the closet, and what did her feelings for Sid have to do with that night? More importantly, where did the hacker get the note from?

The nesting doll of questions had frayed Katherine's nerves to breaking point.

I should have bought and kept a pack of cigarettes.

Samir was travelling. The kids were asleep and the mart was a ten-minute drive. She would be back before anyone could know. She had done that before to pick milk and eggs. But this was her first time doing a last-minute run for a smoke. She always had an emergency stash and once she decided to quit, she never felt the need. Until now.

She picked up the car keys and stepped out. The air outside had taken on an eerie, whispering unreality. But the ghost of her past was more frightening than the faceless threat hanging in the dark. She reached the car and was paralysed at the sight.

A set of green eyes were staring at her.

It's an animal perched on the wall. Stop being paranoid.

She managed to reach the car with her eyes locked to the set of green eyes on the wall. She could do it; fear was only in her mind. She could beat it. But the soft meow of a cat set off a lightning bolt in her heart and shattered her resolve. The neighbour's cat had made her stomach tighten like a fist.

She doubled back home with fear digging a tunnel inside her. The slight movement of the blind, the thud of the door, even her own breath was making her jump out of her skin. Was her guilt manifesting into an abstract fear that didn't exist for anyone else but her?

Katherine was ridiculing and embracing her fears in one breath, like a ventriloquist with two faces, two voices and one body.

Anjali's incoming call ended the rolling tsunami of thoughts.

'Hey, how are you?' Anjali asked. Before Katherine could drum up the courage to blurt out what she wanted to say, Anjali added, 'Busy?'

'I am sorry. Give me a chance to explain, please,' Katherine stammered.

'Let it go. It doesn't matter anymore,' Anjali said in a calm voice.

But Katherine's impulse had taken over. 'The note— I wrote it in high school. It was meant to be his parting gift. But then we landed up in the same college, so I held it back. Soon, he found his first date, and I waited for his little dating game to get over. It always did because his choice wasn't right ever. But then he found you and I knew it was forever. I had torn the note apart. Natasha had seen me doing it,' Katherine explained. She paused for breath and continued, 'I could have told you all this. But it might have changed things between you and him, and possibly between him and me, too. Please don't doubt SK, he knows nothing about it.'

Katherine's heart was beating in her throat. She had never imagined that a feeling she had so tactfully hidden from herself was out in front of Sid's wife and her once best friend.

And that too twenty years too late.

'Katherine, I need to tell you something and I need to tell you now, because if it comes out later, you might think that it happened because of you. We have separated,' Anjali said.

'What separated?' Katherine asked with shock in her voice. She had definitely heard it wrong.

'Sid and me. We are getting divorced,' Anjali reframed her words.

The news of their divorce felt like a clap of thunder in Katherine's ears; it stunned her into a brief silence.

'Katherine, you there?'

'What happened? And are you okay, Anju? I take this is a very recent thing?' she gabbled.

'A month ago.'

'Can't fucking believe it. You guys were so into each other.'

'Things change and you haven't met any of us since forever,' Anjali said.

All the air went out of Katherine's lungs.

Forever?

She had met Sid last year for the high-school reunion, an impromptu dinner planned with high-school friends who were in town that weekend. But why the hell did Sid not tell Anjali about the reunion? Her heart was pounding and her face grew hot. Fear had dampened her recall. She dug deep to unearth the memory. Nothing.

There was a whole night out there that fell through the cracks, and she remembered nothing about it. Nothing at all.

Natasha Gupta Lim
26 Siglap Road, Singapore

In the last two days, Natasha had talked to all of them
and the texture of their renewed conversations felt like
old times. The years between them had melted away,
along with the differences. Should she curse or thank the
person who was harassing them? Because if the drama
continued any longer, they would be best friends again,
once more looking out for each other and covering for
each other, just as in the college days.

Surely, the hacker hadn't counted on that.

'You look lost. What's wearing you down?' Rick
asked. He had paused the movie.

'I just need a weekend,' she replied and smiled.

Her smile didn't reach her eyes. In a beat, Rick would
know that something was bothering her, and the same
discussion would start again. She hated it when Rick played
shrink. She wanted him to hit the play button and let her
breathe; Natasha was happy to roam in her own head. But
before she could request him to resume the show, the buzz
on his phone came to her rescue. Rick headed out to the
balcony, talking animatedly to his colleague.

The boys were in bed, but even so, she thought
she heard footsteps elsewhere in the house. She looked
around; no one was there. She picked up the iPad to check
on the boys and spotted a notification flashing on the
screen. The movement in the boys' room had triggered
the app connected to the security camera in there. She
tapped on the notification and opened the live video feed
of their room. The kids were sound asleep.

However, in the night mode, the camera rendered their sleeping figures in bright green, which had never caught her attention, until now.

Don't let the fear get to you.

She was about to quit the app, discounting it as a false alarm, when the shadow of a woman appeared and disappeared at the edge of the screen.

A gasp got caught in Natasha's throat.

She stared at the screen, waiting for the shadow to appear again. Nothing. She must have imagined it all. But what triggered the app notification if the kids were still asleep?

She was about to get up to check on the boys when Rick's tap on her shoulder startled her. 'You still use this thing? This hovering might just hinder their growth. You can't let your guilt get in the way,' Rick said in a cold voice.

Rick was extremely comfortable with the huge house he had inherited from his grandparents, as a wedding gift. Natasha had also enjoyed the separate allocated floor for the bedrooms, the spacious living room, dining area, kitchen and a huge balcony, until the kids arrived. Rick had installed a couple of cameras to rest Natasha's worries, but her mind always played tricks when the kids were alone upstairs, so she used the camera app to keep an eye on them, especially when she was downstairs.

'Nat?' Rick asked, tugging at her shoulder.

'I will check on the boys and be back soon,' Natasha said and walked up the stairs. They were asleep. No one was there in the room.

I must have imagined the shadow.

Natasha turned back to watch the weekend movie with Rick, but the change of the soundtrack dissuaded her from going to Rick—he had abandoned the movie and was watching a soccer game now.

Worse, he knew what wound he had poked and still he had left her to nurse it. Alone.

She had just changed into her pyjamas when the iPad screen lit up again, flashing a movement-alert message. She tapped on the app and monitored the live feed. Her son Ryan had opened his eyes, causing a green flash to appear and disappear from his face. Her heart kicked in her chest.

Katherine's fears are getting to me.

Natasha quit the security camera app, loaded her Kindle app and read till sleep dragged her down into a familiar nightmare.

In the dream, Natasha had just turned her head to watch the colourful butterfly fluttering its wings— and when she turned back, Ayesha, Natasha's younger sister, was gone. A moment ago, the five-year-old Ayesha was standing on the chair in the balcony, and a split second later, she was hanging on the balcony rail. Natasha could have pulled her back, but she was frozen in fear for a moment too long. By the time Natasha raced to rescue her sister, Ayesha's hand had given up. Natasha looked down and found a pink frock lying in a pool of blood.

She woke up with a startle, rushed to the bedroom to check on her kids. The boys were sleeping fine, but the abstract fear in her heart refused to go away, like a foreboding.

She walked back to her room, but sleep had disappeared from her eyes. She sat on the edge of her bed and relived her sister's death.

That evening, an eight-year-old Natasha didn't need anyone to confirm that her sister had not survived the fall. Everything after that moment had turned blurry. She only remembered her mother's words. 'What did you do, Natasha?'

She had killed her sister. By not pulling her up in time, and by dragging the chair to the balcony, although later, Natasha's mother had blamed herself for not keeping the balcony door locked. But Natasha knew who was responsible for it, and over the years, the burden of her guilt had settled like wet sand over her chest, until she became habituated to it.

This habit, of nursing her guilt, broke after Anjali, Riya and Katherine filled the void Ayesha had created. She had found a part of her sister in Riya, a fraction of her in Katherine, a lot of her in Anjali. But before Natasha could heal forever, Sania's death had stirred her guilt again. And when the twins were born, she didn't sleep well for months, scared that they would choke on milk or on their own spittle, and that she would have to watch them die. Frozen in fear. After all, she had missed her chance to save someone. Twice.

What were the chances of her screwing it up a third time?

Natasha often dreamt of Ayesha. Sometimes her face was Sania's and sometimes it was Ian's or Ryan's. Tonight, she had drowned them all again, one by one.

She overslept the next morning. The kids were with Rick at their taekwondo class. Natasha used the time to sort the toys in the chest of drawers. She had emptied the bottom two drawers to move the art supplies in it, but the boys were back much before she could follow through.

'Mommy, see, I learnt a new move,' Ryan said and straightened his leg to practise the front kick.

'Me too!' Ian said and displayed his front kick.

'Me three,' Rick said. He swirled and kissed her. The kids giggled and copied his move. Rick was trying to patch up. She decided to let go and smiled at him.

'Mommy is playing with your toys,' Rick teased.

'Yup. I was playing hide and seek. Look what I found,' she said and shook a bag full of Lego blocks that she had scooped from the corner of the drawers. Ian leapt and took the Ziploc of Lego blocks from her, and before she knew, the Lego pieces were already on the floor.

'Mommy, one of the wheels is still missing. How will I complete the night crawler?' Ian asked.

'All the wheels are in the top drawer, I will get it for you,' Natasha said.

But before she could get up, Ian tiptoed and pulled open the top drawer of the chest. He held on to the drawer to climb up and look in. Natasha foresaw the disaster an instant before it happened: the tall unit tipped as the bottom two empty drawers slid open. As it began to topple, Ian fell backwards, and in a fraction of a moment, he was going to be crushed. Natasha shoved him away and used her shoulder to stop the unit. The drawer slid out and nailed her on the side of the head.

The last thing she remembered was Ryan and Ian screaming before she lost consciousness.

* * *

'Go slow, babes,' Rick said with a forced smile.

Natasha took in the surroundings. She was ferried to the hospital in an ambulance. The antiseptic sting in the air sent a jolt to her mind.

Where is Ian?

'Ian, what happened to him?' she asked.

'He is fine, at home. You saved him.'

'Ryan?'

'Both of them are at home. Not a single scratch. Relax, can you?'

She stirred in the stretcher bed, impatient and frightened. A quick assessment and she knew that her upper body was frozen in pain and even a slight flinch generated a breathtaking stab of agony. She decided not to move. Moments later, she was taken to the examination room on a stretcher.

'The motion and sensory functions are intact,' the doctor in white scrubs said in English. He then turned around and started speaking in Mandarin, discussing her case with the bunch of junior doctors shadowing him. Natasha had never felt so anxious and out of place. Not even at the family functions at her in-laws' place, where she was the only one unable to speak the language that others spoke; not even when she had no clue as to how many dollars to slip into the ang pao for the first Chinese New Year reunion dinner she had attended.

The doctor's address eased her anxiety.

'Mrs Lim, most likely you have a protruding disc. I have scheduled an emergency MRI to see the extent of damage. Let's hope you have not damaged the disc.'

Before she could worry about the outcome, a nurse was there to take her for a scan. A raw pain in her neck gripped her tight as she tried getting up from the bed. She was about to collapse on the floor when the nurse pushed her into a wheelchair and rushed her to radiology.

The next forty-five minutes were a living hell.

She entered the imaging suite and once again Ayesha's and Sania's deaths came alive in the dark eye of the machine. She could have killed her son, too. If only she had not emptied the last two drawers this morning, if only she had pulled Ayesha back, and if only she had stopped Sania, things would have been different.

The long list of 'if only' scenarios started chasing Natasha, and guilt formed a lump in her throat. She swallowed it.

'Please don't swallow. Else, we will have to do the entire scan again,' the technician reminded her.

But she had to swallow this guilt. Spitting out would mean losing everything. She felt the sting of tears in her eyes.

Is this my karma? Is this pain my penance, an atonement long overdue?

Natasha's results came back, confirming disc protrusion, and she was discharged within an hour. She came home with a white-and-green Parkway East Hospital bag full of medicines. Rick helped her climb up the stairs to their bedroom, while she battled the excruciating pain in her neck and arm.

Ian barged into the room and said, 'Mommy, thank you for saving me and sorry I got you hurt.' He looked mortified.

'No, you didn't get me hurt. It was the unit that fell. Don't blame yourself,' she said, smiling through her pain.

'You know what this means? It means Mommy has no office for the next three weeks,' Rick said in a cheerful voice.

He had wiped away the worry from their tiny faces. 'Yay!' shouted the kids in unison. But they didn't come near her. The boys had either read her pain or were following Rick's instructions. However, Natasha's mother-in-law sat on the edge of the bed, slipped her jade bangle on Natasha's wrist and said, 'Wear this. You will recover before you know. Kids will follow me for dinner. I got chicken soup for you.'

Her uptight expressions meant she was blaming the feng shui of the house for Natasha's accident. She never wanted them to move into this house, and she got back to Natasha and Rick at every chance she got. According to her feng shui-expert friend, this house was a *gui lou* (a haunted house), as it had some evil vibes to it. However, according to Rick, it was all about his mother and grandmother not seeing eye to eye.

Natasha had never bothered about her comment until now, but today the term gui lou had caused an uncomfortable stir in her stomach.

'You saved them. It could have cost them their lives,' Rick said reading her mind. He fed her chicken soup and gave her colourful pills to swallow.

Natasha was asleep before she knew it.

She woke up in the middle of the night with a debilitating pain igniting her shoulders. Some involuntary movement of her hand might have pinched a nerve, sending an electric pain into her neck and her back. She turned her head to wake Rick up and request for another round of painkillers when a shadow standing next to Rick's nightstand caught her attention.

The shadow was dim at first. Unfocused. But as Natasha peered into the darkness, the image shimmered and resolved, snapping to sharpness with an almost overwhelming intensity. She recognized the face and felt an audible drum roll of her heart coming from deep within her chest.

Sania Malik was in her bedroom.

She blinked her eyes in the hope that Sania would disappear. But Sania was as real as Rick beside her. Fear heaved and smashed its way through her body.

Before she could get a grasp on reality, Sania walked towards her side of the bed and offered her the steel jar in her hand. The scream Natasha had been withholding finally broke free and echoed through the bedroom. It woke Rick up.

'Honey, what's wrong?' he asked with panic in his voice.

She pointed to the woman standing by her nightstand. But Sania had disappeared. Her eyes skittered through the bedroom, but Sania was nowhere.

'Did you see a bad dream or is it the pain?' Rick asked, his voice inflected with dread.

'It was a nightmare. A real nightmare,' Natasha said and wiped her tears. Rick flashed a sympathetic smile and planted a tender kiss on her forehead. But it did nothing to calm her. Natasha's mind felt like a wheel yanked out of alignment, steering in a new direction.

Sania's direction.

Sania's ghost had invaded her mind. Hopefully, only her mind.

4

Haunting Sania

Riya Banerjee
Malabar Hill, Mumbai

Riya reread the text sent to her: 'Answers you are looking for are meant to be found within the group.'

Someone was watching her phone screen in real time. Her electronic devices had turned into a landmine. The wire to defuse the explosive was as unknown as the one that would blow her life to smithereens. She stared at her phone's now-dark screen and her own reflection ruffled her. She crossed her hands and rubbed her palms on her arms, but the prickle in her skin wouldn't go away. The fear was breathing through her.

Riya settled her erratic breathing and peeled a yellow Post-it from the stack to list the possible suspects. Sania Malik, she wrote and then struck it off.

A dead body cannot be a suspect, no matter what Katherine says.

Rahim Malik's name again ran a loop in her mind, and the fact that the hacker had stopped her from searching about Sania's cousin only strengthened her suspicion. She curbed her impulse to run a search on Rahim Malik and waited for the cyber security expert to show up soon, so that she could use her devices freely.

However, her nervous energies were in desperate need of an outlet. She picked *Stillhouse Lake* to get immersed in Rachel Caine's latest when the green transparent file kept next to it dropped from the bookshelf. The story arc of 'That Night' had turned into a flickering flame. She had burnt her fingers to light it and now she was going to risk becoming a moth, by going near it. Again.

* * *

That Night: December 19, 1997

'I am here, inside her.'

I had killed it with those words. Anjali and Natasha were as surprised as Sania and Katherine. This was the moment of glory in my tale—a twist worthy of Agatha Christie.

Sania's hand instantly moved away from the coin. She looked at me in disbelief and then her gaze shot at Anjali's and Natasha's faces. She found nothing but shock in there. Katherine had started to shiver.

I laughed a silent laugh in my head and repeated my words, 'I am here, inside her.'

Anjali's frown meant that she was evaluating whether the script had taken a supernatural turn, or my creative mind was doing somersaults. She shot a dagger look and asked, 'So how did you die?'

Her question had handed me a platform and a spotlight. I felt a rush of warm excitement.

'I died yesterday in an accident that happened on the highway,' I said. I was glad that the tedious effort of moving the coin to spell a sentence was out of the way, giving me some creative freedom and speed.

'So what do you want from us?' Anjali asked, her voice still imbued with suspicion.

This was my moment to strike. I leant forward, bugged out my eyes and in a heavy voice said, 'Revenge.' Stark terror stole into Sania and Katherine. Natasha was teetering at the border. Only Anjali wasn't sold.

'Well, can we please listen to your story after you have answered a few of our questions? After all, we summoned you to answer our questions. Fair deal, no?' Anjali asked, flashing her I-know-it-all smile. She was back in her element.

'Life wasn't fair to me. So why should I be fair? It's my turn first,' I said and laughed a croaky laugh. The impact was most visible on Katherine and Sania. It encouraged me to improvise further. 'I am stuck in a purgatory, and the only way I can think of getting out is by getting a few closures.'

Now where did that one come from? I was getting good at this. The look at Katherine's and Sania's faces meant that they were completely sold on the idea of me being possessed. Anjali's eyelids were blinking fast, it was a bonus point, as I had managed to stir some discomfort in her, too. I should have stopped then and there, but the alcohol was bringing the worst out of me . . .

* * *

Riya held the manuscript printout in her hand and paused, reflecting on the question that had run in her mind, like a broken record, for months after Sania's death. Riya was drunk and was on a roll with her story-making, but that night she had crossed all the lines of playing pranks.

It was unusual.

She had always blamed alcohol for it, until now. But what if there was someone else to pin the blame on? What if Katherine was right that someone had possessed her that night?

She tossed the pages on her desk and stood by the window. Deep breathing. She couldn't let Katherine's fears get to her. The clue about the blackmailer had to be found somewhere in the past; all she had to do was to find it and prove Katherine wrong.

Riya picked up the manuscript and began to read again.

* * *

'Okay, let's hear your story first and then we will ask a few questions. Deal?' Anjali asked.

They all looked at me with anticipation. I had always relied on my fertile mind to create instant excuses, especially when we got caught in a situation. But that night, my imagination was running wild. Out of nowhere, I created a story with a paranormal ingredient.

'Last night was meant to be my first dinner date at my favourite restaurant. But my so-called boyfriend, first he missed the skirting on the road and then he sped on his bike, leaving me alone to bleed to death. My parents knew nothing about the date night and how it ended. They think that I was trying to elope. I need you guys to go and tell them the truth and help them find that bastard. He should get the punishment he deserves. And if you don't help me, I will haunt you forever,' I said and looked at Katherine. She averted my gaze and took a sip directly from the bottle.

'Can I have a sip, too? I am so thirsty,' I asked and beckoned Katherine to give me the bottle.

I had to stop her from drinking too much, else she might blow it all. I pretended to take a swig and handed the bottle to Anjali. She had read my mind. Anjali replaced the lid and held it in her hand.

Sania's nervous gaze slid from my face to Anjali's hand. She hid the shock and asked, 'Who brought this to the hostel?'

Anjali took off the lid, poured some whisky in a glass and offered it to Sania. 'Try it. It will drown all your fears.' Our eyes met and I understood that Anjali was making Sania drink so that she wouldn't rat us out later.

And I thought Anjali was getting inebriated!

'Drink,' I commanded in a frigid tone, supporting Anjali in the mission to save our ass.

Sania's pink face turned white at the change of my tone. I had widened my eyes, but I stared just past her head, as though the ghost possessing me did not have full control of its temporary home. All the acting skills learnt from C-grade Bollywood horror movies were put to test in that moment.

But Sania didn't buy it.

'I am going back to my room. These girls called you, and they will make sure you get your revenge. I need to go back.'

Did she have a change of heart or did she understand the game?

'Don't go, else I will chase you till the end,' I said in a hoarse voice and clenched her wrist too tight. Booze was dancing in my head now. Scared Sania took the glass from Anjali and drank to the dregs.

Anjali and Natasha exchanged glances while Katherine shivered and said, 'Please don't harm us. Tell us, what else do you want?' It was the opportunity I'd been waiting for. 'Firstly, I need food to eat,' I said in a calm voice. I waited for Sania to respond but she said nothing. But it gave Anjali some time to recover. She cycled through a calming breath and said, 'But you haven't answered our questions.' She flashed a mean smirk my way.

'Sure.'

Anjali paused to remember the pre-decided question through the haze of alcohol and asked, 'There are rumours about Sania turning into a hijab-clad woman after a heartbreak. Are the rumours true?'

The fear on Sania's face had already satiated my desire for revenge. So instead of coaxing her to reveal the reason for wearing the hijab, I framed my answer around

Sania's question to Ouija about finishing her degree. 'I think that's not the worry ruling her mind. She is more worried about her degree and education, which I am sure she will complete.'

Sania looked up at me with a sense of disbelief, as if I had triggered something dark and dangerous. But oblivious to it all, Anjali was having too much fun in the game.

'Can you read our future too? How about we start with Natasha,' Anjali asked.

I followed the script we had written together while Katherine was in the loo and Natasha had gone to bring Sania.

'Don't always worry about being wrong. A little fun won't harm you. Enjoy this time with your friends. Don't be so serious always,' I said and flashed a warm smile at Natasha.

Natasha looked at me with a piercing gaze, trying to filter the real and the surreal, and Anjali followed the cue. 'What about Katherine?' she asked.

'Your mind is the sharpest of them all, but you are dragged down by your fears. What are you scared of? Ghosts? See they are so harmless. Look at me. Did I do anything to you?' I asked her and hoped for Katherine to get the joke now. But before Katherine could respond to it, Anjali had changed the script.

'How about Riya?'

'What about Riya? She is an open book,' I said.

Anjali wasn't coming that easy on me.

'Why is she not dating Sid?' Anjali asked and flashed an I-caught-you-there smile.

'Because he is not her type. She likes the geeky–nerdy types,' I said, talking about myself in the third person, as if I were really possessed.

Sid had asked me out a couple of months ago, and I had politely declined. There was nothing to dislike in Sid, but he was too vibrant to my taste. Moreover, my idea of a boyfriend was someone who could dance to my tunes or at least listen to them. Sid was not that. He was used to being the sun of every universe, just like me, and there could only be one sun in the universe. Also, I had an inkling about Katherine's feelings. So there was never a decision to make.

'Tell us something about Sania's love life?' Anjali asked, going back to the script again.

I wasn't interested in Sania's love life anymore. I was interested in food. But I tried to make peace with Sania by giving her some food for thought. 'I know something is worrying you. Hopefully, you will find your balance back. Because nobody likes the woman you are turning into.'

My comment had hit bullseye. Sania's milky skin turned beetroot red and a tear fell from her eye. However, by now, Katherine's unease had soured into impatience. 'Let's send the spirit back before it can harm Riya's body any further,' she suggested.

'You guys called me, but that doesn't mean that you can send me back too. I will go when I want to. I want food and revenge in that order,' I said in a cold voice and stared at Sania.

She finally budged and said, 'I can get you food.' Sania's facial expression had changed at the mention of food.

She won't come back was the thought that made me jump out of my quilt.

'Can I come with you and choose what I want to eat?' I asked, placing my firm hand on Sania's shoulder, and followed her.

'You can take all of it,' she said. We walked back to my room with the victory badge.

I stepped back into my room and a wave of sudden dizziness washed over me. Before I knew, I had collapsed on the floor. I came to a moment later and found the four faces staring at me in shock.

'Eat something, quickly,' Anjali said.

Taking the cue, I picked up the homemade pinni and devoured it hungrily. Then, I snatched the mathri and asked Anjali, 'Where did you get these from?'

'You don't remember anything?' Sania asked, a subtle note of shock evident in her voice.

'No. I only remember playing Ouija,' I said.

Anjali gave me some water and an explanation for my hazy recall, 'She must have fainted because of low sugar level.'

'I fainted?' I asked with surprise. The shock on my face was real, and I saw Anjali's brows knitting together for the first time. I had no memory of fainting; my recall of the events was blurred around the edges. Before Anjali could fill me in with the missing details, Katherine's fears had taken over the conversation.

'We need to dispose of this paper properly,' Katherine said with an authority in her voice.

'We need to tear the paper into seven pieces and bury it along with the Ouija—the coin—or else the spirits *trapped in it will find their ways to haunt us with it,'* Katherine added.

'You remember nothing, Riya?' Natasha asked, looking slightly perplexed.

The inability to recall was causing a tingle in my nerves and Natasha had read it too.

'Someone should go and bury the things. Especially the coin. Anjali, can you do that? And when you are downstairs, can you please give the keys to the guard?' Katherine requested and handed the set of keys to her.

'I can come with you to bury the board,' Sania volunteered. She lifted the bottle, poured some whisky in the cup and drank it with determination. She poured some more, handed it to Anjali and said, 'Drink. We will need it. It's freezing out there.'

Anjali gulped it in one swig and they both left to bury the paper and the coin, as per Katherine's instructions, while I relished my hard-earned meal.

'Are you feeling okay?' Katherine asked. Natasha and Katherine were watching me with an eagle eye, mapping my every move.

'Healthy as a horse, Kath. Don't worry, girls. It was an act,' I said and offered them the snacks. But they were nowhere close to being relaxed.

'You cooked the entire story on the go?' Natasha asked, with disbelief in her voice.

'I did. Now you know why I keep saying that I will write a book one day. What do you think?' I asked in a cheerful voice. Katherine let out a sigh of relief and said, 'I won't read it. I hated this story. Every bit of it.'

We chatted for a bit more and waited for Anjali to get back before we could call it a night.

'What a fun night. Hope you left something for me,' Anjali said and snatched the steel jar from me. She took a bite of the pinni and spoke with a mouthful, 'And Riya, you are so right, that girl is a bitch. This all serves her right, but I am just worried. What if she says something to the warden tomorrow morning?'

'And the warden will believe her?' I interjected. 'The warden is busy with her boyfriend, whom she smuggled inside the girls' hostel, against the rules. So, if she questions us tomorrow morning, we will question her back about the men's shoes Katherine saw in her room.'

'In that case, I will take one more pinni. Can you believe it? Sania had so much food with her but she wasn't willing to spare even a tiny bit for Riya! What a bitch she is!' Anjali said and munched on the pinni.

But Katherine was still stuck to the Ouija.

'Who among you was moving the coin?' Katherine asked.

'Me,' Anjali and I said in unison.

Before Katherine could prod any further, Natasha jumped in, 'Where is Sania? Is she in her room?'

'Am I her bodyguard? She knows how to walk back to her room, no?' Anjali asked in a curt voice. I had never seen Anjali losing her calm. But the alcohol had blurred her inhibitions and her facade, exposing the tendrils of anger hidden within. First, she had lashed out at Katherine and now at Natasha. I quickly took over the conversation before it was too late.

'Let us all sleep in one room tonight, like every term-end night. And this is almost finished. A sip each and we can call it a night,' I said and handed the bottle *to Katherine. She took a sip and passed it to Natasha, who refused. Anjali relished the last three sips.*

We crashed on the bed. All four of us with our arms around each other, savouring the moment that stayed with me forever.

We were never together again.

* * *

The trill of the doorbell broke Riya's concentration. She noticed how her heart had detonated in her chest at the chime.

Riya didn't like to be so jumpy.

They had to find the hacker. Soon. The cyber security expert came in and jumped into action. The lines on his forehead made Riya too jittery to concentrate.

'Your computer is compromised, ma'am,' he declared.

'Really? What a discovery! That was the problem I brought to you. You have to give me the solution,' she snapped back, regretting it belatedly.

She had extraordinarily little patience these days, and it was thinning out fast.

'Ma'am, I need to call my manager and check with him as I can't spot the malware added to your system. It's only the unusual data flow that's raising an alarm,' he said and dialled a call.

'I can't start the anti-malware software. It's disabled,' he said into the phone. 'No, I can't start the task manager either.'

Riya looked away from his face to her laptop screen and noticed the movement of the cursor. It was moving on its own. Riya had noticed it a couple of times, but she had blamed it on the old computer and trackpad. But today's cursor movement was different. The unseen set of hands selected the programme and clicked on a folder called 'The Game of Ouija That Killed'.

Riya was stunned.

The folder she had deleted was back.

She turned the laptop screen towards her. Someone was typing. She read the text with the dread of the unknown perched on her shoulders.

'A lot could have happened that night. Want to know? Ask your friends. Anjali is hiding something. So is Katherine. Oh! How about a new hook line for your book: *Each of the friends is hiding a secret guilt about that night. What will happen when the others find out?*'

Sweat crawled down Riya's face in the air-conditioned room. She sat there worrying about the truth, the death, the promise. And now the secret guilt.

The list was growing every minute.

What if there was an iota of truth in the hacker's claim? What if Katherine and Anjali were somehow involved in this more than she thought they were? Her manuscript had opened a can of worms, and now the worms were about to crawl all over her dreams and reputation.

'Don't worry, ma'am. I will help you to clean the computer,' the cyber security guy said, reassuringly.

But Riya's stomach was sick with worry, about to clean itself.

Anjali Kapoor
23 Park Street, London

Anjali had always liked Sid and Katherine as a package—
the non-stop tussle between them was as admirable as
their sticking their necks out for each other. She always
thought that Sid's love for Katherine was like the affection
of an elder brother, but all this time, Katherine had been
in love. Deeply in love.

And this newly discovered information had
discomfited Anjali. She wasn't able to read her own
feelings. Was it insecurity, regret or her own grief clinging
on to everything?

*Was Sid aware about Katherine's feelings? If so, for
how long?*

Anjali caught herself playing the thought-spinning
game again. No way she could pull another sleepless
night; the last two nights had exhausted her. She needed
some sleep to function well at tomorrow's client meeting.
She was alone in office, and the lights in the cubicles had
been dimmed. But she felt safer in her office cabin here
than at home, especially after last night's temptation-
filled encounter with Sid.

She didn't want to end up in bed with Sid and regret
it later. Moreover, her only companions—her phone and
her laptop—were compromised. She picked a safe laptop,
a secured network and an uncomfortable couch over her
comfortable bed.

Anjali changed into a set of pyjamas that she had kept
in her office, popped a melatonin, and relived the events
of her day. Sharing her divorce news with Katherine was

like going for a test ride—the shock in Katherine's voice, her inwardly favouring Sid, the silent sympathy for him and then nothing for Anjali.

They all will react similarly.

But still, she felt courageous, all thanks to Natasha's neutral reaction. Before the tranquilizer could numb her mind, she called Natasha, to bring her up to speed on her conversation with Katherine.

Her phone went unanswered.

Anjali tossed and turned and waited for Natasha's call like an addict waits for her fix. She wanted to stop herself from relying too much on Natasha, but being alone was a feeling so vast, it echoed.

Natasha was the only friend Anjali had for herself. Everyone else in her life was shared with Sid, and claiming them back from him was not an easy feat, especially when he was the favoured one.

An hour went by but there was no sign of sleep. Anjali stirred on the brown couch that had started hurting her the way an aircraft seat begins to hurt on a long-haul flight after the first nap. She wanted to go back to her room, to her bed. But now it was too late for that. Her only hope was sleep, but it had eluded her too. Anjali fished an eye mask from her bag and tried the 4-7-8 breathing technique that she had learnt from her therapy sessions. But her mind again circled back to Natasha.

Something felt out of kilter.

She followed her instincts and texted Natasha: 'Please call me back ASAP.' Minutes passed nightmarishly. She closed her eyes as the discomfort in her chest made itself felt. It grew like a subtle pain; her pounding heart was to blame. She poured a glass of water and gulped it in one go.

Her hands started to tremble.

Not now. Not tonight. Please.

She squeezed her eyelids shut and waited for her breathing to become normal, but the tightening in her throat had intensified. Soon, the room started to whirl around like a hula hoop.

This fear that Natasha is not okay is just a figment of your imagination. Relax.

She had shut her eyes to reduce the stimuli, but her body was still shivering. There was no running away now. She braced herself for a panic attack and did what her therapist had asked her to do—divert her mind. But nothing in the room was good enough to serve as a distraction. She gave up, took out a Xanax and had it. She assessed her fears. They were all about Natasha today. Were they real or was her mind playing tricks with her?

Anjali launched the world clock app on her phone and checked the time in Singapore. It was 10 a.m. How could Natasha miss all her phones and messages? Something was not right. Her heart again started going mile a minute. Xanax wasn't working today.

Or was it a premonition?

Anjali found Rick's number on her cellphone and dialled it. She could feel her heartbeat, quick and shallow, at the base of her throat. She had to calm herself down. Rick should know nothing. She diverted her mind to the happy memories—her frequent business trips to Singapore, Natasha's family holiday in London, Sid's desire to have twins like them and the endless games of soccer in the park near Natasha's house. It brought her palpitations down, and then Rick's calm voice made her burst out with relief.

'Hey, Rick. Nat isn't answering her phone. Is all okay?' she asked in a calm voice.

'Hey, Anjali. Sorry I saw your missed calls on her phone but could not reply. She has met with an accident. A freak accident. The chest of drawers in the kids' room fell on her shoulder, triggering a slipped disc. She is bedridden for a few weeks, I guess. Her arm hurts a lot, so she is away from her phone. Let me see if she is awake, and, in a position to talk.'

Anjali's heart lurched.

Freak accident? Was it connected to any of this?

'How are the kids? How are you managing? Can I talk to her?' Anjali asked, keeping her breathing slow and steady. But she wasn't as calm as she'd thought.

'Don't worry, it's not as bad as it sounds. Wait, I will give the phone to her,' Rick said. She heard his footsteps and then nothing. Anjali could hear her heart beating in her temples; the silence over the phone was that deep.

'Sorry, Anjali. She dozed off. The strong painkillers make her very drowsy. Can I ask her to call you? And don't worry, okay?' Rick whispered. His voice was calm yet tense.

'Can you please ask her to call me back ASAP? Is your mom coming to help with the kids?' Anjali asked.

'Well that's the tricky part. My parents have to fly to Australia tonight, to be with my brother. He is going through a bad divorce. I was supposed to fly with them.

Anyways, I am on leave for the next one week, so it's good that at least I can manage the kids and look after Natasha without bothering about work,' Rick said.

'Call her parents,' Anjali suggested.

She was trying hard to keep worry out of her voice but was failing miserably.

'Won't be my first choice. They are old and sick. But will call if required,' Rick assured.

Anjali felt a compulsive need to be with Natasha, and for a change she acted on her impulse.

'In that case, do you mind if I come and help? At least I can manage the kids after their school hours?' Anjali asked with a slight bit of hesitation.

Rick took a minute to respond to that.

'For now, we are good. You will be the first one to get a call if things go out of control,' Rick assured her.

Anjali's mind again ran in a different direction.

Is Rick telling the truth? Is Natasha not checking her phone? Or he is keeping her away from the phone? Why is he not calling her parents?

Anjali was really fond of Rick. And in this insane moment, she was doubting her best friend's husband for hatching a conspiracy that was picked directly from a domestic thriller.

Not everyone's life is shattered like yours.

Anjali brought herself back to the conversation and requested Rick, 'Please make her call me. I am worried sick.'

'Sure. I will ask her to call you. And don't worry, I am taking good care of your friend,' Rick said. He always teased them both for their legendary friendship.

The call was over, but Anjali's heart was still beating with the same anguish. She reminded herself that it was a freak accident and that there was no need to link the blackmailer to it.

A hacker can't make the chest of drawers fall on her. Or can he?

It was as if the mere thought of the hacker had conjured him back into her life. A message flashed on her phone screen: 'Two can keep a secret only if one is dead. Wish for her to be dead or spill the beans, will you?'

Anjali's chest started to hurt. Her mouth was dry and cottony. Another message barged in before Anjali could recover from the first: 'Btw, you really think hiding in your office can solve the problem. Really? How about facing them?'

Anjali barely read the second message and switched off her phone. Hands shaking, she put a piece of tape on the phone's camera and on the webcams on her desktop and other devices. She shut her blinds as tight as they would go. Staying in the office was not the smartest choice. But going back home at this hour wasn't wise either.

No place was safe now.

Before her thoughts could jumble up with her fears any further, her meds came to her rescue. She fell asleep almost instantly.

Sid is behind all this was the thought that jerked Anjali out from sleep at dawn. She woke herself up and called Sid.

'Hey, how are you?' Sid asked, lovingly.

'You reached?' she asked.

'Yes. Did you wish Ma luck? Today is the opening of the South Delhi Pita outlet,' Sid reminded her. She had completely forgotten about it. A surging tide of warmth left her limp. Tears prickled her eyes. She knew that this separation would damage everyone, but its impact on her mother would be catastrophic. Sid's frequent business trips to India and Anjali's steep climb on the corporate ladder had forced Sid to fill Anjali's shoes in her mom's life. She had never complained.

Not until now.

'Thanks for being there for her. Can I ask you something?' Anjali asked.

'What's with the formality?' Sid asked in a pain-laced voice.

'Do you have a problem with our separation?' she asked almost in a whisper.

He laughed. 'Is that actually a question? And will my answer change your decision? Remember you requested some time away. So I am giving you that. But I love your mom as much as you do. Keep her out of this. Please.'

'Thanks, Sid,' was all she could say without crying. She brought out the divorce papers from her bag and tossed them back into the desk drawer. She needed to sort out the hacker's mess before she could create another one in her life. And then, there was the bedridden Natasha.

Anjali's list of worries was growing bigger and bigger.

The ring on her phone freed her from the clutches of anxiety.

'Hello, Anjali. So, you've heard?' Natasha asked. Her pained voice cleaved Anjali's heart in two.

'You okay, Nat?'

'Yup, in pain but okay. And Anjali . . . Babes, can you enable the speaker and talk? Holding the phone this way might hurt you.'

Rick's voice murmured in the background. It had stopped Natasha from saying whatever she was about to say. It gripped Anjali's attention almost instantly and stirred the suspicion she had buried deep in her.

'Nat, you okay?' Anjali asked.

'Yup. It's a minor injury. Don't worry.'

'You sound in pain.'

'It hurts, Anjali. It hurts a lot. All of it.'

Anjali heard Natasha's sobs and felt something break inside her. Before she could console her, Rick had taken the phone. 'Anjali, the meds are making her emotional, and then there is this thing with her sister that keeps coming back. She's not at her best.' There was frustration, love and concern all rolled into his voice. But Anjali's mind wanted to ignore all of it and place the blame on Rick, simply because there was no one else. Not yet.

'She will be okay. Today is just day one,' Rick assured her.

'Rick, I really want to come and be with her. In any case, I am due in Singapore next month. Will bring forward the travel. If that's okay with you?' she asked.

'Hmm . . . She will definitely feel better around you. So I don't mind you stopping over for a day or two, if you are coming for work. We were in too much stress already, and then this happened. My brother had a mental breakdown because his divorce proceedings got a little messy. Now, as the final hearing of his kids' custody is approaching, he is getting very anxious. The kids want to follow dad to Singapore, but that woman is fighting for their custody,' Rick said. Rick's helplessness and transparency touched Anjali's heart and made her regret doubting him.

'Rick, your brother, he needs you. But Nat needs you too. Stay with her please. And I will see if I can plan a trip soon,' she said.

'Seeing you will definitely cheer us all, especially the kids. So, most welcome. But don't go out of the way. You know that madam doesn't like taking help or favours,' Rick said.

The cheer in Rick's voice made Anjali smile.

She ended the call and studied her calendar, which was filled with meetings. Although this unplanned trip would create a mess at work, all she could think about was Natasha. For once, life had given Anjali a chance to pay Natasha back for all that she had done for her, and she was not willing to miss this opportunity. Not at any cost.

Anjali owed her degree and her career to Natasha.

In the second year of engineering, Anjali's mother had met with an accident. Back then, her divorced mother was working as a cook to sponsor Anjali's education. A slip in the client's kitchen, the hospitalization and the loss of work had drained whatever savings she had, leaving her with no money to pay for Anjali's term fees. Anjali was almost at the brink of quitting the course when Natasha convinced her dad to become a guarantor for Anjali's student loan.

That term, Natasha bought food, books and travel tickets for Anjali from her own pocket money. Anjali's mother soon recovered and resumed work. The loan was paid off too, but Anjali was indebted forever. In the years to come, each time Anjali got promoted, she sent a note to Natasha: 'I owe you this one, too!'

And as luck would have it, Anjali's extensive travel to Singapore had brought her closer to the kids and to Rick as well. The thought of Natasha's kids made her smile and tear up in the same breath. It made her decision easier.

She was going to Singapore today.

She walked from the office to her home down the street. A quick shower and she was ready for the day, not as sharp as ever, yet functional enough to sail through the morning client meeting. She could catch up with sleep on the flight.

Anjali booked herself on the first flight to Singapore, using her personal assistant's laptop while an IT security officer freed her devices from the hacker's clutches. Anjali didn't like acting on impulse. But this one time she was happy to sway, and she was glad that it was for Natasha. At the airport, she texted Rick: 'About to board SIA direct flight. See you.'

Soon after, a new mail notification caught her attention. The sender's email id was the first punch to her gut: WhathappenedtoSania@iotk.com.

The subject of the mail was the second punch: 'Katherine's marriage, how long will it last?'

She read the body of the email, her anger brewing: 'Your marriage is over. Katherine's will be over soon. You couldn't save yours, so save Katherine's at least.'

It was foolish to click on the email attachment, but she did it anyway.

The photo on her phone screen knocked the air out of her lungs. It was a photo of Sid and Katherine.

Lips locked.

The caramel of Katherine's hair and the salt-and-pepper stubble on Sid's chin were enough evidence that it was not a case of the dead walking out of the closet.

It was an old flame flickering in the present, ready to burn everything.

Natasha Gupta Lim
26 Siglap Road, Singapore

Natasha's injury had reduced her to a prop on the margins of her household's morning chaos. Rick was at the top of his game, managing the kids with a new patience, calming the fear that frayed Natasha's nerves.

By mid-morning, Natasha was confident that Sania's appearance was a dream. Her medicated memory might have jumbled up the real and the surreal; maybe she was asleep the whole time and simply remembered a dream as being real. After school, the kids brought her their cute doctor's kit and a new game—Natasha was a patient, and Ian and Ryan were her doctors. Ian placed his toy stethoscope on her chest and frowned.

'You don't have a heartbeat, Mommy,' he said.

'That's because the heart is on the left, silly Ian,' Ryan said.

'Also, because you forgot to load the batteries,' Natasha said and handed Ian the batteries.

The pre-recorded thudding sound on the toy stethoscope got swallowed by their innocent giggles. She patiently waited while the boys read her pulse, checked her temperature with a dummy thermometer and put a sticker Band-Aid on her. When it was time for Natasha's meds, Rick came in, pretended to be a nurse, administered the medicines and said, 'Make sure you let the patient sleep, okay doctors R and I?'

The boys giggled and Natasha relished the undivided attention from them.

Natasha's new role at work had embarked her on a fast-moving train that didn't allow her to take even a single day off. But thanks to her injury, her life had come to a standstill and surprisingly, she was enjoying it. It was only the pain that was unbearable, and it was coming back like clockwork. Thankfully, her medicines robbed her of the pain and of her senses too. The boys were fighting for the toy injection when her eyelids started to droop.

She woke up to the sound of the heartbeat on the stethoscope.

The kids must be in their art class.

Natasha removed the battery from the glowing stethoscope and the room turned pitch dark. She felt her phone on the bed, but every movement in her arm activated a new point of pain. She decided to call Rick instead.

'Rick, are you there? Can you please walk me to the loo?'

She was about to summon Rick again when a movement in the doorway made her stop.

'Rick, help me sit up please,' she requested.

But Rick did not respond. She studied the silhouette approaching her. It was too small to be Rick. 'Teresa, are you here? Are the kids back from the art class?' she asked.

The silently approaching shadow caused a vicious twist of unease in her stomach. Sania was back, and this realization punched all the air out of Natasha's chest. She was lifting herself up to find her phone when Rick warned her, 'Don't try to stand on your own.'

The darkness in the room disappeared as Rick rolled up the blinds using his phone. But Sania was still there, standing between Rick and her. She held her breath and waited for Rick's reaction, but Rick walked in straight, through Sania. Natasha's mind oscillated between shock and fear. The fact that Rick didn't acknowledge Sania's presence meant only one thing—the woman standing in her bedroom was only a figment of her imagination.

Rick could see nothing. She could only pretend that she saw nothing, too.

Rick helped Natasha to sit upright and then guided her to the washroom. She battled the pain caused by the movement and by Sania's presence.

Sania had followed her to the loo, holding a steel jar in her hand. It was the same jar of pinni that they had relished soon after the game of Ouija.

'Don't try to get up on your own. Call me next time, okay?' Rick said, kept the phone near her and walked out. Natasha lifted her phone with a crushing pain in her arm and clicked a photo of Sania. The camera captured nothing, not even a shadow.

Her mind reeled in disbelief.

This is hallucination.

She rubbed her eyes mercilessly and opened them in the hope that Sania would disappear. Instead, Sania had come a step closer.

Was it her guilt or the medications? Or was the woman in her bedroom real?

She looked at Sania's dark-black hair and her milky-white face. The woman in her bedroom was undoubtedly Sania.

I must tell someone. Maybe I have damaged a part of my brain. But what will I tell Rick? Where will I start, and where would it end once I start?

She plucked up her courage to give one detailed look at Sania, but the intruder had disappeared. Natasha switched on the camera app and scanned the boys' room; Sania wasn't anywhere. Natasha connected the dots with painful clarity—the shadow on the baby monitor app, the whistling noise from the monitor, the freak accident, and then Sania herself—all of it was only happening in her mind.

Am I going crazy? Is my brain damaged? Should I stop the medication? Probably I need to tell Rick about it. Maybe I can say that I am seeing my dead sister.

She decided to tell Rick soon after she had done a quick check on the net. She googled 'hallucination after spinal injury' and browsed through the various scientific and non-scientific reasons behind it. With a little more courage, she changed the search words to 'seeing the dead'. A text message came in before she could go through the search results: 'Seeing the dead, is it? Who do you see? Is it me?'

Chills went down her spine. So the hacker was doing all this and was monitoring her phone too. She panicked and phoned Katherine.

'Katherine, I saw Sania. She was in my bedroom. Is it even possible?' Natasha asked. She could hear the hysteria in her own voice.

'What kind of a joke is this, Natasha?' Katherine asked in a loud, agitated voice.

'Kath, I see Sania here. In my bedroom. Offering me some sweets all over again,' Natasha said, jumbling her words.

'It's not funny, Nat. Are you trying to make fun of me? Riya is behind this prank, right?' Katherine asked.

'Please, Katherine. I saw her, twice. This isn't a joke. Can a hacker project an image that is only visible to me? A hologram maybe? Rick was here too, but he didn't see her.' She said, breathing heavily.

'What did you smoke today, Natasha?' Katherine asked.

She couldn't blame Katherine for not trusting her. Her fear-laced words sounded alien to her own ears.

'I really saw her. Not once but twice. And when I googled about seeing the dead, expecting it to be a hallucination, the hacker texted back asking if I was seeing the dead. I have forwarded you the text too. Can you find the sender's location using the text? Kath, I am going mad. I need assurance from you that a hacker can do all this because the Sania I see feels very real, and she has the same clothes on her . . . the one she wore on the day she . . . And can you explain how it is possible that I can see Sania but I can't capture her image on the phone? It cannot be because of my injury, because the shadow of the woman I spotted on the camera was before the injury. Even the whistling sound was a night before the accident . . . Katherine, are you even listening?' Natasha was blabbering.

'Nat, calm down. What injury are you talking about? Can we go through this one by one?' Katherine asked in a panic-filled voice.

Natasha narrated the series of incidents from the lift breakdown to her ending up bedridden and waited for Katherine to make some sense of her illogical deductions.

'The hacker can surely interfere with your devices and network, but making you see Sania is a bit tricky. Can we ask your hubby to take you back for a check-up? Maybe you hurt yourself more than what they think, no?' Katherine asked in a calm voice that made Natasha's tensed shoulders relax a bit. Her reasoning returned, combating the illogical fear, but the realm where Natasha's mind had steered her wasn't a pleasant one.

'No no, I can't tell Rick about Sania. He hates lies, and he had his own mean ways of trapping people in their own lies. Listen, is there a way to check if Rick is behind this? Maybe he somehow knows the truth about that night, and now he wants me to confess. Maybe he is the hacker? After all, he has the passwords to all my accounts, and he might have found a device to project a 3D image of Sania, no?' Natasha asked.

'But why would he go to that extreme to chase the truth? Why would he not confront you instead? Doesn't make sense to me. Most importantly, where did he get to know about that night, and how did he manage to get Sania's photo from those days?' Katherine asked, thinking aloud.

'You don't know him, Kath. He kicked my helper out for a theft of mere ten dollars. Maybe he is trying to chase the truth out of me without making it obvious, the way he caught my helper by deliberately leaving his wallet unattended? I might have mentioned Sania's name while I was being rushed to the hospital after the injury or during the scan. Maybe I said something in my state of delirium. Also, he can always find Sania's photo in my copy of the college yearbook,' Natasha supported her doubts, swallowing the guilt of suspecting Rick.

Katherine took a moment before replying.

'Relax, Nat. You are not thinking straight. Maybe it's nothing but stress. Can you please try and relax? I will check on him, okay? However, I doubt he can actually project a live Sania in your room. Maybe your injury is causing it?' Katherine argued.

'I hope you are right, Kath. But if it is a hallucination, I should see others too,' Natasha argued.

Katherine didn't reply. Natasha tried again.

'Kath, your granny used to talk to the dead. She used to send them back to the world where they belonged, right? Did you learn a trick or two from your granny? Is there a way you can send Sania back? I am scared, dead scared. Real or imagined, these sightings aren't cool. They are killing me,' Natasha said and began to cry.

Katherine jumped in almost instantly. 'I promise you, Nat. We are there for you. Please don't cry. You calm down and rest well. Leave it to us. Hacker or ghost, we will get to it together.'

The confidence in Katherine's voice brought Natasha back to her orbit again. Katherine would explore it all. Unlike her, Katherine didn't need to see the ghost to believe in it.

She drummed up the courage and scanned the room. Sania was not there but her lingering gaze had stayed back. Natasha's mind recoiled at the recognition.

Those wistful and faraway eyes was her last memory of Sania.

* * *

On the night of the prank, a couple of hours after the game, Natasha had spotted Sania pushing open the door that led to the terrace. Natasha's unannounced presence had stopped Sania and the pained look on Sania's face had stopped Natasha from going to the washroom. She had walked towards Sania instead.

Sania's hijab was missing and, in this cold, she was roaming without a headgear. Her gritty hair and her red cheeks should have raised alarm, but Natasha's senses were undermined by alcohol. Yet she had asked, 'Sania, are you okay?'

Sania had bit her lips and replied, 'As if you care.' Anger and despair spilled from her voice. Natasha's woolly mind had connected the dots belatedly.

Sania might have deduced the prank by now.

She tried making peace with her. 'Sania, please tell me what's troubling you? Were you going to the terrace? It will be freezing up there. I can walk with you in the corridor or you can sleep in our room. Come,' Natasha had said and tugged at Sania's elbow.

'How dare you touch me? Leave me alone, you bitch,' Sania had shouted with a slur in her speech. She was drunk, mad and violent. But Natasha didn't budge until Sania agreed to walk back to her room. Natasha walked her to the room and noticed the stench of nicotine enveloping Sania.

'Do you smoke?' Natasha had asked.

'Mind your own business, and tell your bitch friend the same,' Sania had said and closed her room's door on Natasha's face. Natasha had walked back to Riya's room. A scared Katherine was sitting upright on the bed and her fingers were moving along the rosary beads, counting the number of Hail Marys.

'Nat, can you draw the curtain, please?' Katherine had whispered.

Her voice was laced with fear. The word 'HELP' written on the window glass was all smudged with mist, yet it was scary enough for Katherine. Natasha was about to pull the curtain when she had spotted some movement in the woods. A silhouette seemed to be facing her; it was possibly someone looking at her. Natasha had contemplated pointing it out to Katherine but decided against it.

Katherine was already scared to death.

She cupped her hands to get a better look at the woods but found nothing this time. She must have imagined it all. Maybe the alcohol in her veins was acting up. Because it was impossible to spot a silhouette in the fog.

Had she really seen someone or not?

December 19, 1997
Girls' Hostel
Institute of Technology, Kurukshetra, India

I had not planned it, but love happened to me. The love that comes before all the significance of morals. The love that opens a gaping hole inside you. The love that should have suspended your reasoning. But your rationale suspended our love instead.

Don't blame yourself for anything. It wasn't your fault. It was mine. For believing in you.

Alvida

5

Talking to the Dead

Katherine D'Souza
38 City Apartment, New York

Katherine was eight when she first peeped through the hole in the door and saw her grandmother using the Ouija board. She had seen it all—the planchet moving on the Ouija board, the answers written on a piece of a paper and her grandmother reading it aloud for the man sitting in front of her.

Her maternal grandmother was a psychic—a woman supposedly blessed with mystical powers. People dealing with grief and loss would end up at her doorstep to find solutions to the problems that were beyond human control. But Katherine and her brother, Mathew, never believed in any of it, until the tables were turned.

That summer, she was at her grandmother's home in a village near Goa, and the next day was her thirteenth birthday.

'Let's celebrate it in a unique way,' Mathew had said, with mischief gleaming in his eyes. He placed a set of keys in her palm and asked, 'Are you up for it?' The kids weren't allowed anywhere near their grandmother's practising room and that had piqued their curiosity.

However, that summer, Mathew had managed to grab the keys before their grandmother left to attend a wedding in the nearby village. He had taken on the role of keeping Katherine happy very seriously, after their mother's death a couple of years ago. And since there wasn't a way to party in a small village like this, he had found an innovative way to celebrate her thirteenth. A thrill-filled birthday.

Katherine opened the room and found all the neighbourhood teenagers waiting to surprise her. Soon, they all huddled over the Ouija board for some cheap thrills. Katherine led them as she had secretly witnessed her grandmother summoning the dead. She placed the planchet on the board and felt a surge of power. 'Whom do I call?' she asked.

No one answered.

'Come on, guys. One name,' Mathew said.

'Let's summon my aunt,' Vinod, the neighbour's son, said after a long pause.

'What was her name?' Katherine asked in a tone that emulated her grandmother's.

'Jaya Aunty,' he said.

Katherine closed her eyes and recalled every step of the seance to summon Vinod's aunty. Moments later, the coin started to move, providing answers to the questions asked. Vinod broke into a laugh before Katherine could figure out who among them was moving the coin.

'You idiot! My aunt is alive. Stop fooling around,' he said.

They all laughed, packed the board and walked out of the room, relishing the thrill. But the next morning, Mathew woke Katherine up with panic in his voice. 'Kath, wake up. Vinod's aunt met with a car accident last night. She is in coma. He came with his father to seek Grandma's help. She has called us to the living room. He is blaming himself and us for the accident.'

The joy and thrill of last night's adventure evaporated instantly as they entered their grandmother's room. 'This is not a game of snakes and ladders that you decided to play with your friends. You summoned a person who was alive, using the board that holds the power of summoning anyone. Now face the wrath,' she snapped. She was upset, which was a rare sight for everyone at home. Katherine had spent her birthday worrying.

Vinod's aunt recovered in the days to come and lifted the burden off Katherine's chest.

But the fear of the occult had stayed there, establishing its territory in her mind.

'Do you think we were responsible for his aunt's accident?' Katherine asked Mathew one night.

'You are silly. How could we cause an accident? It was just a coincidence, and granny used it to instil fear in us so that we don't go near her room ever again,' Mathew said.

But the fear had set deep within her bones, and whenever she voiced that fear, she got ridiculed the way Natasha had ridiculed her over the phone earlier. But Natasha's ghost sightings had created a paradigm shift.

She was being consulted for fears that hadn't existed for others until now. The fear was getting to them. Or was it really the hacker messing with their minds?

Katherine followed Natasha's train of thought and ran a preliminary search on Rick. His social accounts were all set to private mode, giving away nothing. She decided to hack into his account, just to rule out Natasha's irrational doubt, but before she could act on it, the phone in her pocket vibrated and startled her. Riya's number settled her rattled nerves, but only for a moment.

'How was your school reunion last year?' Riya asked.

'Sorry?' she asked, trying to grasp the reference.

'Okay, let me ask you what I really want to ask. Are you sleeping with Sid?'

Her question snapped the frayed thread of her temper.

'Who told you this crap story? Or is your imagination running away from you again?' Katherine asked with rage pumping through every artery in her body.

'It seems that the hacker knows it all! Check your email.'

Katherine opened her email, scanned the attachment for the virus and clicked it open. A pixellated shot of Katherine in Sid's arms, their lips locked, filled her computer's screen, and brought a wobble to her knees. She had spent her entire adolescent years fantasizing about this one moment, but there was no memory of it being real. The picture on her phone was the only physical proof of it, and it caused a strange sense of revulsion, instead of flickering some old flames.

A wave of recollection passed through her and then it was gone, leaving behind Sid and Katherine sitting by the pool, reliving college days. There was nothing else she remembered. Parts of that reunion night were like a blank spot in Katherine's memory—moments that were lost to the alcohol they'd drunk that night at the poolside bar. No matter how much she tried, she had no recollection of the event.

Not even of the scene that was frozen on her computer screen.

She could have blamed everything else on the evil dead. But this email was way too evil even for revenge. It was too human.

Someone was not only attacking them as a group. They were shattering Anjali and Sid's marriage in an irreparable fashion.

'Katherine?' Riya said. Katherine jumped to her own defence, 'Nothing of the sort happened. This is photoshopped.' Her own voice felt weak with doubt.

Did something happen on the reunion night that triggered their divorce?

She teetered back and forth and then decided to tell Riya about Sid and Anjali's divorce. Riya was quick to overcome the shock; she connected the picture on her screen to their shattered marriage as swiftly.

'So they are getting a divorce because of this kiss?' Riya asked.

'No, they separated a month ago. It has nothing to do with this photo. Anjali didn't know anything about the reunion when I last talked to her,' Katherine explained. She lost her voice and her words in the blizzard of questions that followed.

'If the kiss didn't happen, what all happened between you two? How can you forget what happened that night? You still carry a torch for him, right, Kath?' Riya interrogated.

Katherine still loved Sid, but not in a wanting way. He was a habit that she couldn't quit. However, the picture gave her a twinge of nausea she couldn't explain.

'I remember nothing significant about that night, Riya. Probably, I had a few extra drinks. But I can check with SK. I am sure he would remember,' she said.

There was a contemplative pause, and then Riya was back in her detective role.

'If Sid is behind this, then your call will alert him. So, let's call him when we are sure about his involvement. You never told him about Sania, did you?' Riya asked.

Katherine was unable to keep up with Riya's high-speed processor.

'No. Never. We had promised not to talk about it, and some people remember to keep the promise,' Katherine said, taking a dig at Riya. But Riya was caught up in her own thoughts.

'Do you remember who all attended the reunion night? Someone who clicked this and thought of using it?' Riya asked.

'Seriously, Riya. You don't get it. This photo is morphed. Sid was, and still is, a good friend,' Katherine said firmly. But Riya wasn't in listening mode.

'In that case, it's time to involve the cyber police. What do you say?'

'Involving the police would mean . . .'

But before Katherine could finish her sentence, Riya interjected again, 'First of all, this would be way beyond the statute of limitations. Secondly, it was a suicide. We didn't kill her; we just got her drunk. More importantly, if the hacker thought we killed Sania, he or she would have reported us to the police back then or now. This is blackmail. Let's keep our guilt out of it and not let him or her exploit us to extract something out of it.'

If only Katherine could borrow this clarity of mind and compartmentalize her thoughts and solve the reunion-night problem and the ghost-in-Natasha's-bedroom problem individually. She considered mentioning Natasha's ghost sightings but decided against it. She had already crossed the line by impulsively blurting about Anjali's divorce and was regretting it. She tried damage control. 'Riya, I am not sure if I was supposed to tell you about Anjali's divorce. It was an act of impulse.'

'Is it? Glad I don't share any secrets with you. They will be in the newsroom before I know,' Riya said, probably to tease her.

'We haven't talked for two decades. So you have nothing to worry about,' Katherine continued the banter. They were picking up the lost rhythm between them.

'You can't blame me for it. You didn't accept my friend request,' Riya teased.

'Well, try me now. Maybe I will feel differently,' Katherine said and felt her mood lifting up. She heard a ding on her laptop. It was Riya's friend request. Katherine accepted it and waited for Riya to get a notification.

'Finally, I have at least one piece-of-shit friend back in my life.'

That brought a huge smile on Katherine's face. 'Me too, Riya. Now get lost!' she said, keeping up the charade.

'Oh God, I have missed you,' Riya confessed, and it melted Katherine's heart.

'I missed you too, Riya. But that doesn't change the fact that you are the meanest bitch of us all. Now can I work on finding the hacker, please?' Katherine said and ended the call with a smile. But the smile didn't last long. The thought of the reunion photo pulled her back to the problems knocking on the door.

There was a ghost in Natasha's bedroom, and a hacker in Sid and Anjali's marriage.

She decided to go by 'last-in, first-out'. But the network location test again pointed to a virtual private network. The blackmailer could be smarter than her, but how could one reproduce a live-looking Sania and an old, trashed note?

She ran a quick check on Natasha's husband and found his Facebook account. In minutes, she was into his phone and was disappointed to find nothing. Sid was next. But there was nothing in his account too, apart from the rough draft of the divorce papers and some job applications. He was currently in New Delhi, playing back and forth in emails with some restaurant manager for an outlet opening.

Why would Sid blackmail them and help Anjali's mother in the same breath? But then, if Sid wasn't behind this, who was doing it and why? Was Natasha really seeing the dead? Was Sania actually back to take her revenge in a twisted way?

Riya Banerjee
Malabar Hill, Mumbai

The alarm bells in Riya's head that had been oddly silent began to holler after seeing the reunion night picture. And the trace of guilt in Katherine's voice had given them a distinct shrill.

Someone was heading towards them. Slow and steady. Someone who knew which buttons to press. The hacker was not just a part of their past, he or she was the component of their present, and the revenge planned by this hacker had a concoction of the past and present. He or she had been lying low, collecting evidence to attack when the time was right.

How long had the hacker been waiting to strike? Did the hacker sow the seeds of doubt between Anjali and Sid, and was now harvesting the crop?

Riya's mind again doubled back to the anonymous message sent to her: 'Each of the friends is hiding a secret guilt about that night. What will happen when the others find out?'

Once upon a lifetime ago, she had trusted them with her life. But her association with them had lasted merely three years.

And it takes a lifetime to understand someone, and sometimes you get it all wrong.

Maybe her friends were not the way she remembered them. Maybe one of them or all of them were hiding something. Her primal instinct to first save herself kicked in. She peeled out the Post-it that was fluttering on the edge of her monitor screen and added four more names to the list of suspects—Katherine, Anjali, Sid and Natasha. Rahim Malik, Sania's cousin, was already on the list. She listed the motivation against his name: Revenge.

Riya paused for a moment and filled the blanks in front of her friends' names.

Sid: revenge against Anjali.

Katherine: unrequited love.

Anjali: ?

Natasha: ?

Sid was the only name after Rahim that circled in her mind. It stood out more than Rahim too. Maybe he always knew about that night, but now, with his marriage gone wrong, he was using their guilt to his advantage. Or he might be exploiting Anjali to negotiate the terms of their divorce?

But then, why involve all of them?

Riya's neurons were snapping fast and furious, circling back to Sid and Rahim. She decided to mess with the known devil. Sid.

She texted Katherine: 'Send me Sid's number while I find an excuse to call him.'

'Won't that be odd, to call Sid? And please don't mention his divorce, unless he volunteers,' Katherine texted back and shared the number.

'I will cook up something.'

'Yup. Now that you have an official licence to tell lies, nothing should hold you back.' Katherine replied. But Riya's mind wasn't able to decode Katherine's sense of humour. She sent a question mark to her and got busy with saving Sid's number.

'Authors to me are professional liars who get paid for telling lies. :)' Katherine texted.

Riya smiled at the response and gathered herself to call Sid, and before self-doubt could spread its roots in her mind she connected the call.

'Hi, Sid. This is Riya. Riya Banerjee. Hope you remember me?'

'Of course, I do. How can I forget the most beautiful girl of our batch who said no to me? By the way, a couple of days ago, I saw your book on the newsstand and was wondering whether you still look this pretty or it's an old photo on the book jacket,' Sid teased, chirpily.

The tension in her body abandoned at his uninhibited flirt.

'You are still the same old flirt, Sid. Where are you these days?' Riya asked. She had deliberately avoided the how-are-you question that could end up bringing Anjali into the conversation.

'I am in Delhi for some work. Will be back in London next week. You tell me. To what do I owe the honour of your call?'

Riya had come up with an authentic-sounding reason to call. At least she thought so; it was time to test it.

'Wanted to pick your brain on something. I am planning to write about teenage suicide. Thought if you could contribute,' she said.

'I am still alive, and not at all a teenager anymore,' Sid teased.

His sense of humour was still intact.

'Ha ha, very funny. Do you remember Sania Malik?' She asked.

'Sania Malik . . . the one who jumped from the hostel's terrace?' Sid asked. Sid's pause and recovery were quick but not enough to get unnoticed by Riya.

'Yup. Do you remember anything about her? Anything that could be taken as a sign of depression? Asking you because you were the most well-connected guy in college. Was she dating someone?' Riya asked, not giving him time to think too much.

'Whoa, is this a memory test? I didn't even know that she was in a relationship. Didn't she say no to almost every boy in college? Including me, of course. The guys in the hostel concluded that she was an oddball. But why are you picking Sania? She was close to abnormal in any case.'

Riya had come prepared for that question.

'Sania's death had impacted me immensely. And there was a mystery around it that made me go back to it again and again, so I thought of writing something about it. Never mind if you know nothing. Tell me, how's life been for the last two decades?' Riya asked, changing the topic.

'All good. You tell me where were you and why did you disappear? And tell me what I am dying to hear: Are you still single, ready to mingle?' Sid teased her in his usual singsong voice. He always flirted with Riya, a sweet harmless flirt that made her smile.

'Very much single and at my age, my only hope is a frog who is waiting to turn into a prince charming at my kiss,' Riya replied.

Sid was the kind of friend who brought the best out of Riya's sense of humour.

'Don't tell me that you go kissing every frog on the roadside to find your prince? Call me when you are in London next. I would like to see Riya, the heartbreaker, bending down and kissing every frog on the roadside,' Sid said.

'Wish granted. Let me plan something soon. But promise me that you won't be the same old creepy flirt,' she said cheerfully and ended the call.

Her heart was melting with warmth. She had missed Sid too. His cheesy flirting and his sense of humour. All of it. Before Riya could travel down memory lane, the fluttering Post-it pulled her back to the present. She found the right Rahim Malik on social media and requested for his number. The number came back promptly.

There was a possibility that Rahim was behind all this, but she decided to walk straight into the lion's den. All alone.

'Hello, Rahim. I was your junior at college. Hope you remember me. I need some help or rather information from you regarding some work of non-fiction,' Riya said and paused.

'Hmm,' he said and waited for Riya to finish.

'I am doing some book research on teenage suicide and was wondering if you can shed some light on it by sharing about your cousin Sania,' Riya said and brought the phone close to her ear, as if she could identify the blackmailer from the ebb and flow of his voice.

'We weren't remarkably close. All I remember is that she was okay one moment and jumped from the terrace the next. Khaala had met her a couple of hours ago.' There was nothing in his voice to raise alarm, nor did he sound alert or cautious. On the contrary, he was apologetic for not being helpful.

'Khaala doesn't like talking about Sania's death, else I would have connected her to you,' he said, too eager to please.

'It will be a great help if you can connect me to her . . .' Riya said, adding a little sincerity to her voice. She wanted to end the call and move on to the next person on the list. But he was hell-bent on helping.

'Can I call you back after checking with Khaala? She lives down the road,' Rahim informed. She responded positively and hoped for Sania's mother to dump cold water on his enthusiasm. Talking to Sania's mother would surely send her on a guilt trip.

'Thanks so much,' she said and went back to her notepad. An hour later, a video-call request from Rahim caught her attention. He had taken his helping-a-writer project too seriously. She stalked his Facebook. He was single.

I get it.

Her immediate instinct was to ignore the call, but she answered it and found Sania's mother's face staring at her.

'Ah! It's you. I remember you. But what have you done to yourself? You had such pretty eyes. Too much reading spoils one's eyes,' Sania's mother said with maternal warmth.

Riya fought back tears and the ache of missing her mother. Rahim was lurking behind her aunt, giving Riya no choice but to keep up with the pretence of book research.

'Aunty, I wanted to ask something about Sania's death? How did it happen and why?' Riya asked, treading carefully. She had no intention to poke Sania's mother's old wounds, but asking nothing would have made Rahim suspicious.

'I was in town for some work. So came to visit her and gave food, etc., for you all. The next morning, we received the call.'

Riya wanted to look at the screen, into her eyes, but she didn't have the courage. She pretended to take notes. Tears had started to sting her eyes.

'She was found in the woods, dead. After that, what all happened, you know. The police inquiry and all,' her mother said, speaking the way one narrates a story behind a scar on one's face.

Riya had been struggling with the unwelcome tears in her eyes, but Sania's mother's eyes were dry. Rahim was again on the screen. Was he hanging around for her aunt, or for her? Had Riya fallen prey to his game? She kept up with her charade.

'She left a few suicide notes. Nothing was written in them about her decision?' Riya asked casually. But the mention of suicide notes had changed the old lady's expression, stirring something dark in her.

'Who wants the suicide note? Reet? *Kanjri* Reet asked you to call me, right?' she said and disconnected the phone.

Riya was stunned at the unexpected new finding. The expression of hatred on her face and the curse 'kanjri' meant only one thing: Reet was in some way responsible for what happened to Sania that night.

What had they missed that night? She lifted the manuscript and continued reading it.

* * *

That Night: December 20, 1997

The mess's loud bell announced breakfast, startling me. The table lamp on Katherine's desk was still on, its glare causing a deep pain in my head. I pulled the quilt over and decided to sleep for a little longer, but the warden's summon jerked me out of my sleep. My sluggish mind belatedly registered the pandemonium of voices and sirens.

Something was really wrong.

I recalled the previous night and instantly hid the empty whisky bottle in the depths of my half-packed bag. Katherine was already awake, fighting a hangover too. I woke Anjali and Natasha. They stirred in bed, refusing to get up. But the loud police siren had jolted us all. Or was it Katherine's voice?

'Sania told the authorities about us drinking. Oh god!'

Before the events in the surroundings could pierce through my foggy head, a sharp knock on the door sent my senses on high alert. The cleaner pushed open the door and asked, 'Is Sania here?'

'No, why? Is she not in her room? And why are the police here?' I asked, with my heart beating in my throat.

'She is not here too, madamji,' she shouted from the corridor. She turned back and said, 'Warden Madam has summoned everyone to the mess for a police investigation.'

I shut the door behind me and walked towards them, feeling numb with shock.

Katherine's slow whisper shattered the stony silence in the room. 'Did you guys bury the coin in the backyard? Did she come back with you?'

Before Anjali could answer, Natasha said, 'Maybe she is on the terrace. Last night, I had stopped her from going to the terrace.'

'What time? And why would she go to the terrace in this freezing cold?' I asked. My mind running miles per minute now.

'Maybe a couple of hours after Ouija, but I walked her back to her room,' Natasha said. A frown worked itself on her face.

'Was she pale? Was she looking lost?' Katherine asked. I shot a questioning glance at her as Katherine elaborated, 'Maybe she was possessed by the spirit that visited us last night. Maybe it took her to her house for the revenge she wanted.'

My mind reeled in disbelief. 'Possessed? Are you still drunk?' I asked, conquering my anger. But Katherine was unstoppable with her irrational fears guiding her.

'The Ouija board is not a joke. Spirits can enter into your body through the board and can make you do things that are dangerous for you.'

So, Katherine was blaming the occult for the missing Sania.

'We should go and ask the warden to check on the terrace,' Natasha insisted. She pulled her overcoat and cap, ready to head down, when the warden knocked on the door.

'Did you see Sania last night? She is missing. She left some suicide notes behind. It would have been an open-and-shut case of suicide, but her body is missing. However, there are traces of blood found in the backyard. The police are trying to find the body. I need you all down in the mess. Be brave, girls,' the warden said and walked out, fighting the catch in her throat.

My gaze shifted from Natasha's face to Anjali's and settled on Katherine.

'We have to keep our story consistent: We only saw Sania for a few minutes last night, when she came to give us the food that her mother had brought. You guys turned in early, and Katherine and I studied till late night. We won't say a word more until we know what happened. Sania isn't the kind who will kill herself. So we need to know what happened. Maybe she is hiding somewhere to take revenge on us?' I said.

None of them said a word, but I knew that we were on the same page. We walked to the mess in the hope that no one would notice our hangover. The cop was addressing a bunch of girls, 'Sania is missing. We found her suicide note and some blood in the backyard. My colleagues are searching for her body as we talk. If anyone knows anything about Sania's whereabouts, please come forward.'

I lifted my gaze and studied the cop. He looked sleepy and bored, and his nose was as red as beetroot, despite the layers of clothes on him.

'Here is the tea you requested,' the warden said and signalled the mess cook to hand him the cup.

'Thank you, madamji. My mornings can't start without tea. Your call literally dragged me out of bed. We will be out of your way soon,' he said, sipping the scalding hot tea, and asked, 'Which four girls are on the same floor as the dead girl?'

I noticed the way he mentioned Sania as a dead body.
A spasm of guilt contracted my throat. Before I could
break down, the warden said, 'These four. The most
well-behaved girls of their batch. They keep to themselves
and are found mostly in their rooms. The two of them
must catch a train soon and the other two have an exam
tomorrow. So, if you can please make it quick.'

The cop nodded and asked, 'Did you see Sania last
night?' He was looking at me as if he had already zeroed
in on me as the leader of the pack.

'Yeah, just after Reet, her roommate, left for home.
I had missed my dinner, so on Reet's request, Sania had
come to offer some food that her mom got yesterday,'
I said, using all the might I had to keep the quiver out of
my voice.

'Did she look normal? Did she say anything to you?'
the cop asked, taking another sip of the steaming tea.

'I don't remember anything distinct. She was in
a hurry as we both were preparing for a major exam,'
I managed to say.

'Was she sad or looking upset?' the cop asked.

'She was worried about the exam. But so was I,'
I replied.

The cop nodded and wrote my statement down
on a steno pad, with his fingers popping out from the
fingerless woollen gloves. If I had a quaver in my voice,
he had missed it. Just when I thought everything was
under control, a tear rolled down Katherine's cheek. My
heart leapt in my chest. Her emotions could throw us all
under the bus, but a uniformed cop came to our rescue.

'Sirji, we found a girl's body in the woods, eaten by the animals,' he said panting.

'So, it's an open-and-shut case of suicide,' the cop addressing us said. He finished the last dreg of tea and wrapped up his investigation.

We looked at each other, unable to understand what had just hit us. The cop had left too many questions unanswered, sending my mind into detective mode. Why was he in such a rush to close the case? And if Sania had jumped from the hostel's terrace, how did her body end up outside the hostel's boundary, in the woods? The cop had missed the obvious. Or had he closed his eyes? But any questions asked would have sent trouble our way, so I decided to tame my mind.

'Serve the breakfast,' the warden said and walked away with tears shimmering in her eyes. We sat there, pretending to eat, and then emptied our untouched plates into the refuse bin and bolted back to my room.

Katherine barged in first and began to cry. Her soundless sobs soon turned into a loud bawl that she buried in her pillow. Natasha and Anjali were crying silently. Tears welled up in my eyes and started streaming down my face unchecked.

We were blaming ourselves for Sania's death, guilt and remorse playing musical chairs. Someone had to stop it. I waited for Anjali to gain her composure and take over; she always managed every crisis in the group with a steely calm, be it an injury or unexpected sickness.

But death wasn't something we had experienced before.

'You guys get ready, else you will miss your train,' I said, plucking up the courage to start a conversation.

'Can't leave you alone now. I will go tomorrow, after your exam,' Natasha said.

Anjali was still silent, frozen like a figure in a painting.

'It was a very bad idea to play Ouija,' Katherine said and swallowed a sob.

'As bad as stealing the alcohol from the warden's room,' I snapped back in an equally reproachful voice.

Katherine sobbed and said, 'We killed her. We shouldn't have played Ouija.'

She had voiced our guilt, but she had also added an element of the paranormal to it, and I had no logical explanation to argue with her. But taking the blame for her death wasn't acceptable, not after the suicide note.

'We didn't kill her. We just got her drunk. It was a suicide,' I argued.

'We need to tell the warden,' Katherine said, refusing to budge.

'Tell her what, that the game of Ouija killed Sania? That's ridiculous. We are not telling anything to anyone. It was just a prank. We have all handled pranks and a bit of booze, and it was Sania's problem if she couldn't.' She wasn't thinking straight. I had to steer her back to reality.

'But . . .' Katherine tried to revolt but abandoned the idea.

'One more thing—if we all agree today, we all have to agree forever. This will be a promise to keep for a lifetime. No one would know, not now, not ever. We won't discuss this after this moment. Not with each other or with anyone else. Only if you all can promise, we end it here, else we can go to the warden. But before that, do let me know if I need to remind you what choosing that path would mean,' I said.

'But . . .' Anjali said, fighting a sob. But before she could say another word, I said, 'Your mom is sinking in loan to keep you here. And we might get rusticated from college.'

'I can't think of anything. Right or wrong should have been discussed last night,' Katherine said with a note of blanket accusation in her voice.

'Even if we come clean, things will never be the same. A tiny tear will rip through the fabric of our guilt. She appeared sad. I should have asked her to sleep in our room. I shouldn't have left her alone,' Natasha said.

Before Natasha's guilt of causing her sister's death could be attached to Sania's death, I lifted my arm, palm-up, and waited for the others. Anjali instantly placed her trembling hand on my cold palm and silently pleaded the others to follow. The reminder on her mother's loan had overtaken Anjali's guilt, but Natasha and Katherine were still swaying like a pendulum, unable to pick a side.

Katherine shifted uncomfortably and turned away. But Anjali's pleading eyes had convinced Natasha. We all knew about the financial hardships Anjali's divorced mother was facing to keep Anjali in college.

'Please, Kath,' Anjali pleaded.

And Katherine was left with no choice. She agreed to not discuss the night ever again.

* * *

Riya paused her reading and introspected. There were questions that they should have asked after Sania's death, but clearly their guilt had smudged their thinking. Riya listed them down.

How come Sania's body ended in the woods when she had jumped from the terrace? Did the cop say suicide note or notes? What was in the suicide note that turned Sania's mother abusive, and why the hell did she call Reet kanjri?

If only we did not feel as guilty as sin, if only I had gone back to the hostel after the winter break, if only my friends had worked a little harder to find the reason behind Sania's death.

But it was never too late.

The self-appointed Arthur Conan Doyle on this case was now the Sherlock Holmes, too.

Anjali Kapoor
23 Park Street, London

Anjali was still staring at the pixellated picture of Sid
and Katherine caught in a kissing act when the boarding
announcement started. Her legs felt a slight tremble. She
waited for everyone to board the plane first while she
sat there and reread the hacker's mail: 'Your marriage
is over. Katherine's will be over soon. You couldn't save
yours, so save Katherine's at least.'

*Why is the hacker worried about Katherine's
marriage? Is this photo for real? And when was this
clicked and where?*

The questions felt like a black hole that was rapidly
sucking into it all the light of reasoning. She stood up
and walked to the gate. The phone vibrating in her
jeans pocket caught her attention. It was a text from a
work colleague: 'All okay, Anjali? You cancelled all the
meetings for the next week??'

'Family emergency. I will get back to you. About
to board,' she texted back and switched her phone to
airplane mode before the crisis at work could change her
decision.

Work was an obsession for Anjali. She had never
abandoned it for a day, not even on her vacations. Her
mails went back and forth, no matter wherever she was.

'Wish you were as obsessed about me too,' Sid often
teased her.

He aspired for different things. A house full of kids,
an easy job and partying with friends and family. Anjali's
dreams were different—a spectacular career, her mother's

financial security and then, maybe, kids. And by the time Anjali had got down to the last item on her list, it was too late.

On the plane, the crew's request to switch off all electronic devices stirred a new prickle of anxiety in her. The hacker had developed a habit of working behind her back, and she was about to lose contact with the world for the next thirteen hours. Her only light at the end of the tunnel was the limited network coverage on the flight. However, the three sleepless nights soon caught up with her—she slept, browsed her mailbox and slept again on the flight.

Anjali breathed a sigh of relief when the plane finally touched down at Changi Airport. She rebooted her phone and waited for the signal. A welcome message popped up, in sync with the network signal: 'Welcome to Singapore!! Let's settle some old scores! You and me. See you soon.'

Anjali's mind spun and dived like an out-of-control amusement park ride. There were no digital footprints left behind for the hacker to know that Anjali was heading to Singapore. She had deliberately used her assistant's laptop to buy her ticket. Moreover, she had not told anyone that she was going to Natasha's.

No one except Rick.

Bollocks! Was Rick really behind all this? Had the hacker got hold of his phone too?

The twenty-minute taxi ride to Natasha's home felt longer than her long-haul flight from London. Anything could have gone wrong in the last fourteen hours. She was tempted to call Rick but held back. Once she reached

Natasha's house, she dismissed Rick with a quick hug and waited for him to guide her to Natasha.

'She doesn't know that you are here. Go surprise her. Let's see some light on her face. Shall we?' Rick whispered, keeping up with her pace.

He was excited, a happy excited. He opened the door, anticipating a happy Natasha. But what he saw was the exact opposite. All the light had gone out of her face. Her eyes grew bigger, as if she had seen a ghost. Rick shot a questioning look at Anjali and walked to Natasha.

'Surprise!'

Natasha rubbed her eyes, studied Anjali's face and said in a meek voice, 'Is that you, Anjali?'

'Yes.'

'Oh, I thought I just imagined you too,' Natasha said.

'Imagined her too? Who else are you imagining, Nat? You look flushed? All okay?' Rick asked. His happiness had disappeared.

'I was probably dreaming about something. Rick, I am hungry. Are the kids back? Is Teresa here? Anjali, you need something?' Natasha asked in one breath. Her words bubbling faster than she could speak. Natasha was beside herself.

'Anjali, can I get you some tea and a sandwich?' Rick asked.

Her gut was churning with fear by now. She could not stomach anything, not until she knew what was wrong with Natasha. But she requested for a black coffee, simply to get Rick out of her hair.

'Can you see someone else in the room?' Natasha asked in a slow whisper as soon as Rick left.

'Rick is gone. I will close the door. Tell me what is it.'

'Can you see Sania in the room?' Natasha asked in a timid voice. Her eyes skittered across the room.

'What the hell, Nat?' she asked, trying to keep her tone flat.

'I see her, Anjali. She plays hide and seek with me. She offers me pinni and then disappears,' Natasha said in a breaking voice.

Anjali had to ask again before she could believe what her friend was saying. 'Who can you see?'

'Sania.'

Anjali thought her skewed comprehension was a bitter concoction of jet lag and her meds, but then a suppressed sob heaved out of Natasha and made it all real.

Natasha was scared to death.

Anjali leant forward to wipe the tears from her friend's cheeks. But Natasha had gripped her hand so tightly that the half-moon indentations cut into her wrist. Tears welled up in Anjali's eyes too, but she forced them back.

'When did you start seeing Sania?' Anjali asked, after wilfully suppressing the doubt in her voice. Natasha didn't answer; instead, she stifled a sob.

'Is she here?' Anjali asked in a soft whisper. The question sounded absurd to her own ears, but the look in Natasha's eyes made her catch her breath.

What the hell? Natasha is actually trying to find Sania in the room.

'When was the first time you saw her? Was she the cause of your accident?' Anjali asked.

'After the accident, or maybe before that too, in the kids' room, via the camera,' Natasha replied and looked nervously around the room.

'Can you see her now?'

Natasha shook her head in a customary 'no' and then regretted it. A sharp pain contorted her features. She heaved out something between a sigh and a groan. Natasha's pain caused a shiver in Anjali's back.

'Rick knows about it?' Anjali asked.

Natasha again shook her head and squirmed in pain.

'You daft! Can you stop shaking that bloody neck of yours, else it will pop out of your shoulders,' Anjali scolded her, out of concern. Her love-filled anger brought some light back into Natasha's eyes, the light that had been absent since Anjali arrived.

Natasha's phone alarm went off, breaking the tension in the room.

'Hand me the medicines from the other nightstand,' Natasha requested.

Anjali picked up the white-and-green plastic bag and handed it to her. Natasha craned her neck to find the required medicine from the bag.

'What an idiot I am! Sorry, what medicine?' Anjali said, hiding her embarrassment.

'The white colour one.'

Anjali opened the packet and laughed.

'You utter fool! Most of them are white,' she said and tilted the bag for Natasha to see.

This time Natasha's smile travelled to her eyes.

'Have you ever wondered that they might have names too?' Anjali asked mockingly.

'Come and lie down here with a broken neck and let's play what's the name then?' Natasha said. Anjali fished out the pentagon-shaped medicine but held her tongue; any more corrections and Natasha would curse that the chest of drawers should fall on her too.

'So, what's the name of this pill?' Natasha asked and swallowed the pill.

Anjali raised her left brow and gave a lopsided smile.

'Finally! It's called Perminontle . . . or whatever . . . why can't pharma companies come up with some easier names? Names like George Clooney and Tom Cruise would do some good to the patient, if not the drug itself,' Anjali said light-heartedly and waited for a genuine smile to find its way on Natasha's face.

'Well, till you are cleaning my shit. Let's call it Brad Pitt!' Natasha said feigning a smile. 'You mean Rick is wiping your ass every morning! No way girl, it's only your neck, and I am sure you don't use your neck to clean your backside,' Anjali replied inducing a fake shock in her voice. They both knew that Anjali would do anything for her friend.

A minute later, the kids barged into the room, pumping more love into the air. Natasha snuggled the sweaty kids with her hurting arm. Their fragrance was probably her alternative therapy. A pang of regret jolted Anjali's heart. She had no such fragrance to drown her sorrows in.

'See who's here?' Rick said and placed the food tray on Natasha's nightstand.

'A-Square,' the boys shouted in unison.

Rick had once fed this catchy name to the kids, and after that there was no looking back. Aunt Anjali was 'A-Square' for them. Anjali scooped the twins in her arms and swirled them around. What started as one-time fun had become a ritual.

'Once more, once more, A-Square!' the boys shouted. They giggled and screamed.

But Anjali's eyes were fixed on Natasha's expressionless face. She appeared to be lost in a strange glassy world. The realization struck Anjali like a lightning bolt—Natasha was still looking for Sania. Anjali looked around to find a shadow or a silhouette, but there was nothing.

'She will feel drowsy. Let's go out. Let her get some rest,' Rick suggested.

Anjali carried the twins out and held on to them, not willing to let go of their therapeutic effect on her. The more they giggled, the more she swirled, and they giggled even more, making her ridiculously happy.

'Can we talk?' Rick asked and pricked her balloon of happiness. She had to find a way to get out of it. But dumb confusedness had descended on her mind. Rick's ringing phone came to her rescue. He answered the call, and Anjali used the moment and sped to the loo.

Behind closed doors, Anjali let her facade fall.

As if a pending divorce, a blackmailer/hacker and Natasha's injury weren't bad enough, Sania had decided to walk out of her grave, timing it perfectly. Anjali's cheeks burnt with anger, fear and confusion. She splashed water on her face and recovered her sense of self, ready to face Rick, Natasha and Sania too. She walked out and asked, 'Hey, you wanted to talk?'

'How are you coping? Nat told me about your separation.'

The tightness in her chest disappeared.

'I could be better. But it was my decision to walk out of that marriage, so I guess it's okay.' Rick's concern for her and Sid was written all over his face, but he wasn't the kind who would pry.

Rick is still looking out for her, acting as normal as always. He isn't behind all this.

'How's your brother?' Anjali asked, changing the topic.

'I thought that things were manageable. But my brother had another meltdown, and he is under medical supervision as we speak. My parents are afraid that his ex's lawyer would deem him unfit to take care of the kids. But there is not much my old parents can do to keep him calm. I wish I could be there to see them through this . . .'

Before Rick could complete his sentence, Anjali stepped in. 'Rick, I am here now. If you can go and if Natasha is comfortable with me being around, please go.'

He paused, as if reflecting on the dilemma, to choose between a bedridden wife and a suicidal brother.

'Thanks, Anjali. I will take you up on this offer if he doesn't respond to the new set of meds. Listen, do you mind staying with her for some time? I need to step out for an urgent errand,' Rick requested.

Anjali was glad that the opportunity had presented itself for her to be with Natasha alone.

'She is drowsy most of the time. So you have to be around, in case she needs something. Or you can work from the study. I can hear her from there. The Wi-Fi password is still the same,' Rick said and left Natasha in her care.

Anjali walked to the bedroom and found Natasha asleep. Her hand was raised in an awkward position. She settled on an armchair in the bedroom and scanned the room for an intruder, for Sania. Nothing.

She ran a few searches on the symptoms of slipped disc. Nothing came close to hallucination.

But there has to be a logical explanation to Sania's appearance.

She picked up the medicine bag and started searching for their side effects. Her painkiller was the most likely culprit. A wave of relief passed through her. She closed her eyes and soon the cool air of the air conditioner and the stillness in the room added to her jet lag.

Sleep came over her like a sledgehammer.

'Anjali,' Natasha's voice woke her up.

'Shit, I slept,' Anjali said and stood up, rubbing sleep away from her eyes.

'Help me to get to the loo. Where is Rick?' Natasha asked.

'He will be back soon. You need anything?'

Natasha shook her head. Anjali walked her to the loo and asked on the way, 'Do you think Rick can go to see his brother? Can I manage the kids with Teresa's help? I will take some days off.'

Natasha didn't reply. Walking was difficult for her but the look on her face meant that she was considering it. Anjali added more weight to her request, 'With the blackmailer and Sania in the picture, it's best for all of us that he goes. You know what I mean.'

She helped Natasha on to the toilet seat, closed the door and waited outside. Natasha's pained look had made her disintegrate like a sandcastle. Anjali held herself and said, 'Nat, Brad Pitt is causing this.'

'What?' Natasha asked in an agitated voice.

'I mean the medicine Perminontle is causing the hallucination. We need to tell Rick and your doc.'

Natasha took a moment to reply. 'How do you know?'

'Google Maa! An antidote will help you get rid of these hallucinations, and let me know when you are done. I will come in to clean your shit, literally.'

'Hmmm' was the only sound Anjali heard over the running faucet. Rick was right. Natasha was willing to help everyone, but asking for help was not her thing. Anjali walked her back to the bed and was about to read the search results when the incoming text turned the air in her throat solid.

'How about we start telling some truth to our best friends? Btw, she might have medicine-induced hallucination. But what are you taking to live in the fantasy world? Xanax?'

6

The Forbidden Fruit

Katherine D'Souza
38 City Apartments, New York

Sid and Anjali are getting a divorce.
Riya is writing a story about that night.
There is a blackmailer who is a skilled hacker too.
And Natasha claims that Sania's ghost is wandering in her bedroom.

Katherine didn't have the nerves of steel to survive all this. A single cigarette had turned into a pack, throwing out of the window her resolve to not smoke. She took one final crisp drag on the tailing end of the stick in her hand and relinquished it under her black stiletto.

Katherine drove back home, determined to do what she could do best, other than second-guessing herself.

She hacked.

Her first achievement as a hacker was hacking her brother's email, and then the rest was history. She had strictly adhered to her professional codes by not hacking any personal accounts thereafter. But today, for the second time in one day, she was browsing through Sid's computer, scanning through his folders with a fine-tooth comb.

It felt as unnerving as going through Sid's drawers of briefs.

She contemplated and then decided to hack Sid's phone, too. There was nothing to raise an alarm, though. Moreover, his devices were too vulnerable to be a hacker's device. She ran a quick check on his cloud; no other devices were connected to his account or to his credit card.

But if Sid wasn't a hacker, why was he part of this? *Collateral damage.*

And why was the hacker dragging the reunion night into it? What happened on the reunion night?

She dialled Sid's number to get the answers.

'Hello, KD. Terribly busy, yeah? You have no time to call! How's Sam and my little brats?' Sid asked. But his warmth didn't create an ache in her unhealed wound today. It made her recoil with repulsion instead. The hacker's allegations had tarnished her feelings for him.

She steeled herself and asked sharply, 'SK, what happened on the reunion night?'

The reply came after a pause, 'Which reunion night? Go slow, my bullet train.'

'Last year's reunion.'

'Let's see. Booze. Dance. Fun. Party as usual. But why are you asking me about the night you attended yourself? Are you now wondering what fun you missed, by going back home too early?'

Sid's answer had done nothing to calm her nerves. She reframed her question, 'Did I drink too much? Looks like I had an episode of alcohol blackout.'

'Blimey! You mean you forgot hitting on me and calling me Sam. I had to call Matty to take you home,' Sid said. That sounded more like her. But the picture sent by the hacker would not let her be in peace, not until she had reclaimed her memories, or until someone validated that nothing had happened between them. She tried again.

'So, nothing happened between us?'

Please say no.

'Why are you asking? Are you pregnant and don't know who the father is?' Sid chuckled. But his effervescent mischief didn't do its magic today.

'Sid, answer me please,' Katherine pleaded.

'Do you think I can let something happen between us? Although, it wasn't an easy feat with your stunning new looks and you hardly kept your hands off me. Look, you have a family, and I care about you and them. But Sam is a lucky man, just three drinks and Katherine is ready,' Sid said and laughed a hearty laugh.

Shame live-wired through her body along with a tinge of hatred. For the first time in her life, she wanted the call with Sid to end. He sensed it too.

'KD, what's wrong? Tell me?' Sid asked, lovingly.

Shall I tell him about the hacker? But that would mean telling him about that night.

'What happened between you and Anjali?' She asked and changed the track of their conversation.

'Who told you? Anjali? Did she tell you why she wants this marriage to be over? I don't want to leave any stone unturned, hence asking,' Sid said.

'Nothing much, actually. She just said that you guys want different things from life or something on those lines,' Katherine said and realized that she had not even asked Anjali the reason for their separation.

The silence rumbled like thunder. The lack of jokes meant Sid was hurting.

What did you do, Anjali?

'Win her back, SK. She is hurting too. Do you want me to help you guys?' she asked.

'I am trying. Thanks,' he said and disconnected the phone. Just like that.

Sid was sad and worried; she had sensed it in his voice. Was he desperate too? Was he doing all this to get Anjali back? But he wasn't the hacker, unless he had hired one.

She called Mathew next, to get the reunion night story confirmed. But the call went unanswered. Mathew was a senior-ranked official in the army. He was a loner. Always. But in the last decade his various confidential postings in the army had made Katherine's incessant efforts to keep in touch even more difficult. She called him again. This time he disconnected the call. Katherine called her father and got a similar version of the story. 'You came home too early. Mathew left us in the movie hall to pick you up. You said you wanted to save your energy for my seventieth the next day. And Mathew is out for a couple of weeks—probably for the latest insurgency in Kashmir—barely contactable.'

Her father's words relaxed her rattling nerves. But she still texted Mathew, out of concern for Sid. He could take care of Sid the way she couldn't.

'Hey, can't talk much. Urgent?' Mathew called back and asked.

'Do you know that SK and Anjali are splitting up?'

'No. Who told you? Sid or Anjali?' he asked, distracted.

'Anjali,' she said.

'Did she tell you the reason?' he asked, paying a little more attention.

'Nothing, but I think no prizes for guessing. She is doing extremely well, and he isn't. Sid is hurting, I thought I should let you know. Call him, Mat.'

'Taking his side, as always. Kath, when a relationship goes stale, both are wrong somewhere. So, hear Anjali out too, before you take sides,' Mathew said, patronizingly.

'I did. I talked to both. He is hurting more than her, Mat,' Katherine argued.

He didn't say a word after that. They both knew where the discussion was heading. She had always picked Sid over her brother and it had never bothered Mathew. He adored them both. Mathew had fought only once over Sid, and that was to get Katherine to stop smoking.

'Don't worry, I will call him later in the day. Got to go.'

Katherine was where she had started. No one to suspect. But then, who was messing up with their lives and Natasha's mind? Recalling Natasha's cry for help made her nerves taut with anxiety.

I won't be able to live with myself if something happens to the bedridden Natasha. Hacker or Sania, she could use my help either way.

She acted on instinct and booked a flight to Singapore. The kids got aligned quickly. However, Samir was startled.

'What's on fire there? And how am I going to manage the kids, the household and work?'

But she could think of nothing beyond Natasha's fear-ridden voice.

She pleaded, 'Natasha needs me. Please, this is important for me. Just manage for three days.' She gave Samir no choice but to step in.

Katherine had expected guilt to rip her apart, but as she boarded the flight she felt liberated. For all these years, she had kept her kids so close to her heart that she had forgotten how it felt to be only with herself and think about herself.

She was feeling positive about her decision to go to Singapore until she reached Frankfurt. She switched on her phone while waiting for the connecting flight and the incoming text made her cringe: 'Go back, Katherine. These girls are not your friends. They never were. Don't risk your life for them. Sania.'

The text message triggered an uncomfortable echo inside her.

Is there a real Sania? Is she really trying to tell me something?

She read the anonymous text again. How did the hacker know that she was coming to Singapore? Hacking her devices wasn't impossible, but it wasn't easy too. Her mind was bifurcated—half-worried about the hacker using IT skills to cyberbully them, and half-elated at the thought of facing a professional of the highest calibre rather than an illogical paranormal fear.

She messaged Natasha: 'On my way. Text me your coordinates. See you soon. Katherine.'

There was no point in hiding it now since the hacker already knew her travel plan.

Sania or no Sania, she wasn't going to leave Natasha alone.

This was her atonement for the secret she had kept to herself.

Natasha Gupta Lim
26 Siglap Road, Singapore

Natasha swayed between the real and the surreal
while Anjali's luggage was moved from the guest room
downstairs to the spare bedroom upstairs. The kids were
pleading her to have a sleepover in their room. The giggles
from the hallway made Natasha light with relief. Once
again, she wondered why Anjali had delayed having kids.

She was so amazing with them, and Sid doted on
Ryan and Ian like his own.

It could have saved their marriage.

An incoming text on her phone brought an end to her
chain of thoughts.

'On my way. Text me your coordinates. See you
soon. Katherine.'

Did Natasha really call Katherine, or had she imagined
that too, just like Sania? Natasha's head hung low, heavy
with medication, guilt and shame. She called Katherine
to stop her from boarding the flight, but her phone was
switched off. Katherine had boarded the plane.

*Something must have triggered that drastic a move on
Katherine's part.*

Sania.

Natasha did not believe in the metaphysical, but that
didn't mean it couldn't exist. There must be a reason why
the dead are respected and prayed for, in almost every
religion. Rick's family believed in it. They celebrated
the ghost month by preparing ritualistic food offerings
and burning papier-mâché material items meant for the
visiting spirits of the ancestors. Natasha's own mother

performed *pitrapaksh*, a similar ritual, for her deceased grandparents. However, Natasha had never believed that the dead really came back to visit the earth, but she could have been wrong all along. She looked around and spotted a shadow.

It may or may not be Sania.

Natasha looked away. Anjali had requested her to cope with her hallucinations for another night. They had decided to call the doctor soon after Rick left for the airport. Anjali had convinced Rick to go, and Natasha was glad for it. There was no way she could have explained Katherine's unplanned arrival to Rick without getting him suspicious. Because travelling miles across to be with a long-lost friend was too generous, even by Natasha's standards.

After dinner, Rick came in and handed her the last dose of the day. Natasha took it with the eagerness of a junkie taking her next fix. It alleviated the pain and the thought of Sania. Both. Hours later, Rick woke her up by planting a kiss on her forehead. 'Are you sure I can go?'

Natasha managed to smile and said, 'I am sorry for causing all this. I won't be able to forgive myself if you don't go today. Your family needs you, and Anjali is here. So don't worry.'

Rick's eyes teared up. 'Can you stop blaming yourself for everything? It was an accident, and you stopped it from becoming a mishap. Imagine if you had not pushed Ian away. You were brave, Nat. Very brave.' He planted another kiss on her forehead and left her in Anjali's care.

'Katherine is on her way to Singapore,' Natasha informed Anjali as soon as Rick left.

'What? Why would she come to Singapore? You called her?' Anjali asked in a shocked voice.

'I had panicked and called her. She was supposed to find a solution for me. Next thing I know she is on a flight. Oh God, I troubled her too,' Natasha said and fought back the lump in her throat.

Anjali cheered her up. 'You have the privilege of on-site service. Now, let's see what services she is going to render—hacker or ghostbuster. I am sure the antidote for your med will get Sania out of your world and Katherine would be disappointed, having to focus only on the hacker.'

But Natasha's guilt was sweeping her away. 'I was disoriented and disillusioned when I called her, so much so that I can't even clearly recall what all I said to her,' Natasha said and began to cry.

Anjali sat down next to her and wiped Natasha's cheeks with her thumbs.

'It's ok, babes, we will figure it out. And if we can't, Katherine will. Why not take it as a mini reunion. We will call Riya after your visit to the doctor and see if she can join us too,' Anjali said and flashed a loving smile.

'Did you talk to Katherine about the letter? Is it all sorted?' Natasha asked.

'She is still nursing old wounds, but all okay. She is goddamn late in her confession. But I can't return Sid to her now, because he is no longer mine,' Anjali said, her voice fighting a sob.

'If you think this can still be sorted, we can meet in the Christmas break,' Natasha suggested, hoping for Anjali to open up.

'It's over. Before we know, Sid's mom will find a suitable match for him. A charming Punjabi girl with even more charming Punjabi mannerisms, which Anjali, the current daughter-in-law, can't match,' Anjali said.

'You think you can keep a mother-in-law happy? Try me . . .' Natasha said, but before she could complete her sentence Anjali moved on to the next mission with the steely calm back in her voice.

'Shall we call the doc now? So that Sania disappears before Doc Katherine gets her hands dirty?' Anjali asked and dialled Parkway East Accident and Emergency. As expected, Natasha was summoned to the hospital immediately.

'You look funny with your raised arms resting on your head, looks like someone has punished you,' Anjali said teasingly.

'It's my penance. For killing Ayesha and not taking care of Sania. I could have killed Ian too,' Natasha said. She had never voiced her guilt. Never so explicitly. Injury, pain or medication, or the combination of the three had made her vulnerable.

'You make it sound like you pushed your sister down. Nat, you saved Ian, and you saved him by risking your life. You would have done the same for Sania and Ayesha. I know you. You were a kid when your sister died. Either you should have jumped with her then or you should stop drowning yourself in that guilt now. Stop blaming yourself for everything. And you had nothing to do with what happened to Sania. If anyone is to be blamed . . .' The call for Natasha from the doctor's cabin had cut Anjali short.

'This is an opioid-induced hallucination, more like a neurotoxic effect caused by an overdose. Let's reduce the dose before we change the meds altogether,' the doc said.

The doctor's assurance had loosened the noose around Natasha's neck, but it had placed the blame on Rick. Natasha wanted to count the number of pills before reaching the conclusion.

But the bigger question was: Why would Rick overdose Natasha?

Riya Banerjee
Malabar Hill, Mumbai

Riya again read the questions she had listed. One stood out, blinking like a neon light on the dark highway: Why the hell did Sania's mom call Reet kanjri?

It gave her search a sense of direction. Reet and Sania were always together. They lived in different towns, miles apart, yet they managed to travel together. Even their weekend trips home were well coordinated.

Then why did Reet leave her alone that night? And why were Reet's parents there to get her that night? Why was Sania's mother in town too, especially when Sania still had one paper left? Riya's mind was racing in all possible directions until she reached a place that was forbidden. But it was worth shaking some trees. Something would fall.

Maybe a forbidden fruit.

Riya jotted down the new set of questions storming in her mind.

Why did Reet not wait for Sania to finish her exam as always? Had something happened between them or had something stopped between them? Did a fight between Sania and Reet make her jump from the terrace? But Sania wasn't the kind to end her life for a roommate?

Were they more than just roommates?

Hold on, Riya Banerjee. Go slow. Your thoughts are again sweeping from east to west like a rolling tsunami.

But Riya couldn't stop herself. The series of questions were cutting through the fuzz of her brain. The more she thought about it, the more it made sense. They had got it all wrong. Their guilt had never allowed them to think that Sania's suicide could be anything other than an after-effect of being drunk. But clearly, there was more to the story than what met the eye.

Maybe Reet could help her answer some questions.

Reet and Riya had been Facebook friends for years. They had chatted a few times over Messenger, mostly around the time of Riya's book launch or on each other's birthdays. Reet was also in Mumbai, but somehow none of them had initiated a meeting. Now, Riya knew why.

Reet had something to hide, just like her.

She googled 'Reet Singh' and collected as much information as she could. Which was pretty much everything about her life. Reet had quit her corporate career after her first pregnancy and when her kids started primary school, Reet started a coaching centre. The centre was rated five stars almost everywhere, with special mention of Reet as a teacher. Riya wasn't surprised because back in college too, she had often seen Reet outside the examination hall, helping out someone with some last-minute doubts. Reet was the personification of benevolence, tenderness and intelligence—a perfect concoction for a teacher.

Riya launched Messenger and dialled the call, which was answered in one ring.

'Hey, Reet. Long time no see. How's work?' Riya asked. She chose her words with utmost care. There wasn't a need to alarm her, especially if she was behind this.

'All good. You tell me what's happening? How's writing treating you?' Reet asked.

Riya kept her tone casual. 'Ah! I have been better. I have just entered the market, and my publisher tells me that fiction doesn't sell well. So, planning to make one last attempt at non-fiction before I call it quits.'

'Really? Is it that bad?' Reet asked casually.

'Don't even get me started there,' Riya sighed. 'Anyways, I need a favour from you. I want to write a piece on teenage suicide, and I was thinking of writing a small chapter on Sania. I was hoping if you could share some insights.'

Sometimes catching people off guard reaps more information.

'Why me? Her brother or mother would be the right person to contact, no?' Reet asked.

The sudden change in Reet's tone caught Riya's attention. Reet was being defensive. But before Riya could frame another question, Reet had recovered.

'Listen, I need to go. My next batch of students are here,' she said.

But before Reet could disconnect, Riya jumped in, 'Reet, can we please meet up for a coffee later today? I am kind of desperate. I had submitted a proposal to the publisher and had mentioned about Sania and my proximity to her. I probably shouldn't have done it, but desperate measures, I guess. Can you please give me some facts about her? I realize that I know truly little about her and have made a tall promise to the publisher. Please help me,' Riya pleaded.

The pause was long enough to cause a wave of disappointment in Riya. But Reet surprised her by agreeing to meet. 'Okay. I will text you my address.

But you might have to wait. It's exam time, so I have extra classes.'

In a couple of hours, Riya reached Reet's house, assessed it and concluded that if Reet was behind this, it wasn't for the money. The coaching centre was bigger than Riya had expected.

She must be minting money. Then, what is her motivation?

Reet, with her reading glasses sitting on her head, ushered her into the house. If not for the fine lines on Reet's face, Riya would have passed her off as Reet's daughter. She was still that petite and untouched by age too. Reet sat and tucked her hair behind her ear repeatedly. It brought a flash of recognition. It was an old habit.

Or a sign that Reet was uncomfortable in her skin?

Riya moved towards her, but Reet avoided the hug and settled for a weak handshake instead. Her clammy palm was another giveaway. Reet was nervous but trying hard not to reveal it.

'So, you are writing non-fiction this time? A story on Sania?' Reet asked, breaking the ice.

Riya had to stick to the story. For now. 'The entire book is not about Sania. Just a chapter. I have prepared a framework of questions that I plan to cover across various chapters. More so to deduce a pattern behind suicides among teenagers. And I wanted to seek your help with Sania's chapter, only if that's okay with you?' Riya asked gently. That sounded convincing to her own ears.

'I don't remember much about her. But let's try,' Reet replied. Her eyes avoided Riya's.

'Were you close to Sania? Did she ever tell you what bothered her enough to end her life?' Riya asked, watching her intently with a notepad and pen in her hand, keeping up with the false pretence of taking notes.

'As I had suggested earlier, someone from the family will be the right person to ask,' Reet said. She picked a strand of loose hair from her dress and dropped it on the floor. The youth-filled laughter and the roar of an engine broke their momentum. 'My students,' Reet said and flashed a nervous smile, diverting from the topic.

She had clearly underestimated Reet. But Riya was not willing to give up either. 'Sania's family wasn't forthcoming. I called Sania's mother, but I think she hates Sania for ending her life, and probably for more. And she hates you too. She blames you for her death,' Riya said, adding enough accusation in her tone to shake Reet up.

A wave of unease clouded Reet's face and disappeared like a passing storm.

'Why did she blame you for Sania's death?' Riya asked, this time in a sympathetic tone. It worked better than the accusation.

'I wasn't in the hostel when Sania decided to end her life,' Reet said in a clipped voice. Riya gently brought her to a boil.

'But she also called you kanjri.'

'What she thinks doesn't matter. It never mattered to me. And why is that your concern, Riya?' Reet asked. Riya deflected the conversation, 'Do you know anything about the suicide notes she left behind? I heard that there were more than one. Her mother said that you knew about them. In fact, she was the one who asked me to come and ask you.'

Reet swallowed the shock and said, 'The hostel cleaner told me about one of them. She said it mentioned devils and monsters. Probably Sania was talking about the devils in her head, but the cleaner thought she was talking about the ghosts.'

A cold qualm of guilt assailed Riya. Sania was drunk, maybe disillusioned, or probably Katherine was right that Sania was possessed by evil in a real sense, if it was even possible. But Riya held herself back and asked, 'And the second note?'

'What second note?' Reet asked and looked at her with a storm raging in her eyes.

'There was more than one note. What about the second note? Was it for you?' Riya asked, pushing her limits a bit. Reet said nothing. Riya coaxed her further, 'Her mom thought that you sent me to recover that note from her? What was written in that note and why do you want that?'

Reet again tucked her hair behind her ear, shot a nervous glance at Riya and said, 'I requested for the note because Sania's death had left many questions unanswered. That night, she was a little upset and worried, but not enough to end her life. She was my roommate, so I guess I deserved some answers too.'

The nascent tears gleaming in her eyes shot a wave of hope in Riya. Reet was on the verge of breaking. Riya went for it.

'But why call you kanjri?' Riya asked again.

Reet's tears were flowing unchecked now. 'I received it in the post, a week after her death. I wonder how she managed to post it in the postbox across the campus, in the thick of the night. Did you guys check in on her that night? Did any of you help her in posting the note?' Reet asked.

'Do you remember what it said?' Riya deflected the conversation that could act as a trapdoor.

'I still have the note. You want to see?' Reet said and disappeared with the gait of a defeated soldier. She soon returned with moist eyes and a faded note:

I had not planned it, but love happened to me. The love that comes before all the significance of morals. The love that opens a gaping hole inside you. The love that should have suspended your reasoning. But your rationale suspended our love instead.

Don't blame yourself for anything. It wasn't your fault. It was mine. For believing in you.

So Riya was right. Reet did break Sania's heart, and for years the four of them kept blaming themselves for Sania's death.

'Sania and you were a couple, and she killed herself for you. Did you say no to her? Sania's mother knew about it, right? She called you kanjri because you betrayed Sania?' Riya asked, without bothering too much about being right or wrong.

Reet shifted in her seat, then got up and walked to the window, turning her back to Riya.

'Sania's mother preferred a dead daughter over a lesbian daughter. She calls me kanjri because she thinks that I was the one who gave Sania this "disease". I loved

Sania but not enough to let her suffer. Her uncles were ready to kill her, and her mother thought that marriage was the only cure for Sania's sexuality. But Sania wasn't the kind to give up, so her mother involved the hostel warden and my parents too. That night, I was forced to go with my parents, leaving Sania alone in the room. I came to you because I was worried about her. I thought being with others would help. And she didn't give you anything from the stash because she had just fought with her mother. Sania had promised me that she would sleep over it and act calmly. But the night left her cold and dead,' Reet said, her tears dropping incessantly.

'But why didn't you elope?' Riya asked.

'Because it's not easy to live with a divided consciousness. Sania wanted us to elope, but I didn't want her to throw away everything for us. We were too young to start on our own. However, she didn't care about society, family and friends,' Reet said and broke into a sob.

'I had no idea what you both had to go through,' Riya said. But her mind was not in Reet's sorrow; it was chasing the mystery behind Sania's death.

If we four are not to be blamed, why is someone blackmailing us?

Maybe something else happened that night. Something that has to do with the four of them. Maybe Sania didn't jump; maybe one of them pushed Sania. But then who wrote the suicide notes?

The story had a new twist. The one that would twist everything.

'I need to go,' Riya said abruptly and stood up. Her eyes caught the smiling faces of Reet's husband and two kids in the wooden picture frames on the wall. She had to ask, even though she knew the answer: 'Reet, so is this a compromise?'

'I didn't have the courage to fight. I had lost enough in the first round,' Reet said and closed the door of her house.

Riya hated Sania more than ever now. How many lives had she shattered that night?

But only if Sania had really jumped from the terrace.

December 19, 1997
Girls' Hostel
Institute of Technology, Kurukshetra

I walked back to the hostel building and spotted the back gate under the sporadic streetlight. The tears in my eyes had dried up, and the biting chill in my bones had settled to a light cold of an autumn breeze. The wintry air swirled around me, taking every lick of warmth it could. My hair fell loose about my face, tousled and tangled. I had dropped my headscarf somewhere but going ahead felt easier than doubling back.

I was about to climb up the hostel gate when I spotted the keys shining in the grass. Did I miss them the first time?

I slid my hands between the metal bars, fished out the keys and inserted one in the padlock, which yielded. I went up to my room, holding the tattered me together, reliving the night, and with every recollection, I felt less like myself.

In the washroom, I splashed cold water on my face, hoping the icy water would wash away every remnant of remorse. But I could still see the word 'sinner' written all over me.

My sins required more than a splash.

I undressed and let the icy water burn my skin. I deserved that.

And when my serrated skin couldn't take it anymore, I dressed myself, with beads of water soaking my clothes, serving as a reminder that the world wasn't a warm place, not for a sinner like me.

I walked to my room, unrolled my praying rug and kneeled to ask for forgiveness from Allah. But before I could begin the namaz, her words physically bit into me.

'Women like you have a name: fashisha. Even Allah won't accept you.'

She had quoted something from the Quran that meant nothing to me, but the expression on her face had said everything. I wasn't wanted. By the two women I loved the most—my mother and Reet.

And within the span of a night, I had failed them both. Betrayed them both. There was nothing to live for.

I walked to the stairs, but before I could unlatch the door and free my soul from all the sins by committing one last one, she had stopped me in my tracks.

7

The Haunted Beacon Tower

November 5, 2017
Katherine D'Souza
Changi Airport, Singapore

Katherine landed in Singapore and found a message from Natasha: 'Call me when you see this text.'

Anjali answered Natasha's phone and surprised her.

'Anjali, is that you?'

'Yes, I am here too. Can't wait to see you, madam,' Anjali said cheerfully.

Katherine calmed herself and took in the news. She had spent the last twenty-four hours worrying so much about the hacker and the ghost that she had forgotten about the elusive ghost of memories.

The reunion night.

'How was your flight?' Anjali asked.

Things could have gone from bad to worse in the last twenty-four hours as Katherine struggled to reach Singapore. But Anjali's calm voice was an assurance that they had not. Yet she asked anxiously, 'How's Natasha? Is she okay? What happened to her that you had to come?'

Anjali reassured her in a neutral voice. 'Don't worry. It's all okay.'

Katherine had always admired and hated Anjali's sense of control in the same breath. But she noticed how Anjali was dodging her questions, so she asked categorically, 'She told you about Sania? Is that why you are here? Is Riya coming too?'

Katherine had tried to keep calm like Anjali and had failed miserably.

'Yes, she did tell me about Sania. They are hallucinations triggered by her pain medication. Hopefully, the symptoms will subside with reduced levels of the drug. Rick might have accidentally given a dose extra. We are looking into it. More when we meet,' Anjali said.

Katherine's mind again recoiled back to Natasha's suspicion of Rick. Doing just a quick check into Rick's account was negligence on her part; she should have scanned every mail in the inbox and dug out the dirt on Rick, if any. She wanted to end the call and begin the hacking, but Anjali's words changed the course of her thoughts, yet again.

'I am at her place. We can share the room at Nat's. Come over,' Anjali said.

A pang of jealousy gripped Katherine. How come Anjali got everyone's love—Sid's, Natasha's and Riya's? She too had crossed oceans to come and help Natasha, and Natasha hadn't even bothered to answer her phone.

Katherine got a grip on her emotions and said, 'I have already paid for the hotel, might as well use it. Will come soon.'

She had put cold water on Anjali's warm invite. But she needed some time alone to work on the flood of emotions that were making her go crazy—jealousy was the new one added to a long list. She checked in at the hotel, video-called home and was pleasantly surprised to see Samir wearing an apron and serving dinner to the kids. It melted her heart into a soft blur.

I have never given him a chance to win me over.

The realization came from nowhere. Maybe one day she would feel for Samir the way she felt for Sid. Katherine shook her head vigorously, as if thoughts were a bunch of flies buzzing in her head. It worked.

She hacked into Rick's accounts once again but found nothing suspicious in them. There were a few extra security features embedded into his accounts and devices, but nothing that she could not easily crack, and when Katherine found nothing on Rick, she regretted going against her instinct.

No one would go to that extent to trouble his wife. Unless he was a psycho.

She decided to call Natasha and wipe away her suspicions too.

She texted Natasha: 'Call me back, please. We need to talk before I head to your place.'

The call came in immediately.

'Hey, so sorry Katherine, I get totally zapped out after the meds. How was your flight? Good you decided to rest first. With two jumping jacks at home, you can't get a wink, unless you are drugged the way I am,' Natasha said. She sounded irritable yet warm.

Is she unhappy that I came unannounced? Or is she in pain?

'You can still see Sania in your bedroom?' Katherine asked, skipping formalities.

'I saw a blurred figure in the room a while ago, not fully sure,' Natasha said in a tone of disbelief at her own statement.

'Even after the reduced dose? Did you check with your hubby why he overdosed you?' Katherine asked.

'Rick is travelling. Will call him tonight and check. You checked his computer and phone, right? Anyways, why are we talking over the phone? Come home.'

Katherine said, 'Nat, I will come soon but not now. I am going to meet a cybercrime expert. He used to be a cyber security crime officer at the police force before he started on his own a couple of years ago. He comes with a strong recommendation from a Singapore-based client. If he can't help, we will have to escalate it to the cyber police.'

'What do you mean, Kath? Why do you need someone else to find the hacker?' Natasha asked with panic in her voice.

'Nat, this is organized blackmail. The hacker has cloned our phones. He is using a virtual private network that is difficult to find. Moreover, his computer's unique identifier is buried at all times. I need an extra pair of hands with some dark web experience. Do you think Rick would have the resources and the motivation to do all this?'

'I don't think he can pull an act that expansive. And Kath, your jargon-loaded statements are scaring me,' Natasha said with a quiver in her voice.

'I thought it would be a relief to know that all this isn't a paranormal thingy,' Katherine said and felt a tinge of regret. She had scared Natasha further.

'Kath, I still feel very weird. Like someone is chasing me. Like the freak accident wasn't an accident actually,' Natasha whispered into the phone.

Natasha's words again swayed Katherine's volatile mind, but the taxi notification on her phone didn't allow her to pick sides. 'Nat, just stay put for a couple of hours more. I will be there soon, and hopefully with some answers and some solutions. Till then, you pray and rest. Okay?' Katherine said and heard Natasha's sigh before her reply.

'Cool. And listen, you don't have to share a room with Anjali in case that's what is stopping you. You can stay in my room or she can move to mine.'

'Have to go,' Katherine said. She ended the call and rushed to the taxi stand. In the taxi, Katherine replayed Natasha's offer in her head.

You can stay in my room or she can move to mine.

Was there a real choice? Anjali and Natasha were like soul sisters, always together. Katherine had always felt happy about it, an envious–happy kind of happy, and she had hoped that Riya and her friendship would take that shade too. But it never happened. Sania's death had robbed her of that chance.

The taxi stopped and brought her back to the crisis on hand.

The cybercrime expert ran some searches and found a lead. The hacker had used the airport's network to send the previous text received by Katherine. The expert tried tracking the device, but it sent his search into loops.

'Ms Katherine, this isn't a slip-off. It's a breadcrumb. The hacker used an open network to announce his or her presence in Singapore,' he concluded. After a long pause, he continued, 'I think we should get the police involved. Can your friend come down with me to the police station?'

'My friend is bedridden, so won't bother her until it's required. Let's wait and watch for a couple of hours. Will let you know if anything,' Katherine said and ended the meeting, disappointed. The need to smoke lingered in her stomach like a slow and steady hunger picking its pace. The incoming text accelerated it: 'Last warning! Go back home. You are not needed here. Sania.'

She walked to the nearby Starbucks, settled herself with a mug of steaming cappuccino and requested for the meeting that she had procrastinated on all morning. Then she did what the hacker wanted her to do.

Katherine booked herself on the first flight to New York. If the hacker was monitoring her phone activity, she was willing to hand that bastard some bag of shit.

A web check-in text message would confirm my departure.

She then installed an encrypted sim into a new burner phone that she had picked from Changi Airport and waited for the paranormal investigators to show up. The meeting with the cybercrime expert had led her nowhere, dragging her supernatural fears out in the open.

It's just a backup.

But unlike her previous meeting, she had no clue what to expect from this one. Katherine had reached out to the so-called ghostbusters using a Facebook group. She was surprised to see many such groups working in Singapore. Twenty minutes later, she found herself facing two men in black jeans and black T-shirts who were sitting across the table and describing the process of ghost hunting.

'We investigate the site using these specially calibrated electromagnetic field meters that can detect radiation from unidentified sources. We also use thermal cameras with high sensing capabilities to detect the presence of those from the afterlife. In fact, we have an expedition planned for tonight for our new members. If you don't mind being awake at odd hours, please feel free to join us,' said the taller one.

Katherine was genuinely impressed by the technology and the scientific explanation behind all this. But she was not willing to commit anything on Natasha's behalf. 'Sounds impressive. And what happens when you confirm a presence?' she asked.

'You can move out of that house or get some remedies done. We will take one step at a time,' said the tall man while his partner flashed a synthetic smile.

She thanked them and shared her local number with a promise to revert soon.

The scientific note of the meeting had cleared her head in an unusual way. She had planned to head to Natasha's but decided to go to the hotel instead, playing the game the hacker wanted her to play.

'But you are booked with us for two nights,' the receptionist at the counter said.

'I need to go back to New York, urgently,' she explained and walked out of the hotel.

Katherine needed time and tools to see how far the hacker had penetrated their devices. But right now, all she wanted was to make the hacker believe that she was scared enough to leave Singapore.

She had just boarded a taxi to Natasha's when a message appeared on her screen.

'We need to talk before you reach Natasha's. I think Rick is behind this. This is my new burner phone. I have a feeling he is tracking us all. Meet me at Parkland East, Starbucks. I am heading there. Anjali.'

Katherine read the text again. Her mind split in two. Rick being the hacker made sense and yet something wasn't fitting right. Katherine allowed her mind to leap and bound, and come back with some logic.

Natasha's sightings and her paranoia—Rick must be messing up with her. He must have used the airport's network by accident and not on purpose. And he had threatened Katherine to go back so that he could continue playing with Natasha's mind, until he had achieved what he wanted. For any other hacker, Katherine's location wouldn't have made a difference. But for Rick, it mattered because whatever he was doing at home was about to be caught. And there must be a reason for Natasha to suspect Rick.

Katherine asked the driver to take a detour to Parkland East, almost convinced that Rick was behind this. Her teeth again worked on her lower lip, until it started to hurt. She had bitten it so many times in the last twenty-four hours that her lower lip was wounded.

Or is it a crack caused by smoking?

The tiny size of the island dawned upon her when Katherine reached the beach within ten minutes. The pack of Marlboro on the car's dashboard caught her attention. 'Can I borrow a cigarette from you?' Katherine asked the driver.

The driver nodded and offered the pack and a lighter. She lit one, paid extra for it and walked out of the car park towards Starbucks, smoking vigorously. She dumped the half-finished stick on the metallic part of the green bin and rushed into the café.

Anjali was not there. Katherine belatedly realized her mistake.

Why would Anjali call her here? She could have come to the hotel.

She unlocked her phone to call Anjali and found it in airplane mode. The hacker had severed the communication channel between them.

So, this is a trap.

She disabled the mode and waited for the signal. The incoming text that followed sent a shiver down her spine: 'I am at the Amber Beacon tower. Walk over. 5 mins. Sania.'

She called Anjali, Natasha and then Anjali's burner. Nothing. This was all well planned. Every minute of it. She fished out the pepper spray from her bag and braced herself for an encounter.

Bring it on, dear hacker!

'Which way to the Beacon tower?' Katherine asked a jogger stepping down the pathway. He pointed to the beach shore. The sun had retreated, leaving behind a fiery orange sky that was plummeting to darkness rapidly.

Everything has turned dark in a moment.

The slowly appearing lights on the sailing vessels in the ocean seemed like solar-powered fairy lights coming to life, one by one. She walked to the beach and spotted the striking mustard-yellow tower standing next to a crooked tree. The tree's branches were bent down as if to kiss the lantern room of this abandoned lighthouse. Her eyes followed the spiral staircase and spotted a couple sitting on it. Katherine tugged her luggage on the grass patch, with sweat soaking her black T-shirt.

Her back was covered with static electricity as she approached the tower. Someone was watching her. She turned around, but just then the light in the tower was lit up, warding off the darkness around her.

The couple sitting on the staircase were gone. She looked around, trying to spot them. Nothing. Her heart started beating in every part of her body, and the incoming text made the blood quicken in her veins.

'I had warned you. Now face the music. Come up the stairs, let's talk. Sania.'

The thought lingering at the back of her mind came to her swiftly.

The Beacon tower was chosen for a reason.

She googled the location. The lighthouse in front of her was one of the five most haunted places in Singapore. There were several sightings reported around the tower, sightings of a girl. According to urban legend, a pair of masked attackers had stabbed the girl to death, leaving her lover behind, and now the girl's ghost haunted the tower. Passers-by had often heard a girl's voice screaming for help.

Katherine strained her ears to hear something. Nothing.

Her mind intuitively connected the past and the present. The girl who had visited them on the Ouija night as a ghost had died while she was out on a date, and so had the ghost who haunted this beacon tower. The lovers of the ghosts had survived the night in both the cases. The similarities were too uncanny to be coincidental. She cast a slow glance at the top of the tower, braving herself to climb up the stairs.

She imagined herself all alone, on the top of the haunted tower.

No way I am going up there.

Katherine turned around and broke into a run. But the firm hand on her shoulder had locked her movement. Or was it the weight of fear at the back of her neck?

Anjali Kapoor
26 Siglap Road, Singapore

Anjali was playing with the twins when her phone beeped: 'Katherine is at the Amber Beacon tower. Airport is not far from there. Make her board the flight that she has booked herself on. Else, I will tell what you did that night.'

Why the hell did Katherine venture out alone? What was she thinking? And what all does the hacker know about that night?

Anjali dialled her number, but before it could ring, a voice announced: 'Sorry, your call is restricted.'

Anjali called again. The disembodied voice repeated the message. Her heart shrank, consuming all the oxygen in her body. She left the kids in the helper's care and rushed to Natasha's room. She had dozed off. Anjali was glad for it; Natasha was already on the brink of breaking down, and subjecting her to another crisis might have had a catastrophic effect.

Anjali bolted out and googled the location of the tower. While waiting for a cab, she called the hotel, but Katherine had checked out. It was as though a cold fist was squeezing her heart.

'Please drive faster,' Anjali requested the driver. The minutes in the cab felt like hours, and every call she made to Katherine got the same response: 'Sorry, your call is restricted.'

It's the work of the hacker.

Anjali left the two ten-dollar bills on the passenger seat and ran to the shore and spotted Katherine. Alone.

She winked back tears of relief and sped to her. But Katherine broke into a run. Anjali leapt forward and placed a hand on Katherine's shoulder to stop her.

Katherine's slow, breathy scream set off a lightning bolt of fear in Anjali's heart.

'You didn't call me here, right?' Katherine asked, shivering violently.

Anjali felt like a bundle of nerves herself. But Katherine needed her. She steadied herself and walked her to the concrete bench next to the tower and sat her down.

'This tower is haunted by a dead girl,' Katherine said and pointed to the yellow structure.

'What?' Anjali asked.

'It's a haunted location. See,' Katherine said. She beckoned Anjali to read the text on her phone. Anjali had barely managed to pull Natasha out of the clutches of her fear of the paranormal, and now Katherine was going down the same path.

No ways.

'Kath, the hacker is pushing the right buttons for all of us, and this is a fear tactic to keep you from finding the truth. Don't you get it?'

'But how is it possible that an ex-police officer is unable to find any tracks too,' Katherine said and paused. Anjali locked her eyes and waited for her to continue. 'I also went to the paranormal investigator.'

'And they found it?' Anjali asked with a sarcastic laugh, belatedly realizing her mistake. But Katherine had retreated into a shell. 'Kath, there is no ghost. Okay? There is a hacker. Let's find him or her. All right?' Anjali said, adding more warmth to her voice.

'Hmm,' was all Katherine said, still hidden in her shell.

Anjali decided to divert her attention. Although talking about Sid was like opening a new can of worms, she decided to give Katherine a bigger problem to deal with. It had always worked. At least during the hostel days.

'While we are here, let's get your high-school reunion night out of our hair, shall we?' Anjali asked, keeping her feelings under check. Katherine's reply felt honest yet rehearsed.

'It was dad's seventieth the next day. Coincidentally, Sid was in town. But you were in Dubai for an off-site. Anyways, he arranged an impromptu dinner with a few high-school friends who were in town that weekend. We chatted and drank. There is not much to tell because nothing happened between us, definitely not what the picture sent to you depicts. And Anjali, he is hurting. He loves you a lot,' Katherine said, maintaining eye contact.

But Anjali's mind was chasing a suspicion.

'Were you guys too drunk to not even know what was going on? I am worried about your marriage, Kath,' Anjali asked in a voice that did not feel neutral to her own ears. Katherine shot a questioning glance at her and said, 'I don't think we ended up in bed or kissed each other. That click seems to be photoshopped. I won't forget a thing like that. Would I?'

Anjali parted her lips, then swallowed back her words.

Katherine would be the last person to hear anything against Sid.

'Frankly, I can't recall anything as I was borderline wasted that night. But I called Dad and Sid, and their stories matched. I came home unusually early that night, as I was tired and anxious about the big event next day. You know that I am not a party person. So, it fits the narrative. But what I don't understand is how the reunion night is linked to the Ouija night. And why is the hacker dragging your and my marriage into it?'

Anjali paused for a moment too long and said, 'Nothing is making sense, Kath. Apart from one thing: The hacker doesn't want you to be here. I have been threatened to send you back. So let's go to the airport to receive Riya, and on the way we will figure out what to do. I am calling a cab. Meanwhile, you switch on the location service on your phone so that the hacker thinks you are heading to the airport.' The news of Riya's arrival lifted Katherine's spirits.

'I can't believe that this crisis is actually turning into a reunion that never happened,' Katherine said.

But Anjali's mind had caught on to an idea. It flared and spun. Katherine mumbled something in excitement, but Anjali heard nothing; she was too engrossed in her own head, hatching a plan.

'Is it what I am thinking it is? Do you care to say it, or am I supposed to read your eyes?' Katherine asked, rolling her eyeballs.

'Okay, so the hacker wants you to leave Singapore, right? And the only way the hacker can know this is by monitoring your phone. What if your phone travels but you stay back?' Anjali asked, with childlike excitement in her voice.

Katherine was still catching up when Anjali firmed up her next move.

'You go and dump your phone in someone's bag.'

Katherine looked at her and rolled her eyes again. 'You think I can keep a straight face like you? It was your and Riya's forte.'

They stepped out of the cab and walked to the departure gate. Katherine was quickly calculating the risk.

'But it will get caught at security check,' she said as they entered the gate. Anjali paused near the kinetic rain sculpture to formulate the plan.

'See, that aunty is alone and trying hard to adjust her overweight suitcase. I will go and slip this in. I will play the Indian-helping-Indian card and the phone won't get caught in the cabin bag,' Anjali suggested and gave Katherine no time to react.

'I hope you have a backup for this? Also, send a message to Natasha and tell her that you are going back, as you fear ghosts.'

Katherine did what she was told. She then handed the phone to Anjali and said, 'Mat gave it to me on my birthday.'

'I will buy you a better one. By the way, is he still married to the country or has he found himself a wife?' Anjali asked to distract her. Katherine shook her head.

Anjali walked to the old woman struggling with the suitcase and offered her help.

'I don't mind if you can help me close this suitcase. Thanks,' the old lady replied.

Anjali slipped the phone in, zipped the suitcase and walked away.

'Mat's little reward to her for throwing the hacker on a wrong trail,' Anjali winked. 'You borrow someone's phone and call Natasha's landline and tell her to switch off all her devices, etc. Tell her that you are on your way and then go and help her.'

'I can only help if there is a real hacker monitoring us,' Katherine said. The dread on her face had returned.

The flicker of fear in Katherine's eyes compelled Anjali to pull her into a hug.

'You are stinking,' they both said in unison and broke into a laugh.

Katherine fished out a travel perfume bottle from her handbag, sprayed some on her and passed it to Anjali. 'All that running on the beach, that too with my luggage. And this city is really humid and hot man. Okies, you wait for Ms Beautiful. I will head to Natasha's. See you there.' Anjali's hug had calmed Katherine.

The smile, her model-like curves and her sleek haircut had transformed Katherine into a gorgeous woman.

Had Sid fallen for her new avatar, on the reunion night? Did she tell him something about the Ouija night? And was the hacker's threat really a threat?

Anjali felt worry tightening her stomach. But Riya's smiling face wiped away every fear.

'What happened to your trademark crop tops and skin-tight jeans?' Anjali asked when Riya walked to her in a shapeless high-low cotton dress.

'So, you stalk me on social media?' Riya asked opening her arms for a hug.

'As if you don't,' Anjali teased and hugged her.

She had missed Katherine, but she had missed Riya the most. Riya made her laugh like no one else, and in Sid's absence she needed it the most.

'Switch off all the devices you have and let's get a burner for you and me,' Anjali said.

In the taxi, Riya brought Anjali up to speed with her findings about Sania and Reet. Riya was as articulate as ever, working on the case like a murder squad on the hunt for a criminal.

'Do you think Reet or Rahim could be behind this?' Anjali asked.

'I had the same thought, but I didn't find anything alarming. Rahim connected me to Sania's mother, and Reet trusted me with a secret that she had not even told her family and husband. But let's ask Katherine to check on them,' Riya suggested.

'The hacker knows Katherine's abilities and that's why wants her to go back,' Anjali said and briefed Riya about the Beacon tower episode. But like always, Riya added a new dimension to the story. 'What if the hacker is not scared of her? What if the hacker wants to protect her?'

Anjali's heart skipped a beat.

Sid could scare Katherine and protect her as well. But why was he blackmailing them all, when he could have settled the account with Anjali alone, behind closed doors?

Natasha Gupta Lim
26 Siglap Road, Singapore

The doorbell rang and pulled Natasha out of her slumber. A minute later, Katherine walked in. The glamorous, attractive, lean and toned Katherine. She looked nothing like the Katherine Natasha had known. But underneath her transformed looks, Katherine was still the same soft girl. The WH Smith bags in both her hands were proof of that. The kids had been expecting Anjali, but the books that had come out of the bags compensated for her absence; Dr Seuss had proved to be a fine replacement for Anjali.

'Is she here?' Katherine asked. Her voice was a mix of worry and anxiety.

'No, but I am scared in anticipation.'

The silence in the room had come alive with Katherine's arrival. They could still talk with their eyes, with slight movements of their jaws and with absolute silence too. Natasha always felt that her bonding with Katherine was different from what she had with the other two. Katherine's restlessness and high-on-emotion state always mirrored a part of Natasha's mind. While Natasha hid her feelings in the dark folds of her heart, Katherine carried them on her sleeves.

'I'm Yertle the Turtle! Oh, marvellous me! For I am the ruler of all that I can see,' Katherine read in an animated voice and turned the page while stealing a glance and questioning Natasha with her raised eyebrow.

Natasha shook her head and felt a warm feeling in her heart. Katherine's presence had unrolled a new yarn of emotions, a feeling of loss—the way a kid realizes how much he had missed his lost toy only after finding it.

A teardrop coursed down Natasha's cheek.

'Stupid girl, you will be okay soon,' Katherine assured. The kids began to giggle, and Ian said in a complaining tone, 'Mommy, Aunty used the "S" word.'

'Kath, very bad. Stupid is not a nice word to use,' Natasha warned.

'Mommy used it too,' Ryan said and laughed a hearty laugh.

Katherine brought her hands to her ears and gestured a sorry. Natasha followed.

The house help walked in, interrupting the reading session. 'Come Ian and Ryan, time for bed.'

'Mommy, can we wait for A-Square?' Ryan asked, stalling for time.

'Ryan, Anjali is out for some work. Aunty T will tuck you in.' The boys started whining.

'Mommy, how about Aunty T just helps them brush their teeth and change them into their pyjamas? And then I will tuck them in bed with a quick story about how superman saved an aeroplane?' Katherine asked with a genuine smile.

The boys, who were about to throw tantrums, rushed out of Natasha's bedroom without wasting any time. Katherine's years of handling kids had clearly given her an edge.

'Where is she now?' Katherine asked in a slow whisper when the kids had left.

'She appears and disappears like a flash of light. It's some mind-twisting hallucination, if it's a hallucination at all,' Natasha said. Her words sounded weak and dubious to her own ears.

'Let's hack-proof your house first, and then we will call the ghostbusters to handle the metaphysical stuff, if needed. You hang in there. I know it can be unnerving to see the dead, but tell yourself that it is a hallucination. Meanwhile, can you ask your helper to bring all the electronic devices to you? I hope you have turned them all off, including the Wi-Fi,' Katherine asked, in a professional voice.

She walked out but was back in a jiffy.

'The IP camera in the kids' room, is it offline? It's blinking,' Katherine said.

'I have switched off the Wi-Fi. I can check again,' Natasha said.

'Yes, please. And do not turn on the Wi-Fi,' Katherine said and walked out. Natasha launched the app on her phone, almost convinced that the camera was offline, but saw the kids giggling at the story Katherine was narrating to them.

Natasha deactivated the camera. But it was too late. The hacker must have seen Katherine too. She impatiently waited for Katherine's return.

'Kath, I screwed up. The camera in the kids' room seems to be using some other network,' Natasha said with a tremble in her voice and showed her the screenshot of her and the kids.

Katherine lifted all the devices from the bed and walked out. She came back, closed the door and asked in a slow whisper, 'Do you think Rick can be behind this? Because if your IP camera is still working on a cellular network, it's highly likely that he is the only one who knows that and had planned it that way. Also, who buys a cellular camera for a house?'

Natasha's mind was turning woolly with the meds that she had just popped. She took some time to recall the reason for the cellular camera. 'When we shifted, we had numerous issues regarding the broadband line and then with the optical fibre too, if that makes sense to you. Moreover, on second thought, he knows nothing about us. At least the way the hacker knows us,' Natasha said.

Katherine walked out and came back with her laptop. She hacked into Rick's account yet again and got his location. He was in Sydney. His last login was from a residential property address. She then launched the camera app and asked Natasha to log in.

'There is an unusual data flow. Also, someone has tampered with the settings of the camera using a virtual network. I will physically disconnect the camera,' Katherine said.

She was about to step out when the text on Katherine's laptop made her freeze: 'I see you, Katherine. Now, instead of finding me, find the truth behind Sania's death.'

Riya Banerjee
26 Siglap Road, Singapore

Natasha's duplex house was like a dream. Every piece of
the furniture tastefully picked and every wall of the house
aesthetically accessorized. Riya walked up the staircase
and witnessed Natasha's kids growing from tiny infants
to little boys wearing soccer jerseys.

*It must be a wonderful feeling to relive the same
moment again and again through a photo gallery on the
staircase.*

She wanted to experience this feeling too. The desire
to be a mother had grabbed Riya from nowhere. Had
the knowledge of Reet's incomplete life scratched Riya's
wounds and left them to bleed? Or was it her friend's
complete life that made her feel incomplete? Sometimes
you need to be deprived of something to feel its presence,
and sometimes it's the presence that can make you feel
deprived.

Anjali, who was leading her to Natasha's bedroom,
paused and flashed a quizzical look at Riya.

'This wall is for admiring. Don't be in such a hurry,'
Riya said to drift Anjali's attention away from her face.

'Be my guest. I want to check if Natasha is okay.
Find your way up to her bedroom, okay?' Anjali said and
rushed up.

The mention of Natasha kicked Riya out of her self-
pity. She walked into Natasha's room with a smile, but
Katherine's new, sleek haircut caught her attention first.
She looked stunning in her black T-shirt, blue jeans and a
fresh coat of make-up.

Too stunning, considering what just happened at the Beacon tower.

'Who nibbled your hair? The city mouse or the country mouse? What have you done to our Katherine with the long unruly hair?' Riya asked Katherine.

'Someone has to compensate for the low quotient of beauty in the world. Especially, after you graced the nerdy look. I wish you had focused on writing a good story, though. Your looks won't help you sell the books—not this look. And why the hell did you kill the antagonist in the short story you sent me? I am so disappointed,' Katherine said and gave her a tight hug.

Katherine was always in a rush to fit everything into a single sentence.

'Oh, so you read it already. And what's wrong with killing the antagonist? And why do you always fall for the wrong guy?' Riya asked.

Oops, that wasn't meant to come out that way.

Katherine's expression changed and Riya noticed a shift of emotions on Anjali's face too. Natasha came to her rescue, 'Ah, bitches! No one cares about this bedridden friend.'

'Oh, I didn't see you. Now, that's the disadvantage of losing too much weight. How are you, my loose nut?' Riya covered up.

And they all started talking at once, about everything, but that night. Riya was the one to tie them together with a pact to not discuss that night, but the missing pieces could only be picked up now by breaking the promise and reliving the Ouija night. But before that, Riya decided to clear the fog of suspicion from her head.

'I hate to burst this bubble, but we need to get the hacker sorted. Kath, any idea why the hacker wants you to be missing from the scene?' Riya asked. She had pretended to be normal for long enough.

Anjali shot a warning glance at Riya, which she ignored. But Katherine's eyes were still glued to her screen, running some tests on the devices. Katherine answered with her attention still on the screen. 'Maybe because I reached out to the cyber police? Maybe because I am this close to getting him.'

Riya was weighing Katherine's every word.

'How do you know the hacker is male?' Riya asked.

'I don't. How would I know, Riya?' Katherine asked, irritated yet clacking away at her keyboard.

'Because you just called the hacker "he",' Riya explained.

Katherine lifted her head up from the screen, established eye contact with Riya and said, 'For a moment, I really thought that there was a ghost. Especially, after I finished reading the folklore around the Beacon tower. I swear to god, I saw a couple sitting there a minute ago and then they disappeared into thin air. The hacker or the ghost, someone is playing with my mind and yet he or she is scared of my presence.'

Anjali walked to where Katherine was, as if symbolically picking sides and said, 'The hacker picked that lighthouse to scare you. Kath, you have not shaken a few trees, you have burnt the entire forest. And the hacker is desperate to keep you away. So, I take it as a good sign.' Katherine's perplexed expression meant she was just as clueless about the hacker.

Before Riya could move on to her next agenda, Anjali asked, 'Anything on Reet or Rahim?'

'Nothing at all. Their laptops are clean apart from the porn sites visited by them,' Katherine added.

'Discount that. One is single and the other compromised her happiness,' Riya said. She paused for a moment to swallow the kernel of regret and added, 'Reet claims that Sania posted a letter to her that very night. A letter she had written after they fought. But the exam question is: How did she manage to post the letter to Reet? The postbox was a fair distance from the hostel. How did Sania go there in the night?' Riya paused for breath, lifted her notebook and said, 'Let's go through this together.' She started reading the timeline of that night. She had jotted it together while waiting for the Singapore consulate to process her emergency visa.

Everyone nodded, confirming the series of events that played out that night. They had not talked about that night, but it was clear that each one of them had lived it. Time and again.

A missing link was all they needed to tie the loose threads of the narrative. Natasha provided the first one. 'Riya, was Sania into smoking?'

'Not that I know about. But we can check with Reet. Why?'

Natasha readjusted her hand again on the pillow and said, 'That night, a couple of hours after the game of Ouija, I met Sania near the staircase. I was surprised that she smelt of nicotine. One more thing. I had discounted it as my imagination back then, but it's now worth mentioning that I saw a shadow in the woods that night.

However, the timeline is all mixed up. I can't remember if I saw it before or after meeting Sania. Kath, could it be the dead Sania staring at us from the window?' Natasha asked in a fear-laced voice.

Riya didn't like how Natasha was looking at Katherine to support her irrational fears. She took command before it was too late.

'Anjali, anything strange you noticed when you and Sania went downstairs? Did she smoke?' Riya asked.

Anjali averted her gaze, walked to the window and said, 'That night, I had locked Sania out of the hostel.'

Anjali's stark and naked truth stunned everyone in the room. The hacker's message— *Each of the friends is hiding a secret guilt about that night. What will happen when the others find out?*—flashed like a yellow 'KEEP OUT' sign at a construction site.

So this was the secret the hacker was talking about.

Riya's anger suddenly caught fire. But Katherine was the first one to attack Anjali, 'What do you mean locked her out of the hostel?'

'That night, we'd fought. It started with Sania confessing that she had the hots for Sid. She thought I too had a crush on him. I warned her to shut up, but then she said that Katherine was madly in love with Sid, but Sid was fooling around with Riya. She suspected that Riya and Sid were a couple but were not letting the cat out of the bag. I still kept my calm, but then she said something outrageous. Sania suggested that since we shared clothes and shoes, we could share Sid too, and whoever could make him happier could have him. Including her. I tried keeping my calm but when she insisted on burying the coin and the Ouija paper in the woods instead of the backyard, I just granted her her wish, and locked her out. She had gotten on my nerves with her stubbornness, and frankly, I was too drunk for a rational back and forth.'

Riya blinked as if she had woken up in an alternate reality. 'You locked her out? How? Where did you get the backdoor keys from?' Riya demanded. Her cheeks were flushed with anger.

'It was in the bunch that Kath got from the warden's room. Sania tried a few before getting it right,' Anjali answered, still not establishing eye contact with any of them.

'And the warden was so busy drinking with her lover that she had handed Kath the entire bunch. Holy shit! That means we did kill her. Sania might have died while attempting to get back into the hostel,' Riya concluded.

Katherine jumped in to support Anjali, the way Anjali had supported her a moment ago. 'I don't think so. I am not fully sure, but I have a vague memory of seeing her in the bathroom, just out from the shower, with her skin red from the harsh scrubbing. I might have imagined it but even Nat saw her a couple of hours after the Ouija, right?' Katherine asked.

Anjali walked away from her friends and sat on an armchair with her head in her hands. Riya steadied her racing breath and scribbled in her notepad.

Anjali had locked Sania out. Sania had managed to crawl back into the building, bringing along the stench of nicotine, which she washed away by scrubbing herself vigorously. Natasha had seen a silhouette in the field, and she thinks it was the dead Sania.

I would rather have a root canal than go through this night.

'So now I know why Sania called you a bitch, and why her hijab was missing. I might have met her soon after she made her way into the building. It was a chilly night, Anjali. What were you thinking? And why didn't you tell us about it?' Natasha said angrily.

'Because initially I was too shocked to react, and then you guys started the mud-slinging. Also, you had confirmed that Sania came back to her room. And when a suicide note was found in the backyard, I was convinced that my locking her out had nothing to do with her suicide or death. However . . .'

Before Anjali could complete her sentence, the lights in the room started to flicker.

The pattern in the flicker meant it wasn't a short circuit. Someone was playing with the lights, switching them on and off, purposely.

Before one of them could turn the light off, the loud music blaring from downstairs startled them all.

8

The Presence

November 5, 2017
Anjali Kapoor
26 Siglap Road, Singapore

'Get the kids here, Anjali,' Natasha said in a panic-filled voice.

The words that Anjali had strung together with so much effort, shattered under the blow of panic. *My guilt is my cross to bear.*

Anjali calmed her racy breath and bolted to the kids' room. The music coming from the speaker downstairs in the living room was echoing in an eerie way. She lifted the scared twins, enveloped them in her warmth and doubled back to Natasha's room.

'I am feeling cold,' Ian said. She placed the boys next to Natasha and studied the aircon control panel mounted on the wall. The temperature displayed was sixteen degrees.

Someone had tampered with the aircon too.

Before Anjali could crank up the temperature, the music from the living room went a notch up. Increasing the fear. Slow and steady. Anjali raced down and killed the power to the sound bar. But before she could breathe a sigh of relief, a speaker somewhere on the second floor came to life with loud, ear-screeching static. She sped up to the room, climbing three steps at a time.

The female voiceover announced on the home intercom system: 'All I want from you is to find out the truth behind my death.'

A shiver sliced through Anjali's body. She ran up to Natasha's bedroom and found her shaking vigorously. The kids' loud and panicky wails added more fear to the already sinister night. Riya killed the power to the speaker and the house turned silent.

'Kath, I think the hacker is messing up with the integrated home automation system,' Anjali said.

'But she had already disabled the Wi-Fi,' Riya argued.

'Must be some wireless platform. Kath?' Anjali asked and walked to Katherine. But the red-coloured text blinking on Katherine's laptop screen turned the floor beneath her liquid: *Access Denied.*

'Think of something else. Use some other machine to disconnect the Internet of Things or whatever platform is being used. Stop the hacker, Kath. Kids are scared. Natasha is this close to having a breakdown. Do something for god's sake,' Anjali said, keeping her voice calm.

Katherine stepped out of her stupor, but in the wrong realm. 'Can you see her, Natasha? Is Sania here?'

Natasha shook her head.

'Bloody hell, Kath,' Riya said. She walked to Teresa and said, 'Take me to the main switch board.' Anjali tagged along. Riya opened the door of the unit and asked, 'What the hell is this? A smart circuit breaker.'

Almost everything displayed on the panel was written in Mandarin. But Anjali scanned the board, slow and steady, and then turned the yellow switch up. The house went dark. Riya used her phone's flashlight and picked a set of candles kept on the shoe cabinet in the aisle. Teresa rushed and got the lighter.

'Take this upstairs and on the way light up all the candles you can,' Riya instructed Teresa. The sense of control returning in Riya's demeanour relaxed Anjali's shoulders.

'This needs to be disconnected from the home automation system to get the devices back in action. We need the aircons and the lights at least. Let's put some sense into Katherine so that she can do something about this,' Anjali said and pointed to the control panel next to the switchboard.

Teresa's high-pitch panicky voice could be heard on the stairway as they walked up. 'Flickering light means someone dead is communicating with us.'

Anjali bolted to the bedroom and said sourly, 'Don't talk nonsense. You go and bring a few more candles.'

'It's a strange feeling. I can't see her, but I feel her, like a shadow hovering in my mind,' Natasha said and broke into a sob, supporting her domestic help's findings.

'You will feel better. It's just taking time,' Anjali assured.

But Katherine did not buy it. 'Riya, you really fainted that night just after the Ouija reading, or were you pretending?'

Anjali answered for Riya, 'It was part of the act. No one was possessed. You'd better understand that.'

But Katherine wasn't budging. 'Anjali, a woman had died that night on the highway, not too far away from our college. I read a clipping in the news the next day,' Katherine said. Her fear gave legs to Teresa's.

'Ma'am, my friend in the opposite tower can talk to the ghost. I call her?' Teresa asked.

Things were heading to the realm of the paranormal at breakneck speed. Anjali looked at Riya for support. Riya took the cue and said, 'Katherine, that Ouija night act was inspired by the headline in the newspaper. I had lifted it directly from the newspaper. No one visited us that night, and all this is a hacker's bloody game. Get up and fight it out.'

'But I saw it in the newspaper the next day,' Katherine argued.

'Then you must have got the dates wrong. Now let's go down and get a hang of the control panel and the smart circuit breaker at the main switch,' Riya commanded and tugged at her hand.

Teresa and Anjali rocked the boys to sleep as soon as Katherine had freed the house from the clutches of the hacker.

But a moment later the doorbell rang and shattered the illusion of normality.

Katherine D'Souza
26 Siglap Road, Singapore

The *Access Denied* message on her laptop had closed all
the doors of reasoning in Katherine's mind. It was her first
professional failure in years. Double failure. The firewalls
that she had installed around Natasha's network were
hacked. She was locked out from her computer too.

The way Anjali had locked Sania out. How could she
leave her to freeze in the cold? It was barbaric.

Anjali's truth had shattered Katherine to the point of
no return. The uptight look on Riya's face meant she was
sailing in the same boat.

'Wish disconnecting from Anjali was so easy,' Riya
said while helping Katherine decouple the devices from
the home automation system. 'I can't believe that Anjali
did that to Sania . . .' Riya said. But before she could
complete her sentence, the flash of lightning outside
the window and the thunderclap that followed startled
them.

Her mind had turned into a string of mirror light
catchers, changing reflections at the command of the
wind.

Natasha isn't acting normal. It is time to bring out
the last card.

She stepped away from Riya and texted the
paranormal investigator: 'By any chance, can you come
over now? Urgent. We have had some episodes just now.'

They had mentioned about working late in the night
or early mornings. It was 2 a.m. The hour of the ghost.
Maybe, they were out hunting one.

Her phone vibrated.

'Out for field training. Told you about it. Looks difficult. Whereabouts?'

Katherine was banking on her unusual bonding with the paranormal investigator that morning. They had talked about many things, including her grandmother's Ouija board and her seance practices. She texted the address and pleaded once again for help. The reply came swiftly: 'What a coincidence. We are down the road, at the Kubur Kassim cemetery nearby. Coming now.'

Katherine felt a shiver go down her spine. *There is a cemetery nearby. Was it the same cemetery where Natasha had ended up on the Halloween evening? Did Natasha in some way upset the dead?*

Katherine was glad that she had called the ghostbusters.

'The paranormal investigators are coming now,' she said to Riya and waited by the door intercom. The two familiar faces on the intercom screen made her giddy with relief. But Anjali's response poured cold water on it.

'You crazy or what? Who allowed you?' Anjali asked.

'I had installed the most powerful firewall on Natasha's network, yet it got hacked. I am not saying that it's impossible, but it isn't that easy to mess with the system that has so many layers of protection added to it. And have you ever thought how the hacker manages to be awake 24/7, in three different time zones, monitoring all the four phones?' Katherine argued without bothering about the fear of being ridiculed.

'That's funny, Katherine, very funny. When you couldn't find the hacker, you started blaming it on the ghost,' Anjali said.

'Let them come. Sometimes answers can be found in unimaginable ways. If nothing else, it will help Katherine focus. We need her to be fearless to fight . . .' Riya said and came to Katherine's support. Before Katherine could thank Riya for it, the paranormal investigators stepped in, studying the flushed faces.

'What happened, miss?' the tall one asked, breaking the stony silence.

'Can we get this done with very little noise, if possible? The kids have had a rough night, and my friend isn't feeling very well,' Anjali said, biting her anger.

The investigators requested to see Natasha to complete the legal formalities of running an investigation on her premises. Anjali unwillingly guided them to her. Katherine tried to match Anjali's steps, but Riya stopped her and asked, 'Kath, can Anjali be the hacker? She is too calm for this chaos.'

Riya had echoed Katherine's own feelings about Anjali's calmness. Her allegation felt oddly familiar and helped Katherine fish out a snippet of forgotten memory. Katherine was startled at the recall, which was as clear as the beam of light.

'She is cold, KD. As cold as an icicle piercing one's heart,' Sid had said.

But when? The reunion night?

Her memory became more concrete as she walked up the stairs to Natasha's bedroom.

They were by the poolside, with their toes dipped in water, and Sid's face was morphed with sorrow. Tears had welled up in her eyes. Katherine had looked up at the starry sky to swallow the tears, but a drop trickled down from the corner of her eye. Sid had leant forward to wipe it away, but his lips had found a way to Katherine's lips instead.

The memory of the kiss flashed like a lightning bolt and disappeared. She felt like a traveller lost in a dark stormy night, waiting for another bolt of lightning to give her a sense of direction, or to set her aflame.

While the investigators roamed around the house trying to sense the presence, Katherine drifted inside her head, struggling to recall what had followed the kiss.

Had she somehow slept with Sid or said something to Sid? Was Sid the hacker? Then what were the paranormal investigators doing here?

She followed one of the investigators, who held a tiny monitor supported by a rod. The monitor displayed a bright fluorescent photo. 'We are using temperature theory to investigate a sighting. According to this theory, to manifest, the spirits draw energy or heat from the space around them, causing a temperature drop at various spots. These spots are called cold spots. You want to see the findings?' he asked and grabbed Katherine's attention.

Katherine nodded and did a rethink on her decision to invite the ghostbusters. She could either doubt her professional capabilities or let her fears slide, taking her from the realm of human revenge to that of the paranormal. But the fast-paced events gave her no opportunity to pick sides. A powerful hacker or a powerful ghost, she could pick any, but the adjective wouldn't change.

The face behind Sania was powerful. Immensely powerful.

Was Sid that powerful?

'The screen is peppered with purple spots. These are the cold spots, spots from where energies have been withdrawn. There is clearly some paranormal activity here, but not enough to raise an alarm. What bothers us is that your friend's sightings don't seem to match with that low an activity. I don't think we can claim a ghost sighting in the house,' he said.

Before Katherine could breathe a sigh of relief, Natasha's question knocked all the air out of Katherine's chest.

'How about me being possessed?' Natasha asked.

Riya Banerjee
26 Siglap Road, Singapore

While the investigators searched for the evil presence in
the house, Riya searched for the same in their friendship.
That night, Sania drank because she wanted to. She
played Ouija because she wanted to. But did she jump
from the terrace because she wanted to?

Not Really. She wasn't the kind.

What was the possibility that Sania died while
climbing the wall? What was the possibility that Anjali
had pushed her from the stairs and dragged her into the
woods and left her there? Did Anjali write the suicide
notes too?

'The dead don't walk out of their grave for no reason,'
the investigator said to Katherine. The words resonated
with Riya.

Who dragged Sania out and why? Sid?

Maybe all this while he had guarded Anjali's dark
secret in his heart, and now divorce had freed him, and
he wanted to free the others too.

But why not come out in the open and tell?

Or, Katherine might have blabbered about the prank
night in her drunk state on the reunion night. And Sid
decided to reveal the truth to get even with Anjali. He
could use their fears against them. He knew them all,
especially Katherine.

*But he could have blackmailed just Anjali. Why drag
all of us?*

Or, Sid was there in the woods that night and he had
helped Sania to climb up the wall. That would explain

the stench of nicotine coming from Sania. Did he kill Sania? But then why would he drag out the ghost of his own guilt, after so many years?

Nothing made sense. Riya's mind was running like a computer application active in the background, draining her battery. And the device in the investigator's hand pushed Riya's exhausted mind to dark and uncharted territories.

What if the Sania that Natasha claims to see is real and not a hallucination!

Every single society in the world maintains some form of belief system around life after death. Maybe ghosts are real. Her mother had believed in them; her sister still believed in them. And there had to be a reason for Katherine to believe in them, too.

But before Riya could get a handle on the fear growing in her, Natasha had unleashed another demon hiding within her.

Natasha Gupta Lim
26 Siglap Road, Singapore

Anjali's confession had stirred something violent in Natasha. She feared her own anger, which was vigorously fighting to come out. The violent emotions she was experiencing were so unlike her, as if she was taken over by someone unknown, as if someone was squeezing her skull and controlling her. Before her logical mind could stop her, she had already run a search: Signs of being possessed.

The content displayed on the screen wiped away her doubts.

'The experience started subtly. I felt a strong presence in the very bedroom I slept in. Even in the day, I felt as if someone was following me. There was always someone in my head, telling me things. Evident soft murmurs but not clear.'

It resonated with Natasha's state of mind. The unexpected arrival of the paranormal investigators had appeared like a ray of light shimmering at the end of the tunnel. But when the investigators refuted the idea of this house being possessed, she gave them a new line of research.

Her.

'How about me being possessed?' Natasha asked with a quiver in her voice.

The man in charge paused for a moment, recovered and said, 'Well, there is a possibility . . .'

But before he could finish Anjali interjected, 'You come with me, please? How much do we have to pay them, Katherine?'

Natasha again repressed her aching need to hit Anjali. Was the anger in Natasha driven by some unseen forces, or had Anjali's dark side turned her emotions into a witch's cauldron? Her mind was blaming Anjali for all the mayhem in her life.

Only if Anjali had not locked Sania out.

'Ma'am, we volunteer for this work. This is not our profession.'

'Well, in that case, thank you so much for your time, gentlemen,' Anjali said in a cold voice and showed them the door.

Riya was stunned into silence. Katherine crossed her hands and settled the goosebumps on her arms by rubbing them with her palms.

Was Katherine scared of me?

Natasha looked around nervously. Sania wasn't there. A sigh of relief escaped her lungs, and then her lungs started to work like a bellow again.

What if Sania is inside me?

9

Let Us Do It Again

November 5, 2017
Anjali Kapoor
26 Siglap Road, Singapore

Anjali's heart was revving up. It sounded like the roar of a motor in the still of the night. She had survived the night with a lingering headache. But Natasha's claim of being possessed had brought her own panic attack to a boil. She ushered the ghostbusters out and walked up the stairs with the hope that Riya was in command.

She could use a moment to fight her own demons.

But the night had turned into a rollercoaster ride. Like it or not, she had embarked on it, going up and down. The fear-struck faces in Natasha's bedroom caused another dip, lurching her stomach.

'Nat, your meds are the reason for your hallucination. The pain has made you vulnerable. You are not possessed, okay?' Anjali said, bringing stability to her voice.

Natasha looked at her with hope. She was teetering at the border, waiting for Anjali's logical argument to pull her to the realm of sanity. But Anjali's words and reasoning were sinking fast under the tsunami of her own attack. She wanted Riya or Katherine to spot the cracks in her calm veneer and jump to her rescue.

But they all were sailing in the same boat—the boat that was about to sink.

When no one came to support Anjali, Natasha requested, 'I need to lie down. Anjali, can you please pass me the meds?'

Anjali handed her the meds with a shiver in her hand that was too evident. Anjali needed to get her Xanax. And she needed it very soon.

But she held herself back and waited till Natasha fell asleep. Riya and Katherine had already retreated to the guest room.

Anjali rushed to get the Xanax, and a little later she asked Riya, 'Where is Katherine?'

'In the balcony. Smoking,' Riya replied, with a chip of ice in her voice.

'She still smokes?' Anjali asked rhetorically.

'Tonight, even I wish I could smoke. Why didn't you let the investigators finish?' Riya asked.

Anjali's heart was pounding by now. She took a moment before answering, 'Because all that is bullshit. Because Natasha is just sick, not possessed. I had expected you to come to my support, not succumb to some irrational fear.' She zipped open her medicine kit and popped in a Xanax.

'Irrational fears fill the nooks and crannies of our mind only when our rationale fails. You should have given us a chance to ridicule or accept the facts that the investigator was going to put forward. It was needed for Natasha's well-being, for Katherine's confidence and for my peace of mind,' Riya argued.

The trembling in Anjali's legs meant that the attack was nearing its peak.

'Let me check on Kath,' she said and stepped away from Riya. The need to close her eyes and let this moment pass was getting ahead of her. She did not want Riya to see her like this. She stood at the stairs and looked around for a distraction. Katherine's silhouette and the red dot of the cigarette's flame glowing like a firefly in the balcony drew her attention.

They both could smoke the whole city out. Sid and Katherine.

Anjali's mind circled back to Sid.

Did Sid help Sania in climbing that wall? Did he see me locking Sania out? What else did he see?

Her head was spinning. She reached out to hold on to the stair's railing but crashed on the floor instead. She had hoped for the moment to pass unnoticed, but Riya witnessed it all.

'What happened to you?' Riya asked and rushed to pick her up.

'Nothing. I am fine,' Anjali said.

'Oh! For god's sake, stop acting like you are made of steel. You are wet like a sponge and you are shivering,' Riya said and lifted Anjali up.

'It's a panic attack. I started getting them recently.'

'Are they as recent as your separation?' Riya asked with a little warmth in her voice. But Anjali was beyond framing a sentence. Riya assisted her to the guest room and handed her a T-shirt from her own bag. Riya then turned her face away for Anjali to change. The absence of eye contact gave Anjali some courage to voice her doubts.

'Do you think Sid could do it?' she asked.

'You tell me about it? You lived with him for decades. Moreover, can he do it is not the question. Why would he do it is the question.'

'Lately, Sid had met with some challenging roadblocks on the professional front. He has been drinking a lot and sometimes he becomes aggressive . . .' Anjali said, summoning up courage.

But Riya didn't let her finish. 'Oh, really! So, Sid is an alcoholic, he abuses you, and still goes to your mother's place to help her. And you have hidden this secret like many others? How do I know you are not throwing poor Sid under the bus, especially after all that you did to poor Sania?' Riya asked spitefully.

Anjali looked at Riya, trying to bring out a logical explanation to give her, on what she had done to Sania.

But that night had turned her into a demon—the alcohol had turned her into someone else.

Still, Anjali tried. 'I had left the keys there only. Also, I had planned to get her in a few minutes, but I slept . . . And by the time I woke up, it was too late. I was drunk, Riya,' Anjali argued weakly.

'And you want a divorce with Sid because he becomes aggressive after a few rounds? Seriously, Anjali.'

Anjali's logic, her arguments and the secret buried in her heart lost their structure, seeing Riya's reaction to the little piece of truth she had shared about Sid.

Katherine D'Souza
26 Siglap Road, Singapore

Sid kissed Katherine on the reunion night.

Anjali locked Sania out that night.

And Natasha felt that she was possessed.

Who says that lightning strikes only once? I need to smoke.

But Katherine was too scared to step out of the house. Natasha's huge balcony came to her rescue. She lit the cigarette and inhaled the first puff. Soon, in the circles of smoke, she saw Sid and Sania floating, and then all of them, dissolving into thin air, like a waft of smoke. Was it a premonition or a manifestation of Katherine's fears?

She smoked one cigarette after another, trying to calm her nerves. Stubs of cigarettes layered the balcony grill, resembling her brooding fears piling on one above the other. About to bring everything down. She had lit another cigarette when Riya stepped in.

'You want to finish the whole box, or are you coming up with me now?' Riya snatched the last stick from her. There was more love than anger in her gesture. It encouraged Katherine.

'That night, Sid kissed me, on my lips,' she blurted out with a sob.

Riya's shock was evident in her big eyes.

'Did Sid come inside the hostel that night?' Riya asked, sounding confused.

There are two nights—two nights of betrayal— two nights of faint, alcohol-infused memories that are mildewed with time.

'I am talking about the reunion night, when I met Sid in Karnal,' Katherine clarified.

'So, what all happened? Do you remember now?' Riya asked in a panic-filled whisper.

The tears that Katherine thought had crystallized in her eyes, started to melt. But Riya pinned her to the wall and asked, 'Do you think Sid is behind all this?'

Riya's next question was more head-on.

'Do you think Anjali could have accidentally killed Sania in an altercation, and that Sid had been covering it for years, until he decided to not burden his soul any more? Anjali just had a panic attack. Either she is still hiding something, or her guilt is catching up on her,' Riya speculated.

Katherine's mind followed the lead, harvesting the wild crop of suspicion Riya had planted in her head. Anjali must have accidentally pushed Sania, and she might have told all this to Sid. He must have saved Anjali all these years, but not any more. Not after the reunion night. He was not happy with Anjali, and he had told this to Katherine. She might have said something, pushing Sid to take desperate measures. Maybe this blackmail was nothing but Sid's misplaced feelings.

There was a missing link in the story, bobbing in her subconscious—there but not yet visible. Before Katherine could catch it, Riya said, 'I can't reach Sid. Can you try and check his whereabouts?'

Katherine fiddled with her phone and stated, 'Still in New Delhi. Moreover, his account is very vulnerable for a hacker.'

Am I still taking Sid's side blindly or is this a logical conclusion?

Riya's sad smile that bordered on pity was her answer.

'Let's go up,' Riya said.

In the room, Anjali was perched on the bed, staring at the ceiling with vacant eyes. Katherine felt a compulsive urge to comfort Anjali. But the memory of that kiss came back and triggered a wave of nausea.

There was something ugly about the night, perhaps that's why she had forgotten all about it. But something in her told her that she was this close to bringing the pieces together.

Katherine closed her eyes and waited for her memories to return home and turn the ache unbearable.

Riya Banerjee
26 Siglap Road, Singapore

The reunion tonight was nowhere close to the picnic-under-the-stars kind of reunion that Riya had imagined. Instead, she felt like the protagonist of a thriller, trapped in a haunted house, with three women who were not at all what she had expected them to be.

Anjali and Natasha were both knocked out by their medicines after shoving their mammoth loads of guilt and pain, respectively. And Katherine was lying next to Riya, roaming in the past, trying to pick up the pieces of her shattered memory to make them whole again.

What if it is a case of repressed memory and not of alcohol blackout?

Riya felt a constricting movement in her throat.

It was a mistake to come here—a mirage that had turned into a trapdoor of guilt and lies. She lifted her phone to book the first flight back home, but her conscience stepped in.

You are running away from the situation. Again.

That winter break, Riya had unknowingly put words into her mother's mouth. Her father's stroke, Sania's death and the fear of the truth being revealed had made her stay back. She had guarded her interest back then. She was about to do it again. But this time she was aware of her own feelings.

Stop being selfish, Riya.

But the hacker's message ended her dilemma: 'Good morning, Ri. Can we meet?'

'Who is this?' she texted back.

'You know who it is. I am tired, Riya. Let's get over with it.'

Riya read the text again.

The water has gone way over the bridge. Sania or the hacker, it must end today.

Riya texted back with a sense of resolve building in her veins: 'Where do you want us to meet? When?'

'I want to meet you alone. Considering Natasha's injury, you are my best choice. I don't expect much from Anjali and Katherine.'

Riya's mind reached this conclusion: Sid is playing games. She texted back: 'Okay. Where do you want me to come, Sid? And when?' Riya was convinced that Sid was behind all this, and she deliberately addressed him to catch him off guard. The reply cemented her suspicion: 'Asap. Outside OneKM Mall? Text when you start.'

She decided to play along: 'Okay.'

'Kath, are you sure about Sid's location?' Riya whispered.

'I checked his Gmail. I can hack his phone for a location track,' Katherine suggested.

'Do it now,' Riya said and pointed her phone screen to her. Katherine left Riya's phone on the bed and signalled her to follow her to the washroom. She closed the door and whispered, 'You cannot show up like Wonder Woman on a rescue mission at five in the morning. What if the hacker is armed? Moreover, if the hacker wanted to just talk and solve this, that option was always open. Why exercise it now, after harassing us?'

Katherine's words had instilled in her a fresh fear, but her logical thinking had elated Riya. Katherine was not blaming Sania for it and that was a relief.

Riya texted back, with her heart beating in her throat:

'You have two options: Come out and tell us what you want or wait for the police to get to you.'

But the hacker's reply made her regret her attempt at bravery instantly: 'When all this ends, remember one thing. I gave you a chance, Riya.'

Natasha Gupta Lim
26 Siglap Road, Singapore

Rick's text woke her up. Natasha craned her neck and found her boys sleeping next to her. Safe and sound. The pain in her neck had subsided considerably, too, and so had the feeling that she was possessed.

I was an emotional mess last night. What will they think?

Natasha was glad that Rick wasn't around with all this happening in their house. She again prodded around the possibility of Rick being the mastermind behind it and ruled it out almost instantly. *Rick loves his kids. Rick loves me.*

She picked her phone from the nightstand and read his text message: 'Managed to arrange a private school pick-up for kids. As it is the first day, send Teresa along. I have given them Teresa's number and they will liaise with her. Hope u r feeling better? Call me when awake.'

Her heart was filled with remorse. *I shouldn't hide all this from Rick.*

Tears welled up her eyes. She was about to wipe them when Anjali walked into the room and asked, 'Are you okay?'

'Rick will be so upset. He will never forgive me for hiding all this from him.'

'You are overreacting. This is not equivalent to cheating with an ex-boyfriend. Rick is mature enough to know the difference between an extramarital affair and a prank gone wrong,' Anjali argued.

So, this is how she lived with herself after locking Sania out.

But Rick was not that forgiving. She phoned him and decided to confess before it was too late.

'Nat, babes. You okay? Pain any better?' Rick asked.

'Feeling better. Rick, I need to tell you something that happened years ago at college,' she said, mustering up courage.

'Um . . . Nat, can we talk about it after the hearing, if not that important? I am with him waiting for his hearing.' Rick had cut her off mid-sentence.

In this mayhem, Natasha had forgotten about the court hearing. The call got disconnected, and Natasha distracted herself by helping Teresa, till she left with the kids for school.

'I want to go downstairs to the dining area,' she said, feeling brave, energetic and positive.

Riya instantly appeared in the hallway and assisted her. Katherine was up too or had not slept at all. She was in the study, juggling the HTML codes on her screen.

Hopefully finding the hacker, and not the ghost.

Natasha settled on the dining chair, relishing this little phase of normality. The pain in her neck had increased slightly but regaining mobility had lifted her soul. Anjali handed her a mug of steamy coffee and a slice of toast.

'Do you think Sid can do it?' Anjali asked when the four of them sat for breakfast.

'If in twenty years I couldn't know you, I can't claim a thing about Sid,' she said and turned her face away from Anjali. Natasha was hurt by Anjali's truth, and she made no effort to hide it.

'We all have our own crosses to bear, Nat,' Anjali said and walked to the kitchen with the kids' plates in her hand. The doorbell rang and shattered the accusing silence.

'There is a box for us. It's sent by Sania Malik, shipped from the hostel address,' Riya said with a quiver in her voice, as if she was bending towards the paranormal too.

Welcome to my world, Riya.

'Ouija board,' Katherine said in a panicked voice.

Riya unfolded the note taped to the Ouija board's box and read it aloud, 'Since fear is the only language you understand, let's play on fear. How about a game of Ouija? Place and time I will choose. And this time I will make sure you all come and play. Sania.'

10

The Ouija Night (Part 1 and Part 2)

November 6, 2017
Natasha Gupta Lim
26 Siglap Road, Singapore

The Ouija box had set off a fire-bolt in Natasha's heart. There was something evil about the threat. Anjali threw another furtive glance at the Ouija box and got busy with clearing the table, while Katherine constantly toggled between her laptop and phone, liaising with the cyber security officer, and Riya was on a call with the courier company, trying to find the sender's details. Thankfully, Sania was missing from Natasha's world this morning. But the Ouija box sitting on the sideboard radiated the same haunting presence.

'Natasha, your helper is not back yet. Is it normal?' Anjali asked with a flicker of worry in her voice.

'She must have stopped by to chat with one of her friends,' Natasha said and phoned her.

No one answered. She called again, this time with a thud in her heart. Nothing.

'Check on the kids,' Katherine said, almost instantly, as if reading her mind.

Natasha dialled the school reception, with tears stinging the back of her eyes. Rick's aunt, an administrator in the school, answered the phone. 'Aunty, I just wanted to check if the kids have reached safely, as they took the new bus today,' Natasha said, conquering the fear in her voice.

'I don't remember seeing them this morning. But let me check and revert.'

Rick's aunt would later tell her sister (Natasha's mother-in-law) about Natasha's call, ridiculing her for being paranoid, but that was the least of her worries. The phone rang and brought a sharp taste of danger in her mouth.

'Kids are not at school. They never showed up this morning. They may be at a friend's house,' Rick's aunt suggested.

'Maybe. I will call you again if I can't get in touch with them,' Natasha said and disconnected the call. She called Teresa, again with no luck.

'Can you track her phone?' Natasha asked with panic.

Katherine's dazzled expression was her answer. Natasha had an urge to toss in her pain medicine and drift to sleep. She had often lost her kids in her nightmares and always found them by the end of it. But it wasn't a dream because the worrying realization had already invaded her bones.

'I think it's time to call the police,' Anjali said.

But before she could make the call, Natasha's phone buzzed for attention.

'The kids are with me. Tell no one,' the disembodied voice said and ended the call.

The hacker's words landed on Natasha like a dropped piano. The kids had pleaded to skip school, but she had sent them regardless, in the hope of keeping them away from all this.

I should have kept them near me.

Rick's incoming call dragged Natasha down to rock bottom.

'Don't tell him anything, not yet,' Anjali said.

Natasha pushed the phone towards Anjali and began crying soundlessly.

'Hey, Rick. She just dozed off. What was the verdict?' Anjali asked in a calm voice and tapped on the speaker tab.

'We lost custody. He is in a shambles. Where are the boys? My aunty called Mom and told her that the kids didn't reach school. All okay?' Rick asked.

Natasha wanted to admit everything to Rick, but the hacker's words flashed like a warning.

Tell no one.

'They are in the playground. I kept them at home. Hope that's okay? Natasha wasn't aware of it, hence the confusion,' Anjali lied.

One more lie. A smooth lie.

'Cool. Ask her to call me when awake.' Rick ended the call.

The lookalike faces of Ian and Ryan flashed before Natasha's eyes. The dimple on Ian's right cheek was the only difference between the twins, as she had noticed when she first held them. With every passing day, she had identified more differences between the two pieces of her heart. And now, they had been pulled out from her chest. Natasha walked up the stairs and started dumping valuables in her bag, willing to pay for Sania's death with whatever she could.

But not with her boys.

The trill of her phone shattered her illusion.

'Hello girls, I see that you all are together, just like college days. Now all you need is the hostel to relive that night. So, how about we meet at Brunei Hostel in thirty minutes for a game of Ouija? Remember that the boys are fine, and they will stay fine if you guys do what you are told to do. Sania.'

'This is the hostel,' Anjali said, before the call could get over. She pointed her phone towards them.

Natasha's blood pressure dropped like a stone.

Brunei Hostel was an abandoned building—another haunted location.

Katherine grabbed the phone from Anjali and read the blog article aloud, 'This old, completely abandoned colonial-style building once used to house students from Brunei, who were sent to Singapore to study in the 1950s. But for some mysterious reason, the place was abandoned, and now the building is monopolized by nature. The neighbours have reported sightings and scattered encounters.'

Katherine swallowed, scrolled down on the phone screen, clicked on another such blog and read, 'The compound is not lit, so one of the blogs suggests bringing adequate lighting, just in case our phone's flashlight mysteriously stops working. Also, people have heard raucous sounds of boys playing on the grass field, and women wailing.'

Before any of it could make sense, Katherine had jumped on to the next blog: 'There is an infamous "Dark Pond" within the compound. There are rumours of dead bodies being thrown into the pond.'

Natasha let the fear she had been repressing roll over her. The texture of the caller's voice, which had felt so artificial a moment ago, fell into the nooks and crannies of an unnatural fear, and seemed to acquire an eerie feel.

Can a ghost kidnap her kids and keep them in an abandoned hostel?

She looked outside and felt another blow to her abdomen.

It was about to rain.

Anjali was also looking at the window, pondering the same thought. Soon, the enormity of it caught up with the other two. Natasha let out a sob and said, 'I can't live without them. Cannot. Please help me bring them back.'

'We will bring them back, at any cost. Sania or no Sania,' Anjali said in a calm voice and placed her hand out, with her palm facing up. The bond that had snapped years ago was reconnected as the friends followed Anjali's gesture. The resolute look on their faces meant that they were willing to do anything for Natasha's boys.

Natasha swallowed her throbbing pain and walked to the Uber.

'Are you all going to the Brunei embassy?' the driver asked.

'Tanglin Hill Brunei Hostel please,' Natasha said and turned her face away. The light drizzle falling noisily on the windscreen was competing with her racing heart. Natasha spotted the tricolour at the Indian embassy on the way, and the thought of breaking the news of the kidnapping to her mother sent a shiver down her spine.

She lost her daughter because of me, and now her grandsons too.

Before Natasha could calm her beating heart, the taxi had left the bustle of the city and was paving through the narrow roads lined with affluent houses. The driver zoomed the map on his screen and asked, 'Have you been there before?'

Natasha shook her head, holding back tears.

The Uber turned into a narrow road and the driver asked, 'This one?'

'Yes,' was all Natasha could manage without breaking into sobs. Anjali opened the door and assisted Natasha, struggling with an umbrella in her other hand.

'I don't need this,' Natasha said and rushed to Riya and Katherine. They had already covered the distance without bothering about the heavy drizzle slanting over them. But the steel-grey gate guarded by lock and chain had stopped them in their tracks. There was a red notice board mounted on the gate: Trespassers will be prosecuted.

But Riya was unstoppable. She rushed to the other gate: it stood tall and was secured with a chain and two locks intertwined into each other. The black spray paint on this grey gate was like a graffiti attempt interrupted midway. Anjali pointed to the blue-white crime alert board declaring the number of people detained for trespassing by the Singapore authorities. But getting arrested was the least of the threats today. Moreover, the mid-morning rain had kept the neighbours indoors.

'Not an easy feat to climb this, especially with Natasha's injury,' Riya concluded, after studying the tall steel barricade.

'This place has another entry according to the Internet, as this is a popular dare place. I saw a video on YouTube before we left. A woman was entering this building via the abandoned plot there,' Katherine said. She pointed to the piece of bare land on the right side of the hostel.

'Found it,' Riya shouted and shimmied her way into the building, through a gap in the fence. Anjali and Katherine assisted Natasha to get in. All the neck movement had doubled her pain. She curbed her need to bend in half and let the spasm pass.

Keep going for Ian and Ryan.

Natasha straightened up and observed her surroundings. The windows and doors in the building threatened to fall and bury anyone under their weight. And the dark clouds etched against the sky had added a sinister feel to the setting. The thought of the danger looming on her five-year-old twins was like another punch in Natasha's gut. She fought back tears and covered the distance.

They marched to the stairs leading to the porch and found nothing except someone's scattered belongings, as if dropped and forgotten in a rush.

'The hostel must be behind,' Katherine said and sped to the downslope on the left. Riya matched her steps, leaving Natasha in Anjali's care. They surpassed another abandoned one-storey structure and bolted straight to

the building that looked like a hostel. The sky had turned
ebony black, blocking the daylight.

'I can see some shaft of light there,' Riya said pointing
to the slice of dim light coming from the third floor of
the multistorey building. She bolted to it. The structure
appeared as fragile as a cardboard cut-out. Katherine gave
a nervous glance and followed Riya's footsteps. Anjali
matched Natasha's baby steps and carefully guided her
up the stairs that were covered in moss and creepers.

The stairs were littered with things decayed over
time. There were logs, doorframes and much more,
scattered everywhere. Natasha followed Riya's footsteps
and entered the room. A shiver went down her spine. The
cold breeze was flowing unrestrained in this door-less
room. Natasha looked around in the hope of finding her
kids in there, but all she found was an emergency light
placed on an abandoned tin suitcase. The fluorescent
glow radiating from the lamp highlighted the wall-sized
red-and-blue graffiti. It was a sketch of a demon with red
bulging eyes. Natasha looked away, keeping a check on
her fear of the paranormal. But the view from the room's
window bore an uncanny familiarity: the green pastures,
reminiscent of the woods they could see from their hostel
room window back then.

She walked closer to the window, but Anjali's hand
on Natasha's shoulder stopped her from going any
further. The windowpane was missing, and the window
ledge was barely attached to the wall.

Natasha was about to break into a sob at the thought
of her twins being kept in a place as threatening as this
when the phone kept beside the emergency light made a

beeping sound and startled them all. Riya lifted the phone and read the incoming text that was addressed to her: 'Riya, you will conduct the game. The questions you have to ask are on the chits marked as one, two and three. Follow the order. You will not read the next question until the previous one has been answered. I am sure you don't need a ghost to answer them. Do you?'

Katherine brought out the Ouija board from her bag and hastily placed it on the suitcase. The waft of freshly painted cardboard momentarily overpowered the fragrance of the moss. Natasha walked past the buckets filled with dried up paint, the abandoned brushes, the decayed belongings and observed the seating arrangement created using broken chairs and stools.

A perfect setting for playing Ouija.

Natasha's skin was lined with goosebumps. Was it the draft in the windowless building and her wet clothes, or the fear, or the combination of it all? She wanted to run a frantic search from room to room but sat still instead. The silence around them meant that the kids were not here, and the only way to get to them was to do as told. Katherine had concluded the same.

'Let's play,' Katherine said and placed her finger on the coin. Others followed. Riya unfolded the slip numbered '1', which she found tucked under the emergency light, and read the first question aloud, 'That night you answered each other's questions. Let's see how well you all will do today?'

Knitting her brows, Riya read the question for Anjali, 'Do you know the animal who dragged Sania's dead body into the woods? There is a hint too,' Riya said.

She paused to study Anjali's reaction and read, 'The hint is the note from the therapist: Patient's recurrent dreams are a manifestation of her guilt.'

Natasha waited for the coin to move or Anjali to come up with the answer, but all she could hear was silence rumbling like a whispered threat.

Anjali Kapoor
Tanglin Hill Brunei Hostel, Singapore

Riya read the question again, her perplexed expression magnified in the flashlight of the phone. 'Anjali, do you know the animal who dragged Sania's dead body into the woods?'

A tear dropped, seeming to melt the false fortress Anjali had created in her emotional world. It carried away the stones of pain and guilt, and a confession heaved out of her as she moved the coin to 'YES'.

'That night, I had left the keys on the grass for Sania to open the gate. She could not have missed the keys. And I was planning to get her back in a few minutes. But then I dozed off, and when I woke up in the middle of the night to check on her, she had not returned. I rushed to the backyard with panic jolting my heart. A blood-stained, immobile Sania on the floor left me numb with shock. I panicked and rushed to the warden's room, but the thought of my mother stopped me from waking the warden up. My addled brain convinced me that Sania was dead, but my mother was alive. So, I walked back, found the keys on the grass and dragged Sania out, deep into the woods, hiding the crime and the evidence. I was acting on pure panic,' Anjali said and waited for the trickle of relief that never came.

Anjali wanted to lift her gaze and study the impact of her confession. But her eyelids were burdened with nascent tears of remorse.

However, the hacker showed some mercy by not giving any time to her friends to heap allegations on her.

The warning text flashed on the phone screen: 'Move on to the next question.'

Riya opened the second paper slip and read the next question with confusion embedded in her expression.

'Was Sania Sid's first, Anjali? There is a hint too. The reason why Anjali and Sid are not together is also the reason why Sania ended her life.'

Anjali felt a momentary wash of vertigo, partly in relief and partly in worry.

Sid wasn't the blackmailer. But the blackmailer was after Sid too.

However, before she could place the missing piece in the puzzle, Natasha asked, 'Anjali, what does it have to do with your divorce?'

Anjali felt a swell of painful emotions as the truth took shape.

So Sania was the first one to see the animal inside Sid. But when?

'Anjali, what is it about your marriage that you have not told us?' Riya asked, shaking Anjali.

Anger ballooned up inside Anjali, the anger that had been boiling for ages.

'I didn't tell you or you didn't care to listen. Remember how I was the one throwing your poor Sid under the bus? Do you still want to hear the answer?' Anjali asked in a voice that surfaced the rage brewing in her heart—the rage she should have shown when Sid first forced himself on her, against her will. But back then she was newly married and was madly in love with him. She had ignored it and blamed Sid's act on the alcohol running in his veins. She had been a worse drunk than him.

She ignored the second time, the third, and so on, until she lost count. And by the time she established the pattern, it was too late—she was already an easy victim. Also, Sid's charm had cast a spell on everyone around her. Her mother was charmed; her friends were in his awe.

Moreover, there wasn't a lot to complain about. He was not hitting her, nor was he abusing her verbally. He was just forcing himself on her, whenever he wanted. Sometimes he used his charm, and at other times he simply used his strength and pretended that it was a game.

A game that had gone beyond her marriage too.

'Speak up, Anjali, for god's sake. Her kids are at stake here,' Katherine warned, and Anjali's false pretence disintegrated like a sandcastle.

'Sid has been abusing me forever. The first time he did that to me was soon after the party that his school friends had arranged to celebrate our marriage. That night, I thought a few extra drinks had turned Sid wild. I let it go, as I had done worse things in my inebriated state. But then it became a pattern: party, drink and forced love-making. I ignored that too. However, in the last one year, the occasional episodes had turned into a habit. I tricked myself into believing that he was just trying to establish his territory in the bedroom, as my recent promotions and his job loss had tarnished his shine. But these frequent episodes led to debilitating panic attacks . . .' Anjali dissolved into tears before she could finish her sentence.

The trill on the phone served another reminder: 'Move on to the last question.'

Riya read the last question while shooting a questioning glance at Katherine. 'This question is for you, Kath. You really don't remember what happened on the reunion night?

Katherine D'Souza
Tanglin Hill Brunei Hostel, Singapore

The recall Katherine had been longing for came back with heart-stopping clarity after Anjali's confession.

On the reunion night, Sid's lips had touched hers and she had pushed him away. But before she could walk away, he had pinned her to the wall and tucked her loose hair behind her ear. There was a softness in his action that had melted her, but his words that followed sent a strong sense of revulsion in her veins.

'I always wondered what it would be like, to be in bed with you. Would you know all my moves like no one else?'

Katherine had tried to free herself from his clutches, but his hold was firm yet gentle.

'The more you say no, the more attractive you turn, the more fun you will get. You do that to Sam too, my adorable cat?' Sid had asked in a voice that felt so alien.

Her reflexes were blurred with alcohol, but not enough to mistake this as love. Katherine had felt like a rabbit trapped in a snare. She was about to push him away when Sania's name caught her attention.

'Remember the college days? How much you were in love with me. I would have not known, if not for Sania,' Sid said, planting a lecherous kiss on her neck. She had to use all her self-control to repress the urge to kick him in the groin.

'What did Sania say about it and when?'

Sid had pulled her closer and said, 'The night before she died, I met her near the postbox. She blabbered and gave away all your secrets—who liked whom and all. You girls are all the same; you keep saying no, but in truth all you want is our attention. You remember how Sania had refused my proposal, and that night she played all kind of games with me. And the way you were hugging me a while ago, I know you want me too. How about we play your favourite childhood pretend game: you be the wife and I will be your husband for tonight.'

But before Sid could go any further, Katherine pushed him away with a force she didn't know she was capable of.

'Kath, did Sid force you that night?' Anjali asked and brought her back to the present that was as ugly as the past. But instead of answering her own Ouija question, Katherine had answered Anjali's.

'So that means Sid really raped Sania that night. That is why she ended her life,' Katherine said and looked at Anjali. The silent exchange between them had said everything. But Natasha's mind wasn't able to comprehend anything beyond her kids.

She asked, 'But what has it got to do with my kids?'

Riya shifted impatiently on the tiny stool and said, 'So the hacker kidnapped the kids to take revenge on Sid? But why Natasha's kids? And Sid is not even here.'

The movement on the stairs stopped their hearts. Natasha stood up, about to bolt out of the room, in the hope of finding her kids on the staircase. But the incoming text stopped her. Riya read it aloud with a tremble in her voice, 'The game is not over. You can't get up; else I will haunt you.'

The fear of the unknown that had buzzed like a thrum of locust wings in Katherine's mind turned into a loud, audible roar. The game of Ouija was repeated with too much precision. Who could restage the game without having witnessed it?

The muffled sound of footsteps grew louder, matching the fast thump of Katherine's heart. It brought her train of fears to a screeching halt.

Sid entered the room with a phone in his hand and was taken aback by the faces waiting for him.

'What sick games are you guys playing, blackmailing me for weeks? So, this was your game, Anjali?' Sid said with a frown on his face. The lost-dog look he wore felt out of place. He charged towards Anjali, but Katherine stopped him. 'You bastard, you raped Sania that night. You tried it with me too. And how could you do that to Anjali?'

Sid pushed Katherine away and said, 'I raped nobody. Anjali, what crap have you been feeding them? I did not rape Sania. And Kath, you were all over me that night. You can ask anyone in the party. You can call Mathew and check with him. He knew how drunk you were that night. You had called him to take you home that night, no?' Sid said.

'Did you meet Sania that night?' Anjali asked, still standing where she was.

Sid gave a glance at the graffiti around him and said, 'Yeah, I met her that night. I was out for a smoke when I found her roaming alone on the campus. She said that she was locked out by some mean girls at the hostel, and she didn't want to use the main door as it would put them all in danger, including her. She was drunk and making no sense. However, she was shivering, so I took her to the college building and lent her my jacket. But before I could go and get her a quilt, she pulled me to the floor and started kissing me. And then one thing led to another. Later, I walked her back to the hostel, and she found the keys on the grass. We did cross our lines that night, but it wasn't rape. In fact, it was the opposite. She was hitting on me. She seduced me,' Sid said.

His manipulation of facts broke the frayed thread of Katherine's temper.

'You fucking asshole, like I seduced you on the reunion night?' Katherine shouted.

But before Sid could reply, Natasha said, 'I don't care whether you raped Sania or she raped you. Right now, I only want my boys back, Sid. How could you kidnap them? Please, give them back.'

Sid raised his hand to run his fingers through his hair, a habit Katherine was very familiar with. But Natasha's question caught his hand mid-air. With shock in his voice, he asked, 'Ian and Ryan have been kidnapped? When? And where is Rick? And you think I can do that to the boys? Natasha, trust me, I am getting blackmailed too, and I had no clue that you guys were sailing in the same boat. I have been compelled to come here; you can check my phone.' Sid had managed to blurt everything out in a breath.

'But, if you are not the one blackmailing us, who is? And where are my kids?' Natasha's voice was laced with pain and melancholy.

Logic stirred in Katherine's head, like a beast pulling itself free of swamp mud. The realization alone was enough to drain every bit of colour from her face.

How much am I destined to endure in a single night?

But at the thought of Natasha's loss she was stricken with guilt. It was all because of her. With a crushing sense of shame, Katherine said, 'I think I know who is behind this.'

Anjali Kapoor
Tanglin Hill Brunei Hostel, Singapore

In one night, Anjali had fallen so far down the rabbit hole that a numbness crept through her body. She looked at Katherine's face, her rapidly blinking eyelashes meant she was skirting around a confession. Anjali knew how heavy the weight of remorse felt in the rims of the eyes and how it never disappeared. After Sania's death, she had spent many nights crying, in the hope of getting rid of that regret, but it had stayed there. Back then, it was a choice between her conscience and her mother's life, and Sania's suicide note had made that choice easy, because Anjali had not killed Sania.

Katherine cleared her throat and pulled Anjali back to the present.

'That night, I had called Mathew to pick me up from the party venue. I might have told him about it all. About Sania too,' Katherine said in a low whisper. She bit her lips and winked back the tears. But her reclaimed memory had not derailed Riya's thinking.

'But why would he seek closure on Sania? And why trouble all of us?' Riya argued with a questioning look on her face.

Katherine picked a loose hair from her jeans, dropped it on the ground and confessed, 'Because he must be blaming himself for what happened to her. That night, I had called Mathew to arrange for some food as he was visiting Sid for the term-end party. But the food in the party was over, so I bullied him to give me the whisky instead.'

'So, the hostel warden had no one in her room that night? The bottle wasn't hers? You made up the whole story?' Riya asked. Her face expressed anger and shock in equal measure.

'Yes. She only gave me the keys to make tea. I made up the story to save Mat,' Katherine explained.

Before Riya could react, Natasha asked, 'But then who has my kids? Mathew?'

Anjali stared at Katherine. A night had altered Katherine's universe completely.

Sid and Mathew were the two strongest pillars of her childhood. But the night had unmasked their ugly faces— one was a rapist and the other a kidnapper.

Before Katherine could gather herself together, Sid was shouting orders at her, 'Call your brother and check where Natasha's kids are. What kind of a sick man kidnaps such innocent kids?'

Sid dialled a video call to Mathew, but Katherine grabbed the phone from him.

The phone was answered in three rings.

'Kath, where are you and why are you using Sid's phone to call? Are you with him?' Mathew asked with anger flushing his face red. But Katherine had no time for a decent back-and-forth.

'Mat, why did you do this?' Katherine demanded, fighting back tears.

'Do what, Kath? What are you doing with Sid? And, where are you?' Mathew repeated, this time with anger in his voice. He was in his cabin and was dressed in his star-studded military uniform. But the expression on his face looked like he was in a war, about to shout a shoot-at-sight command.

'Mat, don't act as if you don't know what is going on. I just recalled what happened on the reunion night. And we all know Sid's dirty reality now. I know you are the one behind all this drama to get Sid's truth out—about me and about Sania. But why did you go to that extreme?' Katherine demanded.

'Oh, thank God, Kath,' Mathew said. 'I am so glad you remembered everything. I wanted to kill Sid the very night, but you were drunk, and you were blending the two nights into one, blaming him for raping Sania and molesting you. I waited for you to sober up, but the next morning you had conveniently forgotten everything. I had hoped that you would come back to it after Dad's birthday party was over, but you still acted like nothing had happened, which worried me to death. It wasn't easy for me to level such an allegation against a popular guy like Sid. Especially when you and Dad always chose him over me. So I started tracking him, using an ex-colleague's professional expertise. He had retired from the military's intelligence unit to start a cyber security firm, and I exploited his resources and skills to keep track of things. We also tracked you through the phone I gifted you, as this was the only way to keep you away from him, until I had something concrete on Sid. But I guess . . .'

But before he could go any further, Natasha grabbed the phone and started pleading, 'Mathew, you have got closure on Sania's death, and we all now know Sid's truth.

Now, please return my kids to me. Please . . .' Natasha's shoulders jerked spasmodically as she sobbed.

'Nat, you are also there? And what kids are you talking about?' Mathew asked with shock in his eyes. 'I don't get it.'

'You are not the one blackmailing us? Tracking us all? Kidnapping the kids and forcing us to play Ouija?' Katherine shouted.

'Why would I do that? I just tracked you both to make sure Sid didn't go near you. But why would I kidnap her kids? And how? I had restricted connectivity on deputation. So how could I manage a plan that expansive?' Mathew said. A frown had puckered his forehead.

His words shuttled Katherine into the whispering, unreal world of demons. Before Katherine could blame the dead Sania for it, Natasha asked, 'Then who is the monster torturing my kids?'

The expression on Mathew's tanned face changed from confusion to regret, and the words that followed were like a rockslide crashing down on Katherine. 'Natasha, I am not the monster who kidnapped your kids, but I might have created one.'

Before any of it could make sense, the footsteps in the corridor grew louder, consuming all the silence. The voice pierced through the darkness: 'You did not create a monster, Mathew. You helped me crush a few,' a voice said, and a woman walked into the room from the dark corridor connecting the rooms.

Anjali struggled for a moment to recognize her face, but Riya's shocked voice bridged the gap in her memory.

'Reet, so you are behind this?' Riya asked in disbelief.

The truth Anjali had tried to outrun for years landed on her chest, so heavy she could hardly breathe—Reet's loss had fallen through the cracks.

But tonight, this 'petite woman with the friendliest smile in the hostel' wasn't here to disappear into the shadow.

'Twenty long years,' Reet said, 'every freaking night, I drowned in my mistakes, pursuing the future in time that was enough to lessen my regret. But no time, no logic ever dimmed the feeling of regret and longing in my heart. If only I had not left her alone that night. If only I had the courage to leave my family and my career for her. That night, Sania had not gone home because her uncles might have killed her. But you guys did a better job, by getting her drunk and locking her out. And whatever was left, this devil here destroyed it. He thought that his charm gave him the right to force his way with anyone. She was in love with a girl, Sid. She wouldn't have seduced you. You raped a woman who was already shattered and betrayed; it fuelled her decision to end her life. And to top it all, your perfect match dragged her dead body into the woods for the predators. Did you get a chance to see her photo, Anjali? She was found half-naked deep into the woods. The clothes that she couldn't stop obsessing about were all left in tatters by the animals. The face she took such good care of was all eaten up by animals. But looks like her death wasn't reason enough to leave her alone. The master storyteller of your group decided to cash in on her death too . . .'

Mathew's voice on the phone's speaker cut her off and pulled everyone's attention to Reet's virtual accomplice.

'I wasn't part of this Katherine. I was on a deputation,' Mathew justified.

But Reet was in no mood to take turns.

'But you started this, Mathew, by robbing me of my peace. All this while, I had thought that my walking away from the relationship had shattered Sania's will to live. And when I had finally learnt to live with the ache, you came lancing my infected wound—looking for clues about foul play in Sania's suicide,' Reet said.

'Kath, my ex-colleague helped me dig a little into Sid, to validate how true was your allegation that Sid raped Sania that night, and I was hoping that the truth behind Sania's rape would evoke your repressed memories without harming anyone other than Sid. We just monitored Sid, collecting evidence against him,' Mathew clarified. He was roaming in the room with the phone in his hand, as if he could walk across the oceans to be with his sister. Anjali had always appreciated the way Mathew had taken care of them all. But Reet was untouched by Mathew's love for Katherine.

'You made me call Sania's mother for the suicide note, didn't you? But what you didn't know was that you had unknowingly unpicked the one thread that could unravel the whole tapestry of the past. It was all destined this way, Mathew. You were sent for a counterinsurgency assignment for a reason. Once you were gone, your ex-colleague hacked Anjali's account and then her therapist's, on my instructions. We were looking for clues in Anjali's and Sid's lives. But the notes capturing Anjali's nightmares about her having dragged the dead woman into the woods gave this mission a new spin. One thing led to another and I soon found myself reading Riya's confession-of-crime manuscript,' Reet said and tucked her hair behind her ear.

Her angry voice echoed in the empty space around them. The rain had stopped, and the only sound was that of crickets in the backdrop. Anjali felt a shiver go down her spine. She looked at Natasha, who was trembling in fear too. The look on Reet's face had sent Natasha's mind to dark and dangerous places.

'Where are my kids, Reet? What did you do to them?' Natasha asked with tears rolling down her cheeks.

'They are safe, at your in-laws' house, waiting for your call to go home. It was an easy feat to convince your helper that the kids needed to be away from the house after that scary night. All it took was a message from Anjali's phone explaining to her that you had to rush to the hospital and that you were not comfortable about leaving the kids at home or sending them to school. And then all I had to do was to enable airplane mode on your helper's phone, which was all child's play, as Mathew's ex-colleague had loaded the software on my laptop, giving me unlimited access to all your personal devices. So, your kids are fine, the mother hen of the group. But did you ever think that Sania was someone's daughter too? Natasha, you were the only person in your group whom Sania trusted, and you dragged her into the prank,' Reet said in a voice that hit Natasha like the snap of a rubber band. But the tears in Natasha's eyes softened Reet's tone a bit.

'You can reach your helper now and ask her to go home. I had no intention of troubling your kids. If only

Riya had accepted my request to meet up,' Reet said. Riya helped Natasha in placing the call, but Katherine's mind was speeding like a train in a dark tunnel, covering as many miles as possible. 'So, you created Sania to take revenge on us? But how?' Katherine asked.

'I had messed with Natasha's baby monitor to instil some fear in her, in the hope that she would panic and confess. But before I could scare her enough, she met with an unfortunate accident. Her hallucinations were not my work. It was her system reacting to the opioid. However, I decided to make the most of that opportunity by increasing her dose a bit. All it took was a pretend nurse call to her husband. I played with her fears the way you all had played with Sania's fears. An eye for an eye. But you guys are really something. One is living with an abusive husband; another has conveniently forgotten the truth she had accidentally unravelled; and the meanest in the group decided to rewrite another crap, portraying Sania as mean and snobbish. And the brother who started it all to "protect his sister" and "win Anjali over", abandoned the mission to fight bigger battles, while this bastard kept molesting women at parties.'

Before Anjali could grasp it all, Katherine had fired another question: 'And the note, where did you get that one?'

Reet paused for Mathew to answer. Anjali looked at Sid, who was shifting his weight from one foot to another, with anger tossing and turning in him. Riya was watching Sid too, but Katherine's and Natasha's eyes were glued to the phone in Katherine's hand.

'I had sent it in your folder back then, hoping that Sid would see it,' Mathew said. 'I had already sabotaged a few of his relations for you, hoping to give you what you desired the most. But when he told me that he had fallen in love with the woman I liked, I did what I could, this time for you, Kath, and for me. I sent the note for Sid to read. But nothing of the sort happened. However, I had kept the original copy back where you had hidden your note, just in case this one got lost. I again found it while going through your things at Dad's place, while collecting evidence against Sid. Reet got hold of it from the folder on Sid that I'd shared with her. I thought I was helping her to heal by getting closure . . . but she has clearly gone too far with all this.'

'Seriously, KD, look how twisted your brother's mind is . . . He must have fed you some crap story about the party night, the way he brainwashed my love interests. Nothing happened that night. How can you believe him after this?' Sid said.

But Katherine gestured him to stop and said, 'I wish you had come to me, Mat. I could have recalled that night with your help.'

'Really? When have you ever heard a word against Sid? Your mind had conveniently saved you from the shock, by wiping away the memory of the reunion night. And look at this son of a bitch. He is still denying all of it. What were the chances that you would recall the night? I had burnt my fingers while trying to keep you away from smoking. I wasn't going to take a chance this time. However, my plan wasn't so extreme,' Mathew said with a note of condemnation in his voice.

In the meanwhile, Sid had walked over to Reet, with anger gleaming in his eyes. 'You really are a psycho, just like your bloody girlfriend,' Sid said and raised his hand to hit Reet. But a killing rage swept over Anjali and she pushed Sid with all her might.

'You. I should have killed you the night you raped me for the first time. But I loved you so much that the thought of living without you caused an unbearable ache. It still hurts,' she said and pushed him further away, unable to stop herself. She was boiling with repressed rage.

Sid pushed her back with all the strength in his arms. The blow was too heavy for Anjali to stay on her feet. She crashed against a dangling window frame, which gave way under her weight, taking her along, three floors down, all the way to the ground.

Every night, Anjali had imagined how Sania would have felt while falling down from the terrace.

Now she knew. Exhilarating.

With a thud, Anjali's body touched the soft moss carpet of grass and shrubs, and the minutes that followed wiped away all her senses. Moments later, she opened her eyes and found herself surrounded by people who supposedly hated her. But they were all staring at her with concern and love in their eyes. Sid was there too, with tears rolling down his cheeks—the tears that came every morning after he had raped her.

She wasn't falling for it.

'You, I will not leave you,' he said and walked to Reet. But Riya guarded her. 'Stay away, Sid' she said.

'But . . .' Katherine said.

'She has suffered enough. Reet, go away before it ruins your family too,' Riya said and waited for Reet to step away. Anjali had parted her lips to say sorry to Reet when the paramedics rushed in with the stretcher. Everything after that was a blur of sound and movement.

She woke up in the hospital bed. Her friends were around, waiting for her impatiently. Her neck was trapped in a collar and she had a cast in her hand, but the rest of her body felt lighter than ever. She lifted her left hand and saw the drawings on her cast. Katherine had drawn four girls holding hands. There was something written under it: 'To a fresh and honest start!'

Anjali raised her hand. Riya got the clue first. She placed her palm on Anjali's cast-covered hand. The other two followed, marking a new beginning.

December 19, 1997
Girls' Hostel
Institute of Technology, Kurukshetra

All the love stories were your favourite. Except mine. Because I fell in love with her, instead of him. And my love became a sin in your eyes.

Ammi, you wanted me to be normal. So, tonight I pretended to be normal, by letting his touch morph my feelings for her. But nothing about it was normal. And I cannot live with the ugly feeling it has left behind.

Alvida
Sania

Epilogue

Riya's new book wasn't a commercial success, but it was her magnum opus. And Reet's narration about the denial, the acceptance and the internal conflict, especially after Sania's suicide, were the building blocks of Riya's non-fiction work on sexual orientation and the taboos around homosexuality in Asia.

Riya had also managed to get a copy of Sania's suicide notes from the police record files. Sania's notes to the warden and to Reet were written in a legible handwriting, but the note written to her mother was an unintelligible scrawl; the first two notes were probably written before the game of Ouija, and the third one written soon after her time with Sid.

However, the question whether Sania was raped or not still hung in Riya's head. Sid was serving a five-year prison sentence in London for marital rape and attempt to rape. But he persistently refused that he had raped Sania that night. Riya had a feeling that Sid might have been telling the truth. Sania was going through a realization regarding her sexuality, and probably her divided consciousness had made her love for Reet and her idea of having a crush on Sid both valid. She might have seduced Sid in a desperate attempt to make all the wrongs right.

There was no way to confirm any of it. But one thing was crystal clear: the alcohol in Sania's veins had not made her decide to end her life; it had just fuelled her decision. And this truth had given them all the closure they deserved. Each of them had gone back to her world as a different woman.

Riya had stopped judging people harshly, and, consequently, when Sania's cousin asked her out, she accepted the proposal. All the juicy updates about her romantic tryst with Rahim Malik were shared on the 'Ouija WhatsApp Group'. The group name they decided to keep forever.

Anjali had stepped out of the shadow of her guilt to realize that her friends and family loved her as much as they had loved Sid. There was never an either/or, and it was only her guilt that had belittled her in her own eyes. She moved back to India to live with her mother.

On Katherine's request, Mathew had come to meet Anjali once. There was too much past between them to wash away in one meeting, but Mathew was willing to wait.

This closure had put Natasha's marriage on the rocks as Rick was unable to forgive Natasha for risking his kids. And with every argument, the gap between them widened. They were going through marriage counselling in the hope of mending it all and thankfully, the weekly sessions were helping Natasha to square with her past too.

Katherine rejoined the workforce as the head of IT security. She had finally accepted a full-time position with her fastest-growing client. Riya's suggested self-help list helped her get a good handle on her fears. She wasn't willing to let anyone exploit her metaphysical fears again. However, she still read her astrology forecast every day, the way Reet remembered Sania every day.

Reet created a digital platform for LGBTQ teenagers in India, to educate them on how to handle their divided consciousness in their adolescent years. She trains them for the challenges that come with the acceptance of one's sexuality, focusing on their mental health, so that no one else ends up like Sania.

This initiative has healed Reet in a way revenge couldn't.

Acknowledgements

Atharv and Pradyumn, my adorable boys, thank you for barging into the bedroom at ungodly hours of night—you both are the inspiration for the ghost in this story! Vipin, thank you for pushing me to write a book and for going through every single draft with the patience of a saint.

Juhi, you believed in the story when I had lost faith. Thanks for pushing me. Kunal, thanks for being my best critic and an amazing support. Ma–Papa, thanks for being my pillars of strength, always! Iyra, I promise I will soon write a story for you too!

Many thanks to my loving second set of parents (in-laws) for their blessings, and to Neetu Di, Ashish Jijaji, Bhavya and Shivansh, for being ever ready to bring the moon and stars for me!

My extended family and my crazy set of cousins, thank you all for the endless excitement you have shown. Malik Uncle and Aunty, thank you for being my backup parents in this journey too.

A very special thanks to Basant Sir for showing so much faith in my writing. Milee Ashwarya, a heartfelt thanks for the opportunity! Karan Bajaj and Sidin Vadukut, thanks for being my mentors!

A special mention to the team from the National Arts Council, Singapore, and to the awesome Sarah Cypher for teaching me the technicalities of the craft. Thanks to Jayapriya and her team for their guidance.

My heartfelt thank you to the awesome team at Penguin Random House India. Gurveen, my amazing editor, thanks for believing in me and being my partner in crime. Vineet, thanks for your magical wand that made all my mistakes disappear. Priya, thank you for using a fine-tooth comb to clean the draft further. Antra, thanks for the stunning book cover.

Lastly, *That Night* is all about friendship, and I couldn't have written it without all my friends, from school, college and beyond. A special mention to my college gang—Manisha, Kopal, Lakshmi, Pooja and Sunila—and my 'Old is Gold' gang—Deepa, Divya, Nikki, Preeti, Pragati and Swati. The entire batch of 1997, my seniors and juniors who made college life fun! Chayan, Kopal and Divya Singh, I cherish your selfless friendship. Thank you, my school friends—Aman, Geeta, Shallu, Jyoti and countless others.

Grateful to all my friends and well-wishers in Singapore, with a special mention to Seema, Mitali, Divya Nagarajan and Divya Kalia, for your wonderful support in this journey; and to my tribe in Singapore—the Agarwal, Bohara, Kothari, Singh, Vijan and Khan families.

Above all, my beloved Maamaji, who wanted me to follow my heart and spin a tale. Wish you were here to see your dream translating into reality.